1 MONTH OF FREE READING

at

www.ForgottenBooks.com

By purchasing this book you are eligible for one month membership to ForgottenBooks.com, giving you unlimited access to our entire collection of over 700,000 titles via our web site and mobile apps.

To claim your free month visit:

www.forgottenbooks.com/free768447

ISBN 978-0-483-66833-1
PIBN 10768447

FOREST

OF

MONTALBANO:

𝔄 𝔑𝔬𝔳𝔢𝔩.

IN FOUR VOLUMES.

———◆———

BY THE AUTHOR OF

" SANTO SEBASTIANO,"

AND

" THE ROMANCE OF THE PYRENEES."

VOL. I.

LONDON:

PRINTED FOR GEORGE ROBINSON,
25, PATERNOSTER-ROW.

1810.

FOREST OF MONTALBANO.

CHAPTER I.

IT was near the close of the 17th cen-
tury, that just as the last sad masses
had been performed in solemn requiem for
the departed soul of a lately-deceased venerable abadessa of the convent of Santo Valentino, in the northern extremity of the
kingdom of Naples, a loud and lengthened
peal of the portal bell reverberated along
the mouldering roofs of the antient cloisters,
and rocking, as it seemed, the time-worn
edifice, gave a momentary alarm to the
holy sisterhood, who long had learned to
tremble at every blast of wind, from cherish-

ing the painful apprehension that even each passing breeze might entomb them amid the lapidations of their ruined habitation.

This alarum at the convent gate obtained admission for a courier, who arrived to announce the immediate approach of the new abadessa.

The nomination to the supremacy of Santo Valentino was solely vested in the pontiff. The sisterhood already knew a successor to the late prioress had been appointed, and, in defiance of long-established custom, not of their community; but they dared not appeal; and this impatience for the possession of her new dignity, they promptly pronounced indicative of no amiable propensities in the bosom of their new superior, who came thus indelicately soon to intrude on their sorrow for a departed saint, to bid them beam the smile of welcome ere their tears were dried.

But ere time was afforded for a confidential censure, the unwished-for intruder arrived. Her retinue bespoke the becoming humility of genuine piety, since it was neither numerous nor splendid; but soon that favorable impression, which this propriety of conduct was calculated to inspire, was obliterated, when the dismayed nuns discovered her escort thither, to be Gulielmo, the cardinal patron, the Pope's most valued friend. The gallantries of this cardinal had been more than suspected, and the alarmed purity of the sisters of Santo Valentino, in horror, mentally pronounced the cause of their new abadessa's innovating appointment and of that partially-marked favor, which elected, from the votaries of the world, a prioress for a convent; since the new abedessa had not yet professed the sacred vows necessary for a conventual life.

Every external appearance sanctioned the appalling suspicions of the community; since the air, the form so exquisite in symmetry, the taste, the elegance of her adornments, proclaimed the new prioress of Santo Valentino a being whom the soul of gallantry would gladly pay homage to; but when the nuns, compelled by inevitable necessity, forced to their dissimulating countenances the smile of cordial welcome, and that the intruder raised a thick veil she wore, suspicion vanished, rapidly and forever, from the minds of even the

most fastidious; since her fascinating aspect announced at one glance, that if she
possessed beauty to enchain admiration, she
had virtues to secure esteem; and while
her dazzling charms might awaken envy,
her afflictions must claim the tribute of tender sympathy; for on every line of her
expressive countenance was pourtrayed a
heart laden with sorrows, that admitted no
hope to cheer them.

Sister Olinda, the senior of the nuns, (she
who by the infringement of a custom established right, was the person injured by the
appointment of this stranger,) now charm-
ed from selfish feelings, allowed at once the
pity, the interest she found awakened in her
bosom, to operate uncontrolledly on her
heart; and in the spontaneous benevolence
which that inspired, she gave the hand of
cordiality to the abadessa, while the cardinal, who seemed anxious to escape from
the contemplation of this lovely young woman's desponding melancholy, hastily announced his wish for her commencing her
novitiate on the morrow; and while he
spoke the inflexible tones of arbitary command, his averted eyes, turning from a view

of sorrows he could no longer remedy; told the warfare of his feelings; then with a hurried adieu he fled her presence, and retired to the monastery of Santo Valentino, to reside with the monks of that order during his limited stay in the Albruzzo Ultra.

In conformity with the wishes of the Cardinal Gulielmo, the Lady Constantia Rizzato, for as whom her patent announced her to the community she was now to head, entered upon her novitiate on the morrow, according to the established rule enacted by the formulary annexed to the order of Santo Valentino; and in all the apathy of a mind desolated by the annihilation of every hope of temporal happiness, Lady Constantia exchanged the costume of the alluring world, for the probationary habit of an irremediable recluse.

The boarders of this convent attended at this sad ceremony;—amongst them was a young girl who, not very long initiated in the solemn rituals of a conventual life, and who never before having witnessed a scene like this, was so powerfully affected, both from the humanity of her disposition leading her to feel acutely for the sorrows and sacrifices of such a lovely victim, and from anticipated sympathy, in pained apprehension, of such a pitiless destiny being one day her own, that the officiating priest, even amid the ceremony, loudly and severely reprimanded her; when the poor bashful girl, in alarmed confusion, retired behind the friendly shelter of a pillar, there, unobtrusively, to indulge her tears, if she failed to succeed in her efforts to repress them.

But although unobtrusively inclined, this young boarder was, she had caught, in the moment of her reproof, the attention of his eminence; who contrived to cast many a scrutinizing and inquisitive glance at her, even while she believed herself secure from observation in the ambush she had retreated to; and when all summoned to the refectory to partake of the collation given to the community upon this recent event, Sister Olinda in trembling apprehension, still with eager scrutiny, remarked the riveted gaze of the cardinal fixed upon this young boarder, which with alarm the pious *Mónaca* had made her observations of in the church.

The lovely and unconscious girl, relieved

from every apprehended penance and lecture from the late angry Father Lucian, by that subtle priest, himself presenting her with some of the choicest fruits the rich banquet afforded, promptly recovered a sufficient degree of confidence to raise her eyes from their fear-sentenced station; when the first object that struck her view was the Cardinal Gulielmo, standing before her with a basket of sweetmeats, which he gallantly offered to her and Olinda's acceptance.

Olinda blushed through chagrin; her companion· through youthful timidity and grateful feelings ; and the cardinal, in hurried accents, inquired from the wary sister, " Who that lovely and interesting girl was?"

" She is," replied the nun, " the descendant of an illustrious house; Lady Angelina di Balermo, the only child of the late Duca di Montalbano."

The changed countenance of the cardinal proclaimed sudden illness, and the attentive Father Lucian offering his ready arm, his eminence retreated for air into the grounds, and did not re-enter the refectory until Angelina, by the contrivance of Sister

Olinda, had retired from it; and ere dinner hour arrived, the business of the cardinal patron's various vocations had recalled him to Rome; and every circumstance relative to her momentary disgrace in the church had ceased to be remembered by Angelina, until, as she was returning from vespers, Father Lucian slipped a folded paper into her hand.

Angelina turned pale with affright; and her palpitating heart, with anticipating apprehension, hailed this paper as the cruel mandate for some infliction for her misdemeanor of the morning; and, full of this direful alarm, she hastened to inspect her doom, when, to her utter amazement, she beheld the following lines, traced by the unsteady hand of agitation:—

"Should the interesting orphan, Angelina di Balermo, ever require a protector—an adviser—a friend, she will find all in
                              "GULIELMO."

Angelina had experienced such maternal tenderness from the good Olinda during her residence in the convent of Santo Valentino, that she would have deemed it a crime against gratitude, had she failed immediately to give 'this singular note to her inspection.

.. The alarm of the pious nun was now considerably increased for the safety of her interesting favorite, from having her memory stored with many histories of the former libertinism of the cardinal patron; but he was now drawing towards the vale of years; he might have repented, and she might judge him uncharitably.' How to advise she therefore felt incompetent; and all she was assured it was right to do, was fully to instruct Angelina in the character his eminence long had borne; when the innate purity of Angelina's heart led her to determine, that nothing short of absolute necessity should ever tempt her to seek the alleviation of any future misfortune which might await her from the Cardinal Gulielmo's friendship.

The benevolence of Sister Olinda's heart had led her, the very first of the whole community of Santo Valentino, to pity the apparent mental sufferings of Lady Constantia; and, still more, that benevolence led her, in a very few months, to love, with genuine friendship, the very woman who had been sent to usurp her almost indisputable rights, and wreck her fancy's visions of ambition; and in those few months, although the lovely abadessa could not learn the difficult task of forgetting her direful sorrows, she acquired the sublimer one of bearing them with Christian resignation.

Soon, too, Lady Angelina was perceived to be a most successful candidate for the favor of the new abadessa; who, whether from a recollection of how much that amiable sympathiser was affected by her entering upon her probation, or from any other impellent inducements to friendship, not proclaimed by Lady Constantia, but quickly she seemed to derive no comfort equal to that which Angelina's society afforded her; and shortly her friendship found it's highest gratification in striving, by every means, to mitigate those minor evils of misfortune inflicted by the neglect, or reprehensible parsimony, of those unworthy beings, who had arrogated to themselves the guardianship of Lady Angelina.

The exemplary sisterhood of Santo Valentino had, from the poverty of their funds, been compelled, for several preceding years, to dwell in a habitation scarcely considered compatible with perfect safety to reside in; and, from it's ruined state, repairs were pronounced by every artificer as an ineffectual project; but Lady Constantia, soon convinced of the perils which surrounded her, informed the cardinal patron of them; when permission was graciously granted to her to remove immediately, with her community, to a magnificent castle in the neighbourhood, which, with a large revenue, had been very recently bequeathed to this sisterhood, by a religious noble, lately deceased.

This castle, now consecrated for religious purposes, although most beautifully and romantically situated, seemed dedicated to the most cheerless gloom, which, probably, accounted for the almost universally credited report of it's being infested by supernatural appearances of various forms and terrific aspects; but it was now hoped and believed, by all the *religiòso*, that the piety of the Sisters of Santo Valentino would promptly and effectually exorcise the unquiet spirits; and all the proper forms being complied with, the poor inhabitants of this convent quitted certain destruction in their antient habitation, for the chance of escaping it, by combating and vanquishing a legion of evil spectres in their new one.

CHAPTER II.

WITH trembling apprehension all the domestics and young boarders, with many of the nuns themselves, entered the gloomy and stupendous structure henceforth to be distinguished as the convent of Santo Valentino; but, during the first few weeks' residence in this place of expected horrors, nothing occurred to alarm any of the community, but to the abadessa herself, who had many motives for entombing every circumstance relative to the terror she had experienced within her own bosom; and not a single allusion to it escaped her until thrown off her guard by the dismay of two of the young boarders, who rushed wildly into her presence one evening, and whose panic-struck countenances, and trembling frames, proclaimed; even more forcibly than the incoherence of the sentences they uttered, the magnitude of the alarm, which had sent them to the abadessa's parlour to seek protection.

" Oh! it was the most doleful cry that ever appalled the human ear," said the trembling Clarina.

" It was more a groan from the heart, ready to burst in it's own overcharged anguish," said Laurinda.

" But where did this terrible sound assail you ?" demanded the compassionating Constantia, kindly.

" Oh! Madam," sobbed out Laurinda, " it seemed to issue from beneath our feet; from the spot upon which we then thoughtlessly stood."

" But in what part of the convent were you, when you heard it ?"

" In the grounds, Madam."

Lady Constantia started; her countenance assumed a paler hue than grief had tinted it with, and hastily she exclaimed,

" What ! in the cypress grove ?"

" Oh, Madam ! then you, too, have heard it," replied Laurinda, with a look of

increased dismay; " It was indeed in the
cypress grove. The beauty of the evening
inducing 'us' to venture on the gratification
of our curiosity, by exploring many parts
of the grounds which yet have not been
submitted to the cheering hand of alteration, we, after roving unmolested through
many sombre parts, at length determined
upon summoning all our courage, and to
venture into that gloomy but attractive
structure, which terminates the cypress
grove; and we had just entered it's archway, and were about to descend the steps,
when a kind of half-articulated, half-sup-
pressed sigh, stealing round us on every
side, electrified us at once, and arrested our
further progress, though Lady Angelina
would fain have encouraged us to . . . ."

" Lady Angelina!" exclaimed the Prioress. " Was Lady Angelina, then, with
you ?"

" Oh! yes, and she said it was only the
echo of our own agitated respiration; but,
in a moment more, that dreadfully audible
groan broke on our amazed senses: we
waited for no more, but in wild dismay flew
to your protection;—but—but, we know

not what became of Lady Angelina; I saw her fall to the ground in terror. But do not chide, dear Madam, for it was *our terror* that made us inhuman; we had not power to return to her assistance."

Most powerful was the alarm which filled the sympathising bosom of Lady Constantia, upon hearing that Angelina had been left by her companions, in such a moment, a prey to all the natural horrors which such a situation could inspire; and now, with all the trepidation which varied causes for agitation could shake her frame with, the alarmed abadessa proceeded to the cypress grove as speedily as the almost-convulsive tremor of her frame could admit of.

The cypress grove was certainly one of the last places belonging to her convent which Lady Constantia would then have chosen to explore alone; and when our readers become acquainted with the causes which actuated such reluctance, they will cherish no wonder at the chilling creep which passed over the surface of ner frame; or the violent pulsation of her heart, as she entered this sombre grove, where loudly she called on her beloved Angelina, for whose

safety the most powerful anxiety taught
every other feeling to fade into comparative
apathy,—but Lady Angelina appeared not,
answered not. The abadessa's increasing
solicitude and dismay almost amounted·to
distraction. Onward her anguished solicitude led her, still in fruitless search, until
she began her descent of the steps leading
from the archway, in the building mentioned by Laurinda, when, swiftly glancing her
eagerly-seeking eyes around, Oh, rapture,!
she beheld the·loved object of her alarmed
pursuit, slowly and tremulously advancing
through the massive iron gate of this antient mausoleum, with downcast eyes, and
a countenance flushed by the tints of varied
emotion. The abadessa hailed her; and
the lovely Angelina sprang forward into the
extended arms of Lady Constantia, with a
frame trembling, and a heart bounding in
painful agitation.

" Angelina! my friend! whom have
you seen? What has befallen you?" exclaimed Lady Constantia, gazing intently,
with all the tender expression of the most
poignant solicitude, on the interesting and
intelligent countenance of Angelina, who

promptly replied, although her voice was tremulous from the alarm of her late extraordinary adventures,

"My beloved friend must know all; but let us—let us fly from this melancholy, this terror-inspiring spot—and from every listening ear, would I also lead you."

Together, then, Lady Constantia and her beloved friend bent their faltering steps to the grand terrace belonging to the castle grounds; the immense breadth of which, and distance from any spot likely to contain an auricular witness, well suited it to the purpose of confidential communications; where the lovely abadessa, from the narrative of her not less lovely companion, soon learned a tale of interest, and of wonder; and from that moment they embarked together in a dangerous enterprise; and were surrounded by perils of no common magnitude.

As the convent of Santo Valentino had become extremely wealthy from it's late bequest, united with the great endowments which the abadessa brought with her to enrich it, she judiciously resolved to remove every thing from the castle and grounds of this new habitation which could feed the generally-cherished superstitious influence; for, although extreme beauty marked the situation of this castle, it yet was gloomy to a most dolorous degree. It was embosomed in a lofty, almost impenetrable wood, and the whole of the sombre grounds were filled with every fear-inspiring structure and device, which the dark imagination of melancholy could select, to give to piety a saddening aspect. But Lady Constantia, although the child of dire misfortune, loved to behold religion in a cheerful garb, believing "cheerfulness to be, indeed, the health of Virtue."

The abadessa had brought from the late habitation of the sisterhood all their old domestics; and she soon learned that her projected improvements must be made with the full consent of, or else not under the auspices of, the principal gardener, Cardenio; who, bigoted to gloom and death's heads, by no means approved the innovating plans of enlivening the domains, and admitting, from every acclivity, the most enchanting prospects, to charm the eye, and aid religion, by presenting to view the glorious works of the Creator, surpassing all things in wonderous loveliness.

Cardenio had been long a faithful domestic to the sisterhood he served, whom in consequence the abadessa highly respected; and, not wishing to wound his feelings by any exertion of her own authority, she employed an auxiliary to win him to compliance, her lovely friend Angelina di Balermo, who, with scarcely any allowance to purchase respect, contrived, with only the charms of the most inartificial sweetness of temper, and fascinations of manner, with every attractive virtue of the heart, to win and enchain the affections of each individual in the convent, and could command, with the affections, the ready services of every domestic around her; and to her resistless persuasions, Cardenio found he had not power to say a negative; and soon, by the magic of her spells, she led him on to believe each reluctantly sanctioned alteration, when completed, was the most exquisite of human arrangements.

It was one evening, early in the commencement of this cheering task of improvement, that the works had proceeded so

consonantly ,to the wishes of the interesting
prioress and her lovely coadjutor, during
the whole day, that they were induced to
remain, inspecting the progress of those
auspicious alterations, until the hour for dis-
missing the workmen for the night arrived;
when as Lady Constantia was returning to
the house, she encountered that alarm
which we have alluded to. She had missed
her rosary as she was proceeding home-
wards, when the ever active and obliging
Angelina tripped back to seek it for her;
and the pensive prioress slowly pursued
her way, often pausing to listen for the light
footfalls of her friend, when; in turning to
move on; after one of these lingering paus-
es, she suddenly beheld a man, incased in
grey armor, standing before her, with his
visor down.

The abadessa's heart bounded painfully
with alarm; but she repressed a rising cry
of terror, and, recovering promptly from an
involuntary start, summoned every particle
of courage she could find obedient to her
call, and with, at least, the appearance of
firmness, demanded—" What was his business there?"

" I am glad I have not alarmed you," he replied, in a deep, and fear-inspiring voice, " nor have you any thing at present to apprehend from me; but I must be brief in my demand, and you prompt in your decision, since that arbitrary fleeter, Time, presses for speed. —I am here to demand an immediate asylum for a female."

" Why then did you not, at my convent gate, and in a less formidable shape, make that demand, which was never yet denied by the sisters of Santo Valentino to any being who required protection ?" said Lady Constantia.

" To you I can never appear in any shape less formidable," he answered. " It is not for a female who seeks refuge here, that I am come as ambassador; it is for one whom I must force into your protection. In one of the solitary prisons of your convent must you confine her, until you either compel or lure her into professing the religious vows of your order; and for such important service, any reward you claim, in the power of wealth to bestow, shall be secured to you."

" The mystery which encompasses you

would teach me to fear you, and fly, did not indignation inspire me with courage to hold further parley with you," replied the abadessa, with all the calm dignity of offended virtue; "you did well to conceal your face, when you came upon so disgraceful an embassy. I now know not who has insulted the community which I form one of; but go hence, man, and tell your vile employer, that we immolate no victims here. We are not the sordid tools of violence and villany. We practise no base arts to insnare, or betray; no force to destroy. Our altars are unpolluted by treachery or compulsion; nor can all the wealth which vice could yield us corrupt the integrity of our humble order. The convent of Santo Valentino is not, for your purposes, therefore depart."

"Not until I tempt thee, paragon of firmness! further. Although gold cannot lure thee, because you want it not, cannot *Fear* operate upon this vaunted, virtuous stability of thine?"

"Fear!" she calmly repeated. "What can I fear from you? you can, it is true, here rob me, nay more, can aim at my life, but still you have no power over my integrity."

" I have power," he exclaimed, in the determined tones of implacable vengeance; " I have power, whensoever I have inclination, to annihilate thee, or to blast at once thy fondly-coveted reputation for virtues, which you possess not; and to prove such is my power, doubt longer if you dare ;" and he raised his vizor.

The abadessa uttering a piercing shriek, fell senseless to the ground, where Lady Angelina, returning with the rosary, soon after found her. The armed man was vanished, and no one was near to afford the terrified and affectionate girl the smallest assistance. But those apprehensions for the life of her friend, which first chained her by her loved Lady Constantia's inanimate form, at length urged her to fly to the house for aid. The nuns, boarders, domestics, all rushed forth at the call of Angelina. The now universally-beloved abadessa was tenderly conveyed to her cell, where a succession of almost convulsive fainting-fits continued through the night, and at length terminated in a dangerous illness, which seemed invincible for several days; and when at length she recovered from it, such

an increase of touching sadness seemed
visible in her fascinating countenance, her
thrilling voice, her affecting manner, that
all around her mourned in sadest sympathy for her silent griefs.

CHAPTER III.

IT was upon one of those festivals, which in their commemoration steal hilarity into the convent's gloom, the nuns and boarders of Santo Valentino mingled at the social board; and, in the general-wish for mutual entertainment, each individual exerted their mental stores, and less solid accomplishments, in contributing to the day's amusement, in which the austerity of the cloister (except at customary stated intervals, when the community united in orisons) was suspended, and innocent mirth assumed full dominion, giving, in it's present enjoyment, the happy promise that in after thought it would still be cherished with pleased remembrance.

Amongst the numerous anecdotes related
this cheerful day, one held a place which
told a whimsical tale of early love, when
the observant Abadessa perceiving it's effect upon Angelina was to sadden her ever-
speaking countenance with the gloom of
pensiveness, fixed for a moment the inquiring eyes of wonder on her.

Angelina, conscious of having awakened
the attention and suspicion of the prioress,
blushed at her earnest gaze of scrutiny, and
overwhelmed with sudden confusion, yet
scarcely aware of why she felt so painfully
embarrassed, her eyes instantly fell beneath
Lady Constantia's penetrating ones—a sigh,
struggling for suppression, was distinctly
heard to agitate her bosom—the abadessa's
anxious breast heaved a respondent one in
alarm; and poor Angelina retired to her
pillow that night with the distressing conviction of having certainly awakened, by
her (even to herself almost inexplicable,)
emotion, some suspicion in the bosom of
her friend to her disadvantage; and the succeeding day had numbered but few of it's
hours, when the ingenuous Lady Angelina,

no longer able to exist under 'the shadow
even of suspicion, threw herself into the
abadessa's arms, and " implored," in all
the touching simplicity of genuine inno-
.cence, "to know the cause of that marked
and evidently anxious scrutiny with which
she had regarded her the preceding evening."

" Angelina," replied the abadessa, with
encouraging mildness, but impressive so-
lemnity, " I understood, from the testimony
of your own word, that you had imparted
every incident of your life to me."

" And so most assuredly I did, my dear
Lady Constantia, all, every incident, that I
thought of sufficient consequence to fatigue
you with the recital of."

" O! my sweet friend, could that be
deemed of little consequence by you, which
mere allusion or similitude to could teach to
sadden a countenance of the most brilliant
animation, or steal pensiveness over a mind
glowing with the mirth which reigned?
Alas! my dear Angelina, there is yet some
circumstance untold, which, I fear, you
feel shame to acknowlege — something,

perhaps, which timidity impels you to conceal from your friends."

"Dear madam," replied Angelina hesitatingly, "I—I have no wish for concealment, if I had any thing of certainty to reveal. Surely there could be no allusion in
Sister Marian's anecdote of her niece to
effect the power of sympathy over me; for
it only told of — of love, dear madam; and
that, you know, could scarcely affect me,"
and Angelina's blushes became more brightly tinted.

"Why certainly," returned Lady Constantia, "I may suppose, as well as hope,
it could not, since you have but a short
time completed your seventeenth year, and
have been almost two years in the retire-
ment of this convent. Before your entrance
here, you could scarcely have thought of
love; and since, I may pronounce you have
had no opportunity, as here none of mankind have appeared to you but in the repelling forms of old conventuals."

"In that, dear madam, you are mistaken," replied Angelina artlessly; but with
emotion; "for I have even seen in my se-

-clusion here, the most interestingly handsome man the world can boast of; but there were circumstances attending my accidental view of him, which I felt as an intruder (although an unintentional one,) I had no right to betray, and therefore I concealed the incident."

"Never can I censure that reserve which any honorable feeling dictates," said Lady Constantia; "but Angelina, to return to the pensiveness which attracted, alarmed, and led me to the painful suspicion of your being less ingenuous than I fondly believed you—the anecdote told of the niece of the amiable Marian having, at the age of fifteen, fallen romantically in love—to this anecdote you listened with more than common interest; it robbed you at once of all your cheerfulness; nor could the whimsical method the parents of the young innamoràta devised for curing this weakly-cherished passion beguile you of a mirthful smile."

"Ah! my very young friend, can you wonder at surmises thus awakened? Can you refuse to that friendship, which powerfully interests me in all that concerns you,

to disclose the coincidence this story had
with your feelings, to inspire such sympathy ?"

"Indeed," replied the blushing Angelina, in a voice faltering with the timidity
of genuine bashfulness, " I can scarcely
define the sensations which led to the effect
that awakened your kind and flattering solicitude; but I will try to account for all to
you."

"I believed, dear Lady Constantia —
that is, I mean, I was apprehensive there
might exist some similitude between sentiments which I have cherished for a most
amiable man, and those so imprudently encouraged by the silly niece of Sister Marian;
and that fear made me thoughtful, as in
alarm I questioned my unconscious heart;
but had I not perceived your observation of
my seriousness, and clearly seen you suspected me of something wrong, I should
promptly have reasoned myself out of my
terrible alarms, as an impossibility, as I
have often before done, whenever the suggestion has arisen like an appalling phantom to my view; for well I know his affec-

tions were, long devoted to a most fascinating woman, to whom he was united just
before I was banished from my uncle's castle; and that union, I fondly believed, had
conferred all possible happiness upon him,
until beholding his misery, I had the grief
to conjecture that death too probably had
prematurely torn from him the woman he
adored."

"Beholding his misery! When? Where,
Angelina?" demanded Lady Constantia,
in eager, trembling emotion.

"Before the high altar in the dilapidated
church of our late habitation, I beheld him
kneeling, (a few days prior to our removal
hither,) a sadly, sadly altered, miserable
man!"

"O, merciful Heaven! forbid the realis-
ing of my foreboding apprehensions!" exclaimed the abadessa in trembling emotion;
then, after a successful effort to resume the
appearance of composure, which yet she
could not feel, she gently, but impressively,
added, "O, Angelina! can you persevere
in any reserves to me?"

"Assuredly I cannot, my best friend,"

replied the amazed and agitated Angelina ; but if, in the narrative of my juvenile adventures, I should weary your patience, allow the recollection of it's being in obedience to your wishes to plead in my excuse." !

" When calamitously for many a child of sorrow, as well as for me, my dear, dear father repaired with his legion to give support to the Christian arms in the Morea, he permitted my accompanying my much respected governess, Signora Viletta Tolmezo (whom the living death of immeasurable distance has since, alas ! deprived me of) to visit her family in the republic of Venice, as the contest in the Morea was a Venetian one with the Turks, and therefore constant intercourse kept up from thence with the senate, he could more securely and even expeditiously correspond with me in the republic, than if I remained, during his absence, in Tuscany.

" Amongst my father's vassals had been a man, named Richardo, so attached to his lord, that, a few years prior to my birth, he had rescued him from perishing, in con-

sequence of a sudden eruption of Mount
Ætna, (while my father was visiting Sicily)
at the imminent peril of his own existence;
but in which act of affection, inspired
humanity, his own sight was sacrificed,
and he, alas! became blind for life!

"From that afflicting period, Richardo
was the most respected inmate of the castle
di Montalbano (which, I believe, I before
told you was always our family's favorite residence,) and from that sad period too, all who
loved my father—and that was all who knew
him — became the willing attendants of
poor Richardo; and, from my earliest years,
I shared with his successive faithful dogs
the task of guiding the unfortunate man;
and never, my beloved, grateful father used
to say, ' was his child so dear to his heart
as when paying some part of his incalculable
debt of gratitude to his bereaved friend.'
And, in truth, so fond was my inestimable
parent of seeing me in this employment,
that, when I was only five years old, he had
my portrait taken by the most eminent artist in Florence, in the act of leading the
poor blind, venerable Richardo."

A deep sigh burst from the heart of the abadessa; and a visible agitation vibrated her frame.

" That portrait, so precious to my father, the Duchessa di Montalbano had sold, with all she deemed the lumber paintings of the castle; but no one, I must suppose, thought that picture worth purchasing, since those whom it represented were prized only by my father and those who loved him."

Another struggling sigh burst from the bosom of the abadessa; and, with an air of increased interest, she entreated Angelina to proceed.

" A short period prior to my dear father's unfortunate expedition against the infidels," continued Lady Angelina, " poor Richardo died; and, in his last moments, bequeathed to my especial care my last little companion in his service, a beautiful and affectionate dog, named Fedelio, who had been the sole surviving progeny of his long faithful leader, and had been his unerring guide for three years prior to Richardo's death; and, indeed, I proved a

tender guardian to my little charge until,
expelled from the castle of my forefathers; I
was bereaved of the power of being kind to
any one.

"But I affect you, my beloved friend;
therefore, I will hasten with you from Montalbano; and accompany Signora Viletta,
attended by my charge Fedelio, to Signor
Tolmezo's, where we all met a most cordial
reception; but yet I could find no pleasure,
no comfort there, although all the numerous family of Tolmezo, then, only seemed
to live for my comforts, my accommoda-
tions: but my dear father was gone
to the seat of terrible warfare, and, while
he was in peril, his child could not be
happy.

"The residence of Signore Tolmezo was
most beautifully situated between Treviso
and Venice; it had been a new purchase
since my governess had visited home, and
she was as anxious to become acquainted
with all it's environs as I could wish her;
for in our *tête-à-tête* excursions, in which
we wandered away from the villa di Tolmezo, was now centred my chief comfort;

for then I could unrestrainedly talk of my
father, and rave of his fondly languished-for
return.

" It was in one of these pedestrian expe-
ditions that Signora Viletta and myself,
straying further than prudence sanctioned,
we found ourselves surprised by fast approaching twilight; and, in our eager rapidity to regain the Tolmezo ground, we, in
our natural perturbation, mistook our way,
and by some erring turn found ourselves in
the high road to Treviso. In vain we wandered to regain our lost path, until we were
suddenly surrounded by a numerous gang
of gipsies.

" Our apprehensions were indeed most
powerful, for they seemed a formidable
host; but, contrary to our direfully alarmed
expectations, they merely gabbled over our
future destiny, asked us for some silver, directed us to find our lost path, and civilly
bade us good-night.

" But very far along our regained path
we had not proceeded, when, to my inexpressible dismay, I discovered the absence
of my precious charge Fedelio. In vain I

called, in vain I sought him, until from a
mound, which commanded a full view of
the public road, I found my painful antici-
pations realized; for, even approaching to
darkness as it was, I beheld from thence my
poor favorite in the custody of a gipsy
man; and now, regardless of every fear
but that of losing Fedelio, I flew back to
the public way, and, borne on the wings
of anxiety, swiftly overtook the formidable
troop, and rapidly made my way to the
treasure I sought, when appearing so unexpectedly before the ruthless spoiler, I succeeded in snatching Fedelio to my arms.

" The grateful transports of my favorite
repaid me amply for the exertions I had
made for his rescue; but of short duration
proved our mutual joy; for the purloiner
savagely tore him from me, and swore ' I
should never more possess him.'

" Several of the women now surrounded
me, and as I wept and pleaded for the restoration of Fedelio, and offered them the
whole contents of my purse for his ransom,
they gabbled together in a language unintelligible to me, and still, without cere-

mony, as they gabbled, taking from my dress my different ornaments, as they seemed to attract their fancy; while some of the older ones encouraged me to proceed with them, 'assuring me that at the *osteria* *, which was not far distant, the savage man would be compelled to restore my dog.'

" Thus led on by these delusive hopes, I fortunately, though childishly, had proceeded a considerable length of way, unmindful of the perils which encompassed me, (for the gang, unheeded by me, had turned into a lonely way leading to a gloomy forest,) when a young man, of noble and sweetly prepossessing appearance, with several attendants, all in full speed, on horseback, suddenly emerged from a thicket before us.

Although by this time the fleeting twilight was gliding fast into the sombre shade of night, yet, aided by the coming beams of a rising moon, the whole of the group was perfectly distinguishable, when my appearance, so materially differing from those

* Inn.

who encompassed me, with my supplicating gestures and mournful tones in pleading, attracted this stranger's interest and attention. Instantly he reined in his steed's swift career, rode up gently to me, and, in a voice of melody and benevolence, inquired ' the cause of my distress, and how he could yield me assistance?'

" In the joyful tone of hope, now changed to certainty, I related the nature of my distress, in which I comprised how precious the poor animal was to me, from being the sacred bequest of the blind Richardo to me. .

" The benevolent stranger evinced an increasing interest, and ordering his attendants to enforce the restoration of my dog, Fedelio was promptly given to my fast-locking arms. .

" My gratitude was enthusiastic; and, after my first wild transports of joy had tranquillised into more rational and calm sensations, I artlessly entreated the stranger to accompany me to my governess, and then to the villa di Tolmezo.

" With genuine kindness and urbanity,

he 'promptly, acquiesced in ,my 'requests; and, after making the gipsies restore almost all the articles they had purloined from me, we set out towards, the spot where I had fled from Signora Viletta,' but 'scarcely had we proceeded a mile, when we met 'my almost - distracted governess in pursuit of me.

" The stranger having rescued me from what all considered impending destruction; he was received at the villa di Tolmezo not only with hospitality, but the most flattering welcome. He was but just returned with the victorious Venetians from Peloponnesus, and was then detained in the republic as a witness upon a court-martial, from hastening to convince his parents of his safety, ' whom,' he said, ' resided near Rome; and that he was returning from an excursion to Treviso back to Venice, when he was so fortunate as to extricate me from the danger which seemed to encompass me:' and the subtle family of Tolmezo believing, from his retinue, this stranger a man of consequence, and therefore likely to prove an advantageous alliance for one of their beautiful unmarried females, pressed him, in speculative hospitality, to give up his intention of an immediate return to Venice, and to make the villa di Tolmezo his osteria, at least for that night; and as the court-martial he was detained from his parents by, was postponed for the arrival of other witnesses from the Morea, he assented; but ere he did so, with that propriety which ever marked his conduct, he informed them on whom they bestowed their hospitable kindness, by graciously announcing himself to be ' Fredrico, younger son to Conte di Alviano,' one of my father's dearest friends."

" It was then Fredrico di Alviano! Go on, go on, my friend," exclaimed Lady Constantia; her countenance blanched to the tints of death.

" It was indeed — and, and you know him, dearest friend?" said Angelina, in a voice of interest.

" Yes, *I do know* him!" repeated the abadessa, in a tone of horror.

" Oh, holy Virgin!" ejaculated the amazed, the terror-anguished Angelina,

" what, what of evil can you know of
him ?"

" I am not to be questioned, presump-
tuous girl! Leave me, leave my presence, now and for ever!" exclaimed the
hitherto gentle abadessa, in a tone, and
with a look of vehemence, little short of
phrensy.

Lady Angelina arose to obey with all
the dignity a self-acquittal of meaning to
offend inspired, yet with her affectionate
heart keenly wounded by such unmerited
severity; but, when she reached the door,
her lingering eyes turned on the abadessa,
still fondly hoping to be recalled — one
glance alone changed every feeling to sympathy.

" Oh, my beloved friend!" she energe-
tically exclaimed, " I cannot, cannot leave
you thus."

Instantly the abadessa flew into her extended arms, fell on her neck, and wept
the bitter tears of anguish; which at length
the sweetly-soothing kindness of the affectionate Angelina changed to those of ten-

.derness; when, with a voice softened from every harsh tone of distracted passions, yet broken by powerful emotions, she entreated the promptly appeased Angelina to forgive her.

"Angelina," she then said, "I do know Fredrico di Alviano—I once knew him as a man gifted with every precious store from mental excellence—I now know him for—Oh, holy saints! what do I now know him for? Angelina, sweet sister of my affections, the name of Alviano is treasured in my heart with a power of tenderness that death only can extinguish; yet it is stamped there too with envenomed hatred, with recoiling horror! My miseries, Angelina, deep and direful, admit no consolation; for they are hopeless: even the comfort of participating sympathy is denied me, since, bound by a spell of sacred import to the silence of secresy, I dare make no confident; but by your interesting story, I trust, I shall be sufficiently composed to hear it's termination to-morrow. The name of Fredrico di Alviano I shall then be better prepared to hear; and fear not it shall again overwhelm me with the phrensy of irritated feeling, to lead me into being unkind to you."

CHAPTER IV.

THE abadessa of Santo Valentino deceived herself in her supposition of being suffi-
ciently tranquil on the morrow to hear the
termination of Lady Angelina's little history of her juvenile adventures, and apprehended attachment; for many, many a
morrow glided by ere she could summon
the degree of fortitude necessary to sustain
her through the idea of voluntarily listening to the name of Fredrico di Alviano pronounced : and Lady Angelina, on her
part, experienced no trivial share of reluctance to the task of recommencing a narrative, in which, from Fredrico di Alviano
being the hero of, was so evidently calculated to wound the anguished feelings of her
sorrow-stricken friend.

But at length, in compliance with the request of Lady Constantia herself, Angelina proceeded with her little history, which she commenced in the tremulous accents of benevolence, fearing to inflict pain.

"The deliverer of poor Fedelio," she said, resuming her narrative, "seemed to fascinate every one at the village di Tolmezo; and in return, pleased with the reception he met with there, he cheerfully assented to prolong his stay for several days, although the most anxious to embrace his parents and other friends, after the dangers he had escaped in the Morea, where he, had most honorably distinguished himself among our successful countrymen; for, as you know, perhaps, the Alvianos are Venetians as well as the Balermos. And in this from day to day lengthened visit, I found, in aid of my debt of gratitude, other incentives to awaken my regard for this young man; for each renewed conversation relative to my father, but more and more betrayed how highly he was loved and estimated by Conte Fredrico, who, in all the admiring exultation of his friendship, recounted to me such feats of my parent's prowess in battle, that my heart glowed with the fire of enthusiastic triumph for such a hero being my father; until, in fond and flattered fancy, dwelling on the scenes of glory he had shone conspicuous in; I thought upon the perils he had braved, and learned in tremulous conviction, that the safety of my parent was dearer to my heart than the hero's deeds which fame recorded.

" The conte too had told me, that my father would soon return; but he knew not the decrees of fate — my father never returned to his expecting child: Oh, no; led on by the impetuosity of his valor, he, with his amiable and unfortunate friend, Conte Nicastro, rushed too fatally forward in pursuit of the retreating foe, when, surrounded and overpowered by numbers, they fell — and I — I lost my all!

" Conte Fredrico informed me too, " that his father was about to remove his residence from the villa di Alviano to Bessarno Castle, where, so near in proximity to the Castle of Montalbano, he trusted, from the long existing friendship of our families, we should often meet; and that, there too, he should have .the 'happiness of introducing, as a candidate for my admiration and esteem, the lovely and amiable Lady Violante St. Seviro, his destined wife."

" Yes, Angelina, she was his destined wife — the destined wife of two di Alvi-anos," exclaimed the abadessa : " a parent's arbitrary mandate bound her in the solemn engagements of sacred promise to one — love gave her willing vows to another; and yet — but go on, sweet friend; I will interrupt you no more."

" This intelligence made me most happy," continued Lady Angelina, endeavouring to abstract her thoughts from the perplexing suggestions of speculating wonder, which the mysterious words of Lady Constantia inspired : " for, as he announced his Violante a model of female excellence, I felt assured he had found his counterpart, and therefore his wedded life bore the auspicious promise of every happiness.

" And another thing which added considerably to my pleasure, in the anticipation of the conte's happy union, was awakened 'by the idea of finding in his bride a friend of years more congenial to my own than my dear governess; for, as he said Lady Violante was all perfection, I gifted her in fancy with my favorite age nineteen, when beauty has arrived at the full blossom of it's spring, and the mind is expanding fast into something more than the mere opening buds of mental endowments.

" But too rapidly flew away the short period of Conte Fredrico's visit; but we could not wonder that his wish and ours, for his protracted stay, could not coalesce. His departure was to take him nearer to the woman he adored; but it was to wrest from us a friend we all regarded. He did depart, and gloomy appeared every scene, which he had brilliantly enlivened with the magic of his fascinations; but he left me the bright prospect of my father's speedy return to cheer me — that promised blessing filled up every vacuum in my heart, gilt every scene with Hope's bright burnishing, and by that dearly-cherished expectation I was delusively happy.

" At length the carnival of Venice arrived, but not my father; and, sad with disappointment, I accompanied the Tolmezos to that gay scene; and, young as I was, Signora Viletta took me with the elder and quiet part of her family to partake in a rational degree in the amusements of this festivity, which was celebrated with even unusual splendor, inspired by the triumphant joy of all, from the recent glorious termination of the direful calamities of war.

" It was the second evening of my mingling in this dazzling scene of captivating pageantry, that Signora Viletta, her eldest brother, and myself, observed two *cavalières* land from a *gòndola,* and we each, on the instant, recognised Conte Fredrico di Alviano in one of them; but, although well aware we could not be mistaken, since the form and movements of no other man could so emulate his gracefulness, yet, as this signore was masked, my governess and her brother considered it prudent not to accost him until certain there could exist no mistake; and as the voice would prove conviction, since none could sound in melody.

like Conte Fredrico's, they determined upon following him, to listen for his speaking.

" But as if, in punishment for the scepticism of Signore Tolmezo's prudence, the conte walked on in total silence, apparently busied in attentive observation of the numerous masks who passed; and, by this scrutiny, he was providentially led to perceive a man mingled in the crowd, with an unsheathed stiletto seeking concealment beneath a long mantle he wore, cautiously but steadily following another man, almost bent by senescence, yet venerable in the aspect of his accumulated years."

" The conte's attention was now riveted upon this evident assassin, and was, by that attention, led to pursue his footsteps, as we became the anxious re-treaders of the conte's; and, by this general power of attraction, we were at length all drawn in our succession of pursuit into an almost-deserted street, adjoining Santo Marco's Place, where promptly, by not perceiving his following observers, the bravo aimed the fell blow of death at the bosom of his venerable victim; but Conte Fredrico, with an arm nerved by humanity and valor, averted the pitiless stroke of premeditated murder.

, " But the assassin had two terrible associates, who had perceived Count Fredrico's observation of their accomplice; and had, in consequence, attended our footsteps, and who now, most unexpectedly, attacked the valiant champion of defenceless age; but ere the conte's own companion, or Signore Tolmezo, had time to unsheath their swords in his defence, he had drawn his own, and had wounded one of his antagonists severely in the breast, and had disarmed the other.

" Never, no, never can I forget the valor he evinced in that terrible moment; on the humanity which inspired all his actions in the next; for the moment he had secured himself from the vengeance of his direful opponents, he turned to the further protection of the venerable victim of their sanguinary project; but, alas! while the conte was engaged in his own defence, the first discovered bravo had so far succeeded in his atrocious design as to sheath his stiletto in the side of the old man; but, foiled by the pity of heaven, it had touched no vital part, and weltering in his blood, supported by some benevolent spectators, Conte Fredrico now beheld him; and never in possibility can I describe the tenderness of his conduct to the poor wounded man, or the sweetly-affecting sympathy portrayed on his eloquent countenance; for now his mask was off.

" The poor old wounded man announced his dwelling near, in the very street the direful scene had been performed in; and now every sensation that had agitated the bosoms of the (by this time numerous) spectators all concentrated in recoiling horror; for, as the old man moved forward to gain his home, he recognised in the assassin the conte had wounded—and who had swooned from the agony he suffered— his own, his only son! and now, though direfully convinced that son had conspired with bravos to terminate his life, no power could tear the merciful, the affectionate parent from his miscreant son; but fondly he clung to him, ' promised him pardon for all his offences, would he but look up, would he but let him hear his voice once more.' In short, dear Lady Constantia, all recollection of his own situation was lost in tender solicitude for this dire unnatural son. O! it was a terrible scene to have been doomed to witness! many among the spectators it melted into tears; while others trembled in dismay, on finding there could exist in human kind a wretch so vile in turpitude to spill the blood of his very own parent."

" Did Fredrico tremble? Did no forebodings agitate his soul?" lowly, but emphatically, murmured out the abadessa in a fear-inspiring tone, that vibrated on every sensitive feeling in the bosom of Lady Angelina, who shuddered in appalling conjecture; but, fearing to distress or offend, she hushed the rising tumult in her mind, and answered:—

" He did all that humanity could prompt, all that a heart replete with every virtue could inspire; but I beheld little more of the scene, as Signora Viletta, overpowered by horror, fainted, and was instantly conveyed home by her brother: of course I accompanied them; and from the confusion that prevailed, and from the rapid increase of spectators, the conte never recognised any of us in our masks, and Signore Tolmezo, from the untoward circumstance of his sister's fainting, was so occupied in anxiety for her, that he never once remembered to speak to the conte, or ask for his address.

" Both my dear governess and myself had been too much overpowered by the distressing scene we had witnessed there, to feel a wish for again partaking of the hilarity of the carnival, and we mingled with the revellers no more ; but the other individuals of the family joined in the festivity each evening, but nothing more of Conte Fredrico could they see, nor were their morning inquiries for him more successful; and we all most naturally concluded he had departed from Venice.

" But, ere the carnival was ended, a rumor prevailed that my dear father was returning by a different route from the other troops, and my kind uncle wrote to announce the glad tidings to me ; and nothing now could subdue my impatience to be on the wing for Montalbano. I never felt the inclination to exact obedience from those whom fate placed in a situation that bowed them to submission; but certainly, in this instance, either my wishes sounded arbitrarily, or the kindness of all led them promptly to oblige me, since with rapidity each arrangement for our departure was made, and no one seemed to look even regret for the pleasures I was leading them to relinquish.

" The joyful hope of soon beholding my tender parent illumined each prospect of this glad journey for me; for it was a glad journey to me; since I knew not I was doomed, alas! to meet with sad and direful disappointment, and my fond expectations never, never to be realised!

" On the evening of my first day's journey from Venice, when my companions, Signora Viletta and her beautiful niece, Minora Tolmezo, had alighted with me from our carriage, to view from the summit of a hill we were about to descend the glorious exit of a brilliant sun, Fedelio, who was playfully scampering in Joy's wide range, suddenly began to scent the ground;

and almost immediately disappeared amid the underwood of a closely interwoven copse, when soon the sound of his uncontrolled raptures proclaimed that he had, at no great distance, met a friend.

" A curiosity which we found invincible influenced us all to learn who was the friend thus presented to the view of the joyful Fedelio. Hastily, therefore, we sought out the path explored by him, yet prudently accompanied by some of my male attendants; but many paces I had not proceeded, when it darted into my imagination that, in possibility, it might be my father, when my fluttering heart flew to bid him welcome, assimilating my speed to affection's rapidity of flight, and on whose wings I reached Fedelio's retreat several moments before my companions — when, O Lady Constantia! I beheld poor Richardo's bequest lying prostrate before Conte Fredrico di Alviano, looking up with joyful, and, as I thought, grateful emotion at the conte, who, reclining on a bank of aromatics, was anxiously striving to win the dog into silent greetings, lest he should disturb a venerable monk, who appeared in an untranquil slumber, although tenderly supported in the arms of this benevolent young man.

" In all the trembling confusion of embarrassment at such an awkwardly abrupt interruption, I would have promptly retreated, could I have effected my purpose undiscovered ; but the conte had beheld me in the moment of my appearance, and, by starting in surprise, at once dissipated the slumber of poor Father Marsilio, his preceptor, who had found a momentary respite from pain and mental suffering by a short repose.

" For the conte, accompanied by his preceptor, had been on his journey to the villa di Alviano, to see his parents, and, as the military business which had detained him so long in Venice at length was terminated ; and the conte's own established attendants he had left in Venice, to protect the venerable man whose existence he had saved from assassination, and whose life he had reasons to believe still menaced by the vile emissaries of his unnatural son; and with postillions, guide and *camerière*, recommended by the master of the house where he had lodged at Venice, he and his preceptor had set out about two hours previous to my departure from that city, and about the same lapse of time had intervened between my being thus led to find him, and his having been suddenly overturned by the carelessness of his driver,. where there was no apparent cause for such an accident; and by which unfortunate event, Father Marsilio was severely bruised, and had received some very material internal injury.

" Their guide then led them to the secluded spot Fedelio most providentially found them in; and then set out, with the postillions to the last post, which was at no considerable distance, where, he said, ' he could quickly procure another carriage, or get that which they had been overturned in immediately repaired;' and, at the same moment, *il cameriere* had set out full speed for a surgeon in the neighbourhood, whom the universally-informed guide assured them ' was deemed eminently skilful.'

" The places of the supposed destination of these individuals were at no very considerable distance from the spot where the distressing accident had occurred, yet two hours had nearly elapsed, and not one of them had returned. Suspicions of their integrity had now stolen into the minds of the holy father and his pupil, when many circumstances, which had past almost unheeded by them, recurred in painful confirmation of these suspicions. The carriage contained much of the conte's and Father Marsilio's property, which the former bestowed no thought upon in the moment of afflicting anxiety for his friend; but now they both believed all was devoted to the depredations of those who had taken it away, and that they themselves were probably trepanned into that sequestered spot to become, in the advance of night, a further prey to this apparent plot of villany.

" The poor conte was now in the most distressing perplexity: he believed he had every evil to apprehend from villany; and he had no means of defence, since all the fire-arms had been conveyed away in the carriage and in the holsters of the attendants' saddles, his friend was unable to

move, and he was incapable of leaving him
to his fate.

"Pain both of bodily and mental suffering, with the oppressive heat of the evening, combined in subduing the holy man,
and falling into a train of anxious musing,
he insensibly dropped into a deep, though
uneasy slumber; during which Conte Fredrico discovered, in terrible conviction of
their peril, the marks of newly-shed blood
sprinkled on the grass beneath his feet, and
staining the shrubs around him; and soon
these dreadful sensations of alarm were
powerfully augmented; for, in gazing around
upon this horrible confirmation of his direful fears, he suddenly beheld, glaring from
amid the roots of the aromatics upon which
himself and friend rested, a pair of immense
human eyes.

"Conte Fredrico commanded sufficient
self-possession not to start, or betray any
symptom whatever of observation, although
little doubting that the bank on which he
sat was the covering sward of a subterraneous retreat of brigands; nay, perhaps
the sepulchre of those whom they had im-

molated : but promptly he now resolved that the moment he could suppose the robber had descended from his reconnoitring post, to snatch Father Marsilio in his arms, and, in defiance of inflicting increase of pain by the movement, to bear him into the open road, and there to seek for assistance from some haply passing traveler.

" In the moment almost of his forming this intention, the appearance of Fedelio dissipated his agonising alarms; for he brought with him the certain hope of instant succour. Yet still he beheld the glaring eyes; yet retaining his firmness even in the joy of expected deliverance, he warily betrayed no emotion to influence his appalling observer until my appearance dissipated his caution.

" You can readily imagine, my dear Lady Constantia, that it was not in that direful place I learned all the particulars of this singularly-perilous situation; and having heard of the destruction my providential arrival most certainly removed Conte Fredrico and his venerable preceptor from, can you wonder that the conte not only ex-

pressed, but felt joy, at seeing me : **but**
still, unknowing the numbers of the am-
bushed brigands, in alarm for my safety;
as well as his own, he with prudent precipitance hurried us all to the carriage, where
we placed the suffering father as commodiously as possibility would admit of; and
in which we now, for the poor monk's sake,
slowly proceeded; but the heiress di Montalbano had then safe escort in numerous
attendants, and we had nothing in the form
of banditti to apprehend.

. " The place of my night's destination
was the villa of one of my father's friends,
il Marchèse di Castrioto, where I knew every
friend of mine would find a cordial welcome,
and the holy father tender and efficient
care; thither therefore, with the approbation of my governess, I invited him and the
conte to accompany me. The distance to
the village was so inconsiderable, and it's
promise of every comfort for Father Marsilio so alluring, that my proposition was
gratefully acceded to."
. " Flattering indeed was the reception
given by *il marchèse* and *la marchèsa* to me,

and most benevolently kind their welcome
to Conte Fredrico and the reverend sufferer:
and at this villa awaited my arrival a letter
from my dear uncle, ' announcing to me,
that so vague and unsatisfactory he found,
upon investigation, the reports relative to
my beloved father's change of route, that he
recommended my remaining at the villa di
Castrioto until he could send me more authentic information, lest, by proceeding, I
should miss the earliest opportunity of em-
bracing my dear father.'

" In pursuance of my uncle's advice,
which I' was in the pleasing habit of implicitly attending to, I remained ten days at
the villa di Castrioto, in the constant society
of Conte Fredrico di Alviano, when the
more I saw of him the more my admiration
of his external graces was awakened; and
the more causes I found for conviction, of
his mind being the precious repository of all
human excellence: but in those short days,
beguiled by the magic of Conte Fredrico's
fascinations of half their hours, I first caught
a glimpse, and with dismay it flashed upon
me, of the real disposition of Minora Tol-

mezo; but, even then, no presentiment
whispered an anticipating sound of what
that disposition could induce her to perform, or how deep was the plot laid by her
and the males of her subtile race, ere she
became my companion on this journey.
But then most glaringly she evinced an
anxious wish (even urging her to overstep
the boundaries of delicacy's sweet and becoming restrictions) to monopolise the whole
attention of Conte Frederico, and, though
perfectly informed of his sacred engagements with Lady Violante, to ensnare his
affections, and lure him from his constancy;
even ill-concealing her spleen, at his civilities to me; which, from his attachment to
mo dear father, and from the circumstance
of his being, through my means, so cordially
received a guest at the villa di Castrioto,
would have been impossible for him not to
pay me.

" But on the tenth evening of my visit at
the villa di Castrioto, a courier arrived from
my uncle, to announce his having obtained
some farther intelligence, of a more satis-

factory nature, and he thought I might pursue my journey home.

" Nothing now in existence could restrain my impatience to be gone, and as early as the convenience of the marchese and marchesa would permit my feelings of urbanity to appoint the hour, I recommenced my way to my loved home: for hope told me, there would my beloved father be, to meet his child; but hope proved a delusive flatterer.

" The gratitude of Conte di Alviano to me, for proving, by the ordination of merciful Providence, the means of rescuing him and his friend from what he had reason to suppose inevitable destruction, so filled his heart, so softened it to kindness for me, that, in the moment of separation, it awakened more evident regret at parting from me than from either of my companions, and that awakened new cause for spleen in Signora Minora; for the tone was malicious in which she said, shortly after our departure from the villa di Castrioto.

" ' I fear Conte Frederico di Alviano is a

mere man of the world; for I perceived his attentions were always proportionate to the rank of the person he paid his unmeaning adulations to.' "

" There she wronged him," said Lady Constantia. " He then was guileless; and the attentions he paid you were the spontaneous effusions of his heart. He believed you a something almost beyond even mortal perfection; and he gave you homage as to a seraph sent from the spheres, to show how sweet, how fascinatingly sweet, could prove the combination of beauty, youth, and heaven-formed innocence."

Lady Angelina now blushed, in joyful surprise, and her heart fluttered it's gratitude for an eulogium she almost hoped was but the repetition of what Conte Fredrico had uttered; but, in timid bashfulness, anxious to turn from a suggestion she felt had too much elated her, she rapidly changed the theme of their conversation to the direful disappointments she was doomed to encounter at the Castle di Montalbano.

" Alas! my friend," she continued, "no beloved father awaited me there. My heart, my arms, expanded in vain; I had no father to fill them—oh! no, only some of his adherents, who had attended him to the Morea, had arrived; and instead of my father, they brought me a letter from him, written before the last day's battle, and final victory of the Venetian arms. It was a sweet kind letter — Oh how affectingly sweet and kind! Yet with almost anger I received it; for I was irritated by disappointment. It was but a trifling gratification as a substitute for my beloved father's presence, and I received it not, as I ought to have done, with sacred reverence; for it was the last address of my last parent to me."

"That dear, and now for-ever-venerated letter I cannot show you, beloved friend; for as the first of all my heart's prized treasures, I had placed it in the very centre of a highly-valued casket (it had been my mother's own), to make the companion of my exile. In it were no treasures but such as were so to an affectionate heart. It contained the portraits of my parents; an ode addressed to me on the first anniversary of

my birth, by my sainted mother ; a journal,
copied from a kind of diary, kept in chalk,
by poor Richardo, of the first year of his
calamity; with all the letters my kind indulgent father and my uncle had ever addressed to me. To me this casket and it's
contents were more precious than the
estates I was bereaved of; yet the Duchessa
di Montalbano rudely and unfeelingly
wrested them from me, on the morning I was
banished from my late father's palace."

The flush of indignation that glowed upon
the cheeks of this amiable and lovely young
woman, at the recollection of the unmerited insults she had received, soon found a
refreshing shower steal softly over it, spring-
ing from her heart, in sad remembrance of
all she had loved, and had been torn from.
But hastily chasing those unbidden drops of
pained affection away, she continued her
recital, in an assumed voice of cheerfulness,
which a strong exertion of firmness had procured for her.

" My sainted father's last letter was written
in that tender language of fond paternal affection, in which he always addressed his

child. After giving me the sweet and soothing comfort, of assuring me of his perfect health, and of his flattering hope (alas! how fallacious was that hope), ere many weeks elapsed, to embrace his child again; but he never more embraced her—never, never. Oh! why do I thus increase your sorrows with mine? I was only to tell you of Conte Fredrico, and still, still I wander into a repetition of my griefs.

" In that letter of my sainted father, dear Lady Constantia, what do you think he said? Why, he bade me ' seek out the expected inhabitants of Rossarno Castle, the moment of their arrival there; but from all to select out Fredrico di Alviano, as the individual amongst them he most wished me to regard.

" ' I would have you, my child,' this now-sainted parent said, ' to venerate this young man, for his eminent virtues. I would have you cherish him in your affection with a sister's love, for his excellence claims your highest esteem, and your gratitude will aptly pay him the incense of it's most lively inspirations. Yes, my Angelina, your gratitude! for you owe him some, and I, knowing the attachment of my child to me, can well imagine how incalculable she will deem the debt, in the dread hour of battle, Angelina, when death gleamed in sanguinary horrors around me, and had too surely aimed it's mortal shafts at many a valiant hero, the intrepid Fredrico di Alviano saved your father's life, my child, at the imminent peril of his own.'

" My beloved friend, now you know that this Fredrico saved the life of my parent, you cannot, no you cannot wonder, that my interest, my regard, my veneration for him, should have arisen to the very summit of enthusiasm. No, surely no; and whatever may since have been his fatal errors, I will still find in the heart of gratitude a vail to hide them from my view; and still must that grateful heart proclaim it's conviction of his not meriting all the censure which may, alas! have fallen upon him."

" Impatient became my inquiries for the arrival of the expected inhabitants of Rossarno Castle, but they came not while I was heiress of Montalbano, and when I became no longer the heiress of my ancestors, I had no means to evince my gratitude to any one — I no longer possessed a home to entertain the preserver of my parent in — I had lost my father, and all was lost to me —"

"But, although I was no longer a being of any consequence in the world, the amiable Fredrico forgot not the regard which, as my father's child, he felt for me; for I know that he and his parents made many and many a fruitless effort to obtain an interview with me; but the new Duchessa di Montalbano frustrated all their kind and friendship-inspired projects."

"At length, dear Lady Constantia, a very short period prior to my expulsion from the castle of my uncle, the duchessa one day informed me, with a kind of mysterious exultation I could by no means account for, 'That Fredrico di Alviano was to be united on the morrow to Lady Violante.'

"No," exclaimed the abadessa, in trembling emotion; "the direful morrow never arrived to unite Violante and Fredrico."

"Not united!!! — Lady Violante and

Conte Fredrico not united!!" exclaimed Angelina, starting in amazement, and blushing with sensations she had yet to learn the definition of. " But I believed they were, dear friend," she tremulously added, " and my sad heart ceased for a moment to sorrow for it's own woes; for, in truth, it did rejoice at hearing of this union — ' For now,' I mentally said, ' Fredrico, the preserver of my father, will be happy.' "

"Happy!" repeated the abadessa, in a tone of solemn wildness, that struck with the chill of horror to the heart of Angelina, " Fredrico can never be happy — not here — not hereafter!' "

The feelings of Lady Angelina were dreadfully tortured; but, with a successful effort at self-possession, she arose from her seat, filled out a glass of water, and carried it to the abadessa.

" Beloved friend, revered, respected Lady Constantia, drink this," she mildly said; " let it's effect assist in recalling your firmness, your recollection, your submission to the decrees of Providence. That Fredrico di Alviano can never be happy here, I have,

alas! too many presaging fears for it's sad
truth to doubt; but of his happiness hereafter, who? what mortal can pronounce?
Behold the pendant cross upon your bosom!
what does that proclaim? The sufferings of
a Mediator, who died in anguish, that the
repeated sins of man might be forgiven!
Remember Fredrico what you once knew
him; and, remembering that, can you
doubt of his repentance? If indeed he has
sinned, and if a contrite penitent, who
can disbelieve forgiving mercy may await
him?"

The trembling abadessa drank the water
—her fleeting senses returned to their boundaries; when, struck, by the mild fascinations of Christian charity, presented to her
recollection by Innocence officiating as it's
priestess and it's votary too, she meekly
sunk upon her knees, and, with pious fervor, prayed for the first time that Fredrico
di Alviano might repent and be forgiven:
and, while sinking to this sacred employment, the lovely Angelina silently withdrew, and softly closing the door, bent her
pensive steps to her own chamber, there to

mourn for the misfortunes of her interesting friend, and for the still more dreadful ones of Fredrico di Alviano, which thus cruelly subjected him to the dire suspicion of having committed inexpiable crimes.

CHAPTER V.

WHEN at length the restored composure of the sorrow-stricken abadessa permitted her to request the conclusion of Lady Angelina's narrative, her lovely friend continued.

" The sudden flush of joy, which glowed on my cheeks, it's uncontrolled irradiation from my eyes, on hearing of the approaching marriage of those I believed long and fervently-attached lovers, awakened the most powerful curiosity in the mind of *la duchessa*, who was warily observing me, and who imperiously demanded what had occasioned that aspect of joyfulness in me.

" 'Your intelligence,' I replied; 'for it is joy to me to hear that Conte Fredrico's happiness is to be insured to-morrow.'

"Her comment on my answer, was—a blow! given with all the phrenzy of a maniac. Yes, Lady Constantia, it is too true, the low-born Minora Tolmezo dared to strike the offspring of Theodore di Montalbano: then, then indeed was his daughter humbled.

"Under the protection of the benevolent abadessa of Santo Valentino, I have never had occasion to betray one great leading fault in my disposition, pride: but, indeed, dear Lady Constantia, I am, alas! very, very proud. I knew it not in the days of my prosperity, but when I became poor, and was insulted, I discovered I was haughty to excess, easily irritated, and slow to be appeased, by those who ceased, for one instant, to remember the respect which, as the child of such a father, I, claimed from all.

"The rank my dear infatuated uncle had raised Minora to, did not shield her from my contempt, as a being too much beneath me, to condescend to resent the indignity she had insulted me by, to her; but not in Christian charity forgiving the trespasses of others, I—oh! Lady Constantia, I am indeed ashamed to tell it to you, but never have I ceased repenting of that terrible fault—I reprehensibly complained, in the bitterness of my wounded pride, to my uncle, of the insult the child of his brother had just received; when he, ever fondly attached to that brother, and parentally partial to me, most highly resented the duchessa's misconduct; so thus, most improperly, I caused a serious disagreement between him and his most ill-chosen wife.

" Almost immediately after this unfortunate *discórdia*, which I strove with all my power to efface from my dear uncle's remembrance, and restore amity to where it should for ever reign; he became alarmingly ill, and shortly after fell into that state of weakness, in which he lost the energies of his once-animated mind: then it was the duchessa announced her prospect of adding to my uncle's happiness by progeny, then it was that she and her subtile relations planned my exile.

" By the death of my beloved father I

had lost my right, as heiress apparent to the Montalbano possessions and titles; and by this promise of expected progeny to my uncle, I was likely to be excluded from my presumptive also, and then, though only in expectancy of my total exclusion, the Tolmezos treated me as if the intervening heirs were born; and I was cruelly expelled from the castle of my forefathers, and to the then inconsiderable, and consequently obscure, convent of Santo Valentino, I was privately banished; where, under your protection, I have found, that could I forget a tender, beloved, indulgent parent, could I banish from my remembrance the direful misery I witnessed, as the anguished portion of the amiable Fredrico di Alviano, and could I cease to see you the drooping child of irremediable affliction, I should have learned that I could still be happy."

When Lady Angelina paused, as if come to the final close of her narrative, the lovely Constantia threw her arms around her, and tenderly pressed the interesting girl to her bosom—

" Oh! that I could indeed make you

happy !" she gently said—" then, then
you would not have a grief to sorrow for. But, my beloved Angelina, you
have not yet informed me, by what means
you came to behold Fredrico di Alviano in
our late convent. But mark me, Angelina, I only wish for as much information
on this subject (remembering how you before alluded to something of an interdict),
as the genuine feelings of honor you possess
may sanction your revealing."

" Then that dear friend may now be all :
for as you know Conte Fredrico, know the
errors, perhaps crime, he is accused of,
even sanctioned by honor, in the pure es-
sence of Gratitude's best feelings, I will announce all that I witnessed, in the full conviction of it's supplying more than presumptive proof of his perfect unblemished innocence.

" Before your example taught me resignation, and your kindness contentment, I
often wandered alone to the church, to
kneel at the shrines of our blessed saints, to
implore their intercession for my being inspired with fortitude, to bear misfortune

E 5

without feeling it so very poignantly as I
did, and to pray devoutly for the repose of
my dear father's soul.

"One evening, while I was thus seriously, thus awfully employed, my thoughts
were suddenly recalled to sublunary apprehensions, by the sound of quickly-advanc-
ing footsteps. I know not why it is that
we should feel any sensation like shame
at being discovered in the private performance of our sacred duties; but certainly I
experienced something like such an inexplicable emotion, and instantly started from
my knees, and sought concealment amid
the mouldering rubbish that time had thrown
from the ruined window which you may remember in the shrine that joined the great
altar; and scarcely had I effected my
purpose, when I beheld a man rapidly approaching through the aisle which led immediately from the house.

"The distraction of his air and movement led me at once to believe him a pursued assassin, who had flown thither for
sanctuary; but as he drew nearer, the wildness, inspired by mental anguish, which he

evinced, changed my supposition to that of his being an unfortunate maniac, broke from those who had him in their care.' I know not which suggestion dismayed me most, my heart tremulously bounded with sicken‑ ing apprehensions, and my short and un‑ equal respiration became difficult to silence into the stillness that would not betray me, when this terror-inspiring object I recog‑ nised to be—Fredrico di Alviano: but, oh! direful fate, how changed!

" The Conte Fredrico, whom two years since I had left at the Villa di Castrioto, in all the bloom of health and beauty, smil‑ ing in all the animated vivacity of a man greatly, deservedly happy, now stood be‑ fore me, pale, haggard, attennuated, with agonizing grief, horror, and despair, legi‑ bly, touchingly portrayed upon every line of a countenance eloquent in proclaiming the feelings of his heart.

" Grief at this piteous, unexpected 'tran‑ sition, enchained my every faculty, and I possessed no longer power to fly, or to an‑ nounce my presence. Immovably trans‑

fixed by horror and amazement, I remained
to behold a scene that can never, no never
be effaced from my remembrance.'

'" Conte Fredrico' arrived in a line with
the altar, beheld it, and instantly stopped,
arrested by it's view. How in one moment
did every worldly, every turbulent passion
cease, or, changing their nature, all
swiftly concentrate into reverence for the
great object before him. Upon his knees
he meekly sunk to pray—to pray: oh!
how devoutly did he pray ! The influence
of the sacred intercourse soon was visible ;
the Christian's resignation diffused itself
in mild affecting calmness over a countenance so lately distorted by despair, tran-
quillising it to a submissive serenity, that
promptly thrilled to the heart of sympathy ;
while by degrees his grief-dimmed eyes
emitted rays so bright, so resplendent, they
seemed beams of the sublimated fire of virtue, sparkling in consciousness of some
heroic greatness, approved by him whose
holy spirit could alone inspire it ; and as
he arose from the altar, a smile beamed over

his countenance, a smile so sweet, so celestial, it surely was formed in heaven, and only given to innocence to wear.

"Conte Fredrico now moved from the altar, and from my sight, with dauntless tread, with resignation and firmness, inspired by that consciousness of meriting heaven's favor, which only the truly good can ever know.

"From that hour, my friend, I was convinced the amiable preserver of my parent's life was unfortunate; and from that hour my increased interest for him became almost painful to my heart, for in it was mingled an unceasing anxiety, a melting tenderness, which the happy Conte Fredrico had never awakened.

"And now, Lady Constantia, you do know every incident of my life, every secret of my heart, and know the motives I had for feeling interested in the anecdote of sister Marian's niece. I before had believed every sensation I experienced for Conte Fredrico were all inspired by gratitude and pity; but when I heard an almost

child could love, I was—I now find courage to confess it to my friend—I was
alarmed; I trembled, and feared I had
been deceived by my security, and that
it was possible I had incautiously, imprudently, and, alas! reprehensibly, permitted a premature passion to steal into my
unsuspecting heart, for a man whose affections I had always known were devoted
to another, and who was long, as I supposed, the husband of that very woman of
his choice."

Lady Angelina now caught the hand of
the abadessa with tremulous grasp, and
panting with painful emotion, while her
eyes sought the ground, and her cheeks
were suffused with the brightest glow of
sensitive bashfulness, she eagerly, but
touchingly entreated her " to prove indeed
her friend, by not deluding her, but, as she
knew all, to tell her faithfully, unhesitatingly, if she believed her attachment to
Conte Fredrico more than the inspirations
of gratitude and pity: if she believed her so
unfortunate as to have heedlessly given

her tenderest affections to a man whose heart had been long and irrevocably devoted to another."

But ere the equally-agitated abadessa could reply to this affecting appeal to her friendship; a lay sister entered the apartment with a packet, which had just arrived by express for the abadessa of Santo Valentino.

Lady Constantia opened and perused the packet, when the flush of surprise at receiving it, was quickly succeeded by the pale hue of death, sudden agitation heaved her bosom, tears filled her eyes, and throwing her arms around the alarmed Angelina, she mournfully exclaimed—

" Friend of my choice, and gentle soother of my sorrows, I am, alas! doomed to lose you. You are demanded from me; and I ought to rejoice, because it's promise is auspicious to your interest; but I love you too well to endure, without a murmur, the afflicting pang of parting with you. But your uncle recalls you, and I lose my beloved, my interesting Angelina within one hour."

A letter from the Duchessa di Montalbano announced " the duca being dangerously ill; that he had obstinately refused to
follow any medical advice, until he should
see his niece again; and that, therefore,
the Lady Angelina must set out for the
Castle of Montalbano in one hour after the
delivery of that letter, and under the escort
of those sent to conduct her to the presence
of her uncle:" and in this mandate to the
abadessa, was a letter to Lady Angelina
herself, couched in the following terms.

" Angelina di Balermo,

" At the earnest request of your
dying uncle, I have been induced graciously
to forgive your past unprecedented inso-
lencies to me, and to grant you admission
once more beneath the roof of my castle.
You therefore cannot but, in justly-
awakened lively gratitude for this my unpa-
ralleled kindness, come unaccompanied by
your former unbecoming supercilious arrogance, and, from my condescension, learning to be grateful, acquire the necessary
knowlege of your own dependent situation;

and, remembering the respect you owe your superiors, come in meek humility, bending with that just submission, which, as my right, I am determined to exact from all beneath me.

" If you really possess that affection for, the now almost idiotised duca, which you have hitherto so loudly, and diligently proclaimed, and professed to feel, you will not delay (although you have now no numerous vassals to expedite your moment of departure) your setting out, with those whom, I have kindly sent to conduct you thither, in one hour after you receive my command for hastening to my castle.

" I am henceforth, as you deserve it,

" Your kind,

" And condescending aunt,

" MINORA DI MONTALBANO."

Montalbano Castle.

The gentle and affectionate Lady Angelina was too sensibly affected by the intelligence of the dangerous indisposition of an uncle whom she sincerely loved, and by the agonizing thought of being torn from her beloved friend, Lady Constantia, and the amiable Suòra Olinda, to attend to the unfeeling insolence of a letter that made her weep, although it did not make her angry, and with streaming eyes she set about the sad preparation for her almost instant departure; a sad preparation, which the sympathising tears, and unrestrained lamentations of her numerous friends in the convent were not calculated to cheer.

At length the dreaded moment for the departure of the universal favorite arrived, and even the inspirations of Piety's submission to affliction could not restrain the general burst of grief that now echoed through the convent's wide range; for Angelina, their friend, their companion, their sympathiser and consoler in trouble, their participator in joy, their example in patient acquiescence beneath the correcting rod of adversity, their peace-maker, their earthly treasure, was tearing from them; and old and young, superior, nuns, boarders, and domestics, all, all believed " they ne'er should look upon her like again."

But ere the highly-afflicted abadessa

yielded her beloved Angelina in solemn trust to those unwelcome beings sent to escort her to Montalbano Castle, she charged her, " never to forget, that in her she had a zealous affectionate friend, in the Cardinal Gulielmo a powerful protector, and in the Convent of Santo Valentino a home."

Eloquent were the thanks of Angelina, for they sprung from her grateful heart, and as they descended to the parlour where the companions of Lady Angelina's journey waited for her, she again entreated the abadessa " to remember her sacred charge; to forget not the mausoleum."

" Fear me not," said Lady Constantia, solemnly. " And do you forget not this my last admonition,—exterminate, with all the powers I know your mind is gifted with, the unfortunate but tender attachment you have unconsciously cherished; exterminate it, as you prize your every hope of happiness, since Fredrico di Alviano is unworthy of your love !"

The heart-chilled Angelina now entered the grated parlour with her agitated friend, and there beheld Father Ezzelino di Tol-

mezo, uncle and confessor to the Duchessa
di Montalbano; Anfania, a favorite woman of la duchessa's; and a monk, who
seemed so lost to worldly cares and ceremo-
nies, that he sat with his arms folded across
his breast, with his head bent towards the
ground, and his cowl o'ershadowing every
feature of his face.

.. Solemnly and affectingly the lovely
abadessa gave up her inestimable charge,
into the especial care of Father Ezzelino.
The moment for departure was arrived;
the carriage, attendants, luggage, were all
in readiness; Lady Angelina heaved her
last sigh on the bosom of the weeping abadessa and Sister Olinda, gave to their grief-
chilled hands her last grateful and tremulous pressure, attempted to articulate some
tender messages to the weeping friends she
had just bidden adieu to in the refectory;
and Father Ezzelino was bearing her away
in his arms (for grief, and unwillingness yet
to go, had robbed her of the faculty of
walking), when the hoodwinked monk approached the powerfully - affected abadessa—

" Doubt you longer my power of vengeance?" he lowly said, raising his cowl.

" Treachery!" Lady Constantia shrieked;
and ere she could accomplish her intention,
of snatching Angelina from Father Ezzelino, who had borne her from the parlour,
her terror-struck feelings deprived her of
respiration, and she fell into the arms of
Sister Olinda in a swoon; from which she
did not recover till Lady Angelina was too
far distant from the Convent of Santo Valentino to be recalled.

CHAPTER VI.

LADY ANGELINA distinctly heard the abadessa shriek, and felt almost assured she heard her articulate a sound like " treachery!" but although uncertain of the latter, she was convinced of the former, and struggled to get free from the confessor, to return to her friend; but the ungracious priest's strength was too potent for her to extricate herself from his firm grasp.

" It is only the hysteric shriek of romantic grief," he sternly said. " She, as superior of a pious community, ought to have her thoughts too sublimated to allow such temporal trifles to discompose her serenity ; and you, most boastingly-dutiful young lady, I should have imagined, would have felt more of that vaunted duty and affection for your uncle, than thus to wish to linger with a friend of yesterday, to protract, and thereby render abortive, the power of medicine over his complaints, since well you know he has been seised with the maniac caprice of refusing the aid of medicine till he beholds you, cruel and ungrateful girl as you are."

Lady Angelina, feeling this reproof was not altogether unmerited, blushed in shame, restrained the impressive wish of flying back to the arms of her kind friend, suppressed the violence of her parting sorrow, and Father Ezzelino had no longer reason to reproach her for unwillingness to proceed with the rapid speed of dutiful impatience, to attend the couch of her invalid uncle.

The varied unpleasantness of her reflections so occupied the mind of Lady Angelina, that many hours had passed away in traveling, before she observed that the hoodwinked monk had not formed one of the companions of her journey; but not feeling any interest about him, she forbore to make any inquiry relative to his absence, or in any way to attempt the dissipation of that gloomy silence which Father Ezzelino seemed determined to persevere in; since the carriage was loaded with books of science, and he devoted himself diligently to intense study, or at least the appearance of it, nor once bestowed a look, a word, or even the most trivial attention, upon his lovely charge; and if an inadvertent observation, or spontaneous exclamation escaped Anfania's lips, he silenced her at once by a stern rebuking frown.

But at night, when they arrived at their place of destination for repose, Anfania resolved to make ample amends for the restraints of the day, and to give her talking faculties a double share of indulgence, for the long and gloomy embargo laid upon her precious words by Father Ezzelino. The chamber in the inn they stopped at, allotted for Lady Angelina, contained two beds, which the arbitrary confessor ordered to be occupied by her and this favorite abigail of the duchessa's; who so well was tutored by her lady, that, taking from Minora her tone of respect for Lady Angelina, the moment they entered the room for the night, she burst at once into a torrent of insolent familiarity.

"Thank Heaven!" she exclaimed, "my girl, we are at last left to ourselves, to have our sociable chat together, and I am sure I want recreation, after my dull and fatiguing journey to that convent after you; where the infatuated noodles made as much fuss at parting with you, as if you really were somebody, a something worth grieving after. The saints be good unto me! but there was as many lamentations at parting with you, as much weeping and wailing, as if you were taking all the endowments of the Institution away with you. Just like the fools about Montalbano, who howled for weeks after you and your charities; as if you left no soul behind at the castle to give a canting word of cheap comfort to the afflicted, or the alms of ostentation to the poor. But, as I said, ' you might as well be away for them as not, since you no longer had a mite yourself to bestow.' "

Angelina, well aware of the impertinence

she was doomed to experience from la duchessa and her satellites, had wisely resolved
to meet them all with the weapon most
likely to foil them—silent contempt. She
therefore now listened to Anfania with an
appearance of the most provoking philoso-
phic indifference, although her heart was
sensibly affected by this disclosure of the
grief of the vassals around Montalbano at
losing her, whom they had indeed known
from her earliest days as the gentle almoner
of benevolence, " with a hand open as day
to melting charity."

Anfania next proceeded to criticise Angelina's night-cap and traveling dress, until that lovely being, taking up her rosary,
calmly and piously sunk upon her knees, to
perform her last duty of the day to her
Creator, and all whom her religion taught
her to address, ere she sought repose.

Anfania was severely mortified at this most
unexpected interruption to her premeditated
strains of impertinence; for, dreading some
unpleasant penance by the award of Father
Ezzelino, should she profanely disturb her,
she (although most unwillingly) forbore to

do it; but the moment Lady Angelina arose from her sacred employment, she eagerly exclaimed,

"The duchessa is in the family way again; and the wise ones say, ' she certainly will have twins this time.' You know, I suppose, the lovely Lady Minora is dead? Oh! she was a beauty! and those who remember your infancy say, she set off the gold cradle, and all the fine things your fickle fortune delusively nursed you in, considerably more than you did; and that I can readily conceive, for you could have been but an ordinary sort of a child, inclining to rickets, I doubt not, or worms, or fits, or something."

Angelina had not before heard of the death of her infant cousin; and although sincerely grieved that her uncle should have experienced so severe an affliction as the loss of his child, would not encourage Anfania's familiarity by any comment upon her communications, but still persevered in silence, listening to an infinity more of impertinence, until, wishing to regulate her watch, she inquired of Anfania "if she could tell her exactly the hour?"

" Fiddle de dee! about hours !" exclaimed Anfania, " I am telling you about
your family, and you are so unnatural as
not to attend to me, when I am giving you
the pleasure of hearing of your relations.—
I can tell you, that your dear uncle is grown
more frightfully hunch-backed, more fanciful, more ridiculous, and more weak in
body and mind than ever. And, for my
part, I hope, if he does not betake himself
speedily to a better world, that they will
adopt the excellent plan they have had in
contemplation, and at once take out a sta-
tute of lunacy against him."

The chilling shock of horror thrilled to
the affectionate heart of Lady Angelina, on
hearing that such a project of consummate
villany was suspending over her beloved
uncle; yet she suffered not the feelings of
her mind to betray themselves, and still apparently uninterested, she hastened to bed,
as if anxious to seek repose.

" For then," said Anfania, who continued speaking, " the duchessa need not be
under such restraints; she might then have
all her own family about her, and then she

might go where she pleased, and do as she
pleased; and so she ought; for she ought
to be indulged in every thing, to recom-
pence her for marrying such a fright: she,
the finest creature the sun ever shone upon,
sacrificed to a hunched-back lunatic! for
what signifies his titles and riches; she
might have done much better; for, now in
her twenty-third year, she is come to the
full blaze of her beauty, and it is quite dazzling to behold her; and she dresses with
such taste too, and so superbly: Lud! what
a contrast there will be between you! The
clumsy jewels of the old duchessa your mother are all new-set most magnificently, and
she wears them in such profusion, so beautifully dispersed about her drapery, adorn-
ing them, not they her, and looking all the
time like the rising sun in resplendent glory;
while you, you! will look by her like a
shabby star, endeavouring to twinkle through
the clouds and murky vapors of a foggy
night. Ah! she is so perfectly the queen
of love, that every one is of opinion she
might have married some king or emperor
at least, since every man who sees her is dis-

tracted, for her. There, for instance, is
Conte Fredrico di Alviano has literally gone
crazed for her. Ah! many and many a
letter I have carried from her to him, to re-
ject his suits of love; so, when he found she
really would not listen to him, he cared not
what became of him, and so in despair
plunged slap into all the enormous crimes
he has since committed. And there too is
the Prince di Belcastro, whom your old
plotting father meant to insnare for you, has
become her voluntary slave, and has been
led so far by his love in pursuit of her, a
already to ask for the reversion of her hand
when the poor shattered animal her husband
dies."

This torrent of invidious impertinence
had, as it was intended, it's full effect upon the sensitive heart of Lady Angelina.
Keenly and indignantly she felt the disre-
spectful, the irreverent terms in which her
beloved heart-homaged parents were mentioned; the idea too that her mother's
jewels, which she had long been taught to
look on as her own, should be thus degraded
in the adornment of the worthless Minora,

was a source of deeply-felt mortification to her; but the inflicted wound that rankled most painfully was contained in the allusion to Fredrico di Alviano.

" Was it, could it be in possibility, that what Anfania related was true? Could the superficial acquirements, the blandishments, and inferior beauty of Minora di Tolmezo have seduced his affections from the peerless Violante St. Seviero (whom suspicion led her to identify in her beloved abadessa of Santo Valentino), and ultimately plunge him into the perpetration of crimes? Alas! alas! and had Fredrico di Alviano really committed crimes? Oh! it was, it surely was impossible." And now the heart-rived Angelina, wishing to indulge in uninterrupted meditation upon the possibility of Fredrico di Alviano having really committed crimes, affected deep and overpowering drowsiness, and soon so well counterfeited a profound and tranquil slumber, that the enraged and disappointed *la cameriera;* after striving with all her might to awake her by her noisy movements, and flashing the candle in her face, found herself com-

pelled at length to the dire penance of silence for the remainder of that night.

The succeeding day's journey was performed to the infinite annoyance of Anfània,
in as profound a silence as if the holy father
Ezzelino was preparing himself and party
for the solemn community of La Trappe;
and so the next was passed; and indeed
each day, until the evening of the last one
of their journey, when, as twilight was making rapid advances towards the approach of
night, and that they had for some time entered into the romantic and extensive Forest
di Montalbano, Ezzelino condescended to
inform Lady Angelina, that, ere they proceeded to the castle, he must call at the
monastery of San Stefano, to take up the
justly-celebrated physician, Father Jeronimo, whom the Duca di Montalbano had
consented to see as soon as she arrived at the
castle.

The holy father, in the innovating character of a speaker, directing the postillions
fo proceed up an acclivity, from the summit
to which branched off a path-way to the
Dominican convent, they slowly and cau-

tiously obeyed; when Ezzelino alit, and ordering the carriage to a mound, the situation of which he took infinite trouble in pointing out to the attendants, and where he ordered them to await his return; then desiring one of them to accompany him to the monastery, as the way to it was lonely, he hastily entered the path in view; and the carriage slowly wound it's way to it's place of stationary destination.

Almost immediately upon their arrival at the mound, Anfania, after looking earnestly around for some interesting object, declared she beheld the chimnies of her mother's cottage, and that she would avail herself of the confessor's absence to run and see how she did, as she had left her very ill when she set out for Santo Valentino. Then requesting one of the three remaining attendants to accompany her, she sprang from the carriage, ran down the declivity; and, with the companion she had selected, soon was out of sight.

Angelina perfectly remembered that Anfania's mother had a cottage in the vicinity of San Stefano, and had heard her speak of

her mother's illness repeatedly, during their
journey from Santo Valentino; so that she
experienced no degree of surprise at the step
Anfania had taken; although she did of
alarm, at being left alone in the carriage in
such a lorn, fear-inspiring situation; and
now the meditations of Angelina became of
no very pleasing aspect, since the sombre
appearance of the scene around awakened
the busy recollections in her memory's stores
of many a tale her nursery's legends had
presented to her infant ear, of the cruel ex-
ploits of dire banditti in that very forest.

The heart of Angelina now throbbed
painfully the passing seconds of Father Ezzelino's protracted absence. She had heard
the chimes of San Stefano's announce the
departure of three quarters of an hour, and
yet he came not, neither did Anfania re-
appear; and, in those tedious moments of
actively-anxious observation, as she looked
from the carriage, she beheld the postillions,
who were hired with the horses at the last
post, in earnest consultation, and the two
attendants warily scrutinising them with
glances of alarmed and alarming suspicion.

At length the chimes of San Stefano's announced another quarter of an hour was gone for ever; when instantly a distant whistle was heard, and a responsive one, more approximate, distinctly given.

Instantly the two attendants flew to their horses, for they had alighted, when they commenced this stationary service, remounted, and placing themselves with a presented pistol by each postillion, commanded them at their peril not to move, or answer these signals of villany.

The apprehensions of Lady Angelina now were fast horrorising to dismay, when, in the moment of fearful alarms, a man in the habit of a Dominican lay brother advancing, almost breathless with the apparent haste he had made, hailed the attendants with a demand, "If that was the Holy Father Ezzelino di Tolmezo's equipage?"

Upon being answered in the affirmative, the lay brother proceeded to inform them 'He had been sent to announce that Father Ezzelino being detained longer than he had expected, by the absence of the reverendo pàdre Jeronimo; he desired the carriage might go round to the convent-gate, and there to wait for him, as a place of more security than the spot they were in."

The postillions were ordered to proceed; when they sullenly desired to be instructed in the way, since they knew not one step of it: the attendants now declared their inability to afford such necessary information, since they had only been taken into the service of the Duca di Montalbano a very few days preceding their accompanying Father Ezzelino upon that expedition they were only then returning from, and they knew nothing of that part of Tuscany they then were in.

"A precious set of fellows, I must confess, to be employed by travelers," replied the lay brother gruffly, "to know nothing of geography beyond the longitude of your noses: so I must prove your polar star, and trot myself into a consumption in the service of hopeful ignorance."

"You need not endanger your precious health either, mèlto amorándo fratéllo in Cristo," replied one of the postillions sarcastically, " since there is a seat on the luggage in the front of the carriage that your reverenza may occupy."

The fratello bounded into the seat he was jeeringly invited to; the carriage moved slowly down the declivity from the mound, then took a winding way through a rugged and narrow defile, so limited in breadth that the horsemen could not continue on each side of the carriage, as they before had done, but were compelled to retreat behind it; but a little anxious for the safety of Lady Angelina, and a great deal for their own, they kept as closely after it as the badness of the road, and the darkness of the fast-coming night, would admit of.

The way along this defile seemed endless to Angelina; for the moments are tedious which are passed in alarm: but at length the horses seemed to start forward from the slowest motion of necessary caution into the winged speed of the fleetest coursers, darted over a draw-bridge, which was raised on the instant the carriage cleared it, and ere the following attendants, not aware of the sudden spring forward, could prevent their being cut off from the power of proceeding.

The moment poor Angelina heard the resounding noise of the actuating machinery of the heavy portcullis, anticipating horror struck with direful force upon every faculty of her dismayed senses; and, in all the wild tumult of anguished terror, she looked with almost phrensied eagerness for objects to confirm or dissipate her direful apprehensions.

But, alas! no hooded friar met her view; nothing to indicate an entrance to a monastery; for here, on the instant she looked from the carriage-window, she beheld a mustachoed centinel of formidable aspect, armed for warfare, who, obtaining the friendly signal from the leading postillion, sounded a bugle shrilly, to announce to the other guards the approach of expected guests.

The agony of Angelina's mind seemed now to threaten the annihilation of her senses, when the carriage stopped, a door was opened, and she beheld a man of grace-

ful appearance, who instantly vaulted into
the vehicle, and placed himself beside her.

"Fear nothing, most interesting, most
fascinating Lady Angelina," said this intruder, in a voice of melting kindness:
"although the aspect of alarm surrounds
you, although the appearance of many ills
encompass you, believe my power here is
absolute, and that I, can and will protect
you from every evil which can in possibility
assail you."

"O! speak not ambiguously to me,"
faintly articulated the parallised object he
meant to comfort: "tell me, O! tell me
where I am? what evils await me? and
how you can secure me from this threatened
danger! Tell me, tell me all! convince me
my gratitude is your just claim, and in true
sincerity it will pay it's debt."

"Let the most solemn and sacred bond
the heart of an honorable man ever conceived, now guarantee my faith and my
power to protect you," he impressively replied; "but not until I have the happiness
of seeing your naturally alarmed spirits resume some degree of composure, can I

venture to disclose to you all that you require."

"Composure! O, heavenly saints! when shall I acquire composure?" exclaimed the agitated Angelina, bursting into convulsive tears, and sobbing bitterly, heart-rendingly. From the time this intruder entered the carriage, it had proceeded up a sort of mazy, winding acclivity; and now having reached the summit, and entered upon a platform surrounded by a rampart, which concealed the dwelling from the view of those below, it stopped before the door of an apparent fort, or kind of military habitation.

CHAPTER VII.

As the sounding of the bugle had announced their arrival, a tall, majestic looking woman, whose attenuated form and sallow complexion proclaimed ill health, opened the house-door, and came forth to receive them: her dress was neat, but in it was singularly combined a mixture of Fancy's chaste taste and phantastic wildness. She appeared to be about forty years of age, but neither hope nor fear could find encouragement from her countenance; since in that was legibly portrayed the unvarying calm of apathy; or if, to an accurate observer, a change was ever visible, it was in the unsettled expression of her eye, that told the secrets of an unsound mind.

She now stood at the door like an automaton, mechanically to take and put away the small packages delivered to her.

Angelina's intruding companion now descended from the carriage, when light fully
shining on his face, she discovered him to
be the very attendant who had accompanied Father Ezzelino to the convent — a
man who had, during their whole journey
from Santo Valentino, evinced the most
marked and earnest solicitude to provide for
her comforts, and to bestow every attention
upon her which the humble station he was
placed in could sanction; and, by thus
awakening her gratitude, had led her to
bestow more observations on him than she
otherwise would have done.

"Mother," said this young man, tenderly bearing the terror-anguished Angelina from the carriage; "Mother! come,
assist me to comfort this treasure I have
brought you."

"Comfort!" she repeated; "your father is not returned, Orsino; he is gone to
the deep waters, to look for that man they
murdered amongst them: and where am I
to find comfort? I thought you, too, were
gone on some bad mission, and then I

needs must begin to slaughter lambs my-self."

"Hush! hush! you must not talk thus," said Orsino; "you know my father per-mits it not. Come, come, dear mother, lead on to the parlour, and then look at, and welcome this treasure I have brought you."

The woman now obediently preceded Or-sino, who led the trembling Angelina to a neat parlour, where, as apprehension had enervated every faculty, she sunk into the nearest seat she came to, unable longer to stand beneath her burden of horrorised alarms; when Orsino's mother, for the first time looking at her, eagerly approached her:—

"Are you Hermione?" she anxiously exclaimed. "O, no! I see now you are not. O, no! you are younger, and haply more beautiful than she was: but she was my child, and I thought her lovely. But she is gone, gone; that terrible conte.— the very being who made a villain of her fa-ther, he seduced her from me, and swift he buried her in the grave of penitence."

Angelina, although nearly subdued by horror, and anticipating apprehension of the event of all the mystery which surrounded, and had entrapped her thither, could not but spare from her own anguished sorrow the feelings of benevolent sympathy for that direful calamity, which had thus, apparently, bereaved this wretched woman of her reason.

" You distress Lady Angelina by indulging in this wild loquacity," said Orsino, tenderly taking his mother's hand. "Come, come, dear mother, exert your firmness, recal your recollection; you know, when my father comes, he will not suffer it."

" O, no!" she replied, " he will not suffer me to feel. I must not remember what I was — what I am — on her who is lost to me. — No, he would transform me into a statue of insensibility, and so I appear before him; but still I have a heart, not callous as his is. — O, no! on mine all is stamped, and yet it is not broken. And so I distress you, and you weep for me, young and pretty thing; but keep, keep your tears for your own woes; for you will want a river of them if you should come to know Fredrico di Alviano, since all who know him may rue the day they ever breathed in this world's vale of misery!"

The wretched maniac had now conveyed a blow to the heart of Angelina she was little able to sustain: the shudder of receding life crept through her frame, the pale hue of death stole over her beauteous countenance, and only for the timely and humane exertions of Orsino, she certainly must have fainted.

When Lady Angelina had recovered from her threatened indisposition, so perfectly as to admit of Orsino's quitting her, without apprehending danger to her from his absence, he left the room; first desiring her " not to fear his unfortunate mother, who never injured any one."

His mother smiled mournfully on him as he now departed, then seated herself by a table, upon which she rested her aching head, and closing her eyes, soon seemed to lose all traces of her sorrows in her accustomed semblance of apathy.

But very long poor Angelina was not

doomed to the sole society of this terror-inspiring companion, (for, notwithstanding Orsino's assurance, she could divest herself of fear, when thus left to the mercy of a confessed maniac,) since half an hour had scarcely elapsed from the moment Orsino had retired, until a most strikingly handsome and elegant looking young man, dressed in the garb of taste and affluence, entered the room, and hastily approaching the trembling, heart-rived captive, with an air of tender courteous kindness said: —

" Would I could see you bereft of your alarms, Lady Angelina, since here you have nothing in the form of danger to apprehend."

This man's appearance had awakened a sensation of wonder in Angelina's mind; but now his voice did more — it made her start and color with astonishment; for by it she discovered that it was Orsino, despoiled of his mustachos and disguising domestic's habit, who stood before her, and who now proceeded, by the alluring graces of his conversation and suavity of his manners, to beguile her of her evident alarms; but, while this fascinating mode of conduct in some degree tranquillised the agony of her terrors; it could not lull her sorrows. She felt herself the outcast of her house, thrown by the villany of her foes into some dreadful snare, to separate her from all who pitied and could befriend her; or, at least, if not by forcible detention to conceal her from her friends, to throw a dire stigma upon her fame, which would as effectually sever her from honorable society for ever; for, was she not carried off by a young and handsome man, of captivating manners; and although he was in (at best) but an equivocal situation in life, who could say it was not an elopement with her own concurrence? By the poor maniac's testimony, the father of the family she was thus insnared by was a villain! a murderer! and what had she to expect? Nothing but evil. What had she to hope? Nothing but that the mercy of heaven would quickly terminate her life, since that life seemed now devoted to inevitable wretchedness.

But from this direful contemplation of anticipated misery or death, Angelina was

at length aroused by the precipitate entrance of Orsino's father, followed by another man, when promptly she perceived that
the aspect of neither afforded even the semblance of a balm to alleviate the anguish of
her direful terrors.

Orsino's father was in stature far, far
above the common height of men, and his
form perfect in it's model of athletic symmetry was now disfigured by the savage
dress he wore, which seemed well suited to
display the powerfully muscular strength of
his limbs, for the apparent purpose of inti-
midating, or rather dismaying those whom
in his hostile pursuits he judged it expedient
to subdue. The contour of his head was
exquisitely fine, and ornamented with black
curling hair, trained in the antient Roman
form. His countenance, bronzed with the
unimpeded influence of many a summer's
sun, might be deemed beautiful, if beauty
could be moulded in a terrific cast; yet upon it no eye could seek to rest, but in mingling horror and apprehension find the resistless impulse to turn it's gaze away, and then
to wonder what assemblage of features and

expression could, in the absence of deformity, so disgust the sight, so appal the
heart? Yet it was a face which most une-
quivocally proclaimed strong intellectual
powers; and the acuteness of his large, dark,
and penetrating eyes, bore further testimony
to the depth of his mental endowments; but
the general intelligence it conveyed was almost impossible to develope, so spontaneously it's character arose, so rapid was
it's variations; for, ere you could read it,
it's import was obliterated by a new page of
Art's formation, even still more indefinite,
or haply too abstruse for the common capacity of man to comprehend: it spoke in the
multipled tongues of Babel, and none could
understand their meaning, unless this great
master of Feature's language wished to be
intelligible; then could he gift with almost
magic's power his countenance with expression, and teach it to speak without the
aid of sound in all the fluency of unambi-
guous impressive eloquence.

The companion of this fear-inspiring man
appeared as the most perfect model of deformity, which nature in her wayward fancies

had ever huddled together from the refuse of her stores. His large and squarely-formed head was stubbled over with bright red bristles, making a long, thin, pale visage still more ghastly by it's contrast; for his face seemed blanched by horror at the turpitude of the mind it indexed. His nose, large and hooked, curved over his indented lips, whilst his small grey eyes, set in the oblique direction of deep-designing cunning, scanned and leered in half-closed observation for unsuspecting prey to entrap in the toils of villany.

These men of conspicuously savage exterior entered the parlour without the ceremony of noticing any one in it, until Orsino, in trembling emotion, announced to his father, " that Lady Angelina was present."

The father laughed exultingly, tapped Orsino congratulatingly on the shoulder, exclaiming, " Ho! ho! my amorous boy! this tell-tale agitation proclaims how you approve my project;" then turning to his hideous companion, unfeelingly added —

" Go, Scaltro, gaze on the intended

danghter-in-law of the polite Salimbini, and
speculate, in mortifying repinings, on the
manifest illustration of dame Nature's par-
tialities, in giving y_ou_r formation to the
unskilful Laplander, to distort with his
clumsy chisel into a bad resemblance of his
countrymen's worst form; while to the Cir-
cassian artist, of superlative skill, that creature you behold was given to be moulded
in the most exquisite mould of all their
vaunted beauties."

The savage Scaltro, nothing affected at
the humiliating contrast so rudely presented as a speculation to him; now did as he
was bidden, unconsciously advanced quite
near to the horrorised Angelina, and stared
oppressively at her; for Orsino dared not to
reprimand him for it, since it was done by
his father's command: but the poor maniac,
in some undefinable eccentricity of her malady, seemed now at once to lose all fear of
her husband, while some ideas of propriety
and urbanity floated in her mind.

"Salimbini!" she said, "in the society
you mingle with you have lost every refinement you once possessed — lost even the

courtesy of a gentleman to a stranger, or you would not suffer, much less encourage, this monster of uncouthness to so distress this lovely unfortunate. Alas! Salimbini, who, in the besotted ruffian I have the grief now to call husband, could recognise the once boasted representative of kings and heroes. Who in you could now discover the once almost worshiped favorite of an admiring world. Fie! fie! amend — to-bed, and get you sober."

Scaltro, thus unexpectedly rebuked, withdrew his gaze from Angelina; but in Salimbini's rage (which now burst forth in cruel invectives against his hapless wife, for daring to reprehend him), Orsino first perceived his father was in one of his often repeated fits of inebriation, just in that irritable state when the libation to Bacchus had been only sufficient to affect the brain, without any exhilaration of the spirits; just in that state when all the brutal propensities of his fierce nature were ready to be awakened by any contradiction into action, and to coalesce in amity or good fellowship with no one but those inclined to sacrifice more deeply with him at the shrine of the jolly son of Jupiter and Semele; and Orsino, there-fore, anxious to save his unfortunate mother from violence, hastily challenged his father to taste with him a flask of lachrymæ Christi, which he had lately become pos-sessed of.

It was a wine of which Salimbini was par-ticularly fond ; and the pleasure he felt in the idea of Orsino having obtained some for him, dissipated at once the threatened storm, and introduced upon his brow a tran-sient sun-beam.

The flask was soon produced, and sooner emptied by Salimbini and his associate; when the former jovially exclaimed—

" Come, Scaltro, we'll make a night of it, and each man swallow his half dozen in drinking success to Orsino's sposalizio; for since my boy is so enamoured of the girl, he shall not be disappointed ; and, by Plu-tus, they shall give us a warm portion from the duca's coffers, to fee us for not betray-ing their villany; unless my discoveries are crowned with success, and then I shall take from their hands the power of feeing us."

"Done!" cried Scaltro; "I'll not flinch from a dozen flasks drank in so good a cause: but when comes the sainted d—l, Father Ipocritóne, to tie the happy knot?"

"If chance directs him hither to-night, it shall be done; if not, to-morrow you shall summon him."

The projects of villany relative to her, which each passing moment became more and more revealed to her anguished apprehension, increased the trembling horror, the mental agony, to direct torture in the palpitating heart of Lady Angelina, who now sat with her chilled hands clasped, her streaming eyes raised up to heaven, like the wan and speechless child of hopeless despair.

At length Orsino, convinced that his father was seriously intent upon a Bacchanalian revel, considerately persuaded his mother to retire; and summoning a female domestic, ordered her " to conduct Lady

Angelina to the chamber prepared for her reception."

This chamber was upon the same floor with the parlour, and, though small, was neat, and might have been considered comfortable by any inhabitant who was not, like Angelina, a heart-rived captive in it. The walls were only white-washed, but around it were suspended many gaily painted pictures of saints and martyrs.

From this chamber the terrorised Angelina promptly saw, as she gazed around in heart-saddened despondence, there was no prospect of escape; for it contained only one window, that was thickly grated, and was placed most aukwardly about seven feet from the ground, and close to an angle of the room. Her attendant thither had not an idea of courtesy, therefore made no offer of assisting Lady Angelina to undress; but, believing all that could be required of her was comprised in conducting her thither, almost immediately withdrew, leaving Lady Angelina alone, to meditate upon the conspicuous horrors of her hopeless situation.

The tumultuous agony of her thoughts

for some moments forbade any connected train of musing upon the direful calamity of her destiny; but when reason, collecting it's powers, succeeded in unchaining it's faculties from the dominion of fear, it's first proof of renovated energy was it's leading her to her knees, to implore, and by the fervor of her unaffected piety to merit, the protection of the guardians of the helpless. From her knees she at length arose with renovated firmness; for her reliance rested where the Christian's hope had found an adamantine basis; and under the sacred influence, (which only could remand the affrighted energies of her mind back to their active station,) she first examined the door, to try what security from alarm that could afford her, when, to her inexpressible joy, she found that all the fastenings annexed to it were withinside, and not a moment now was lost until she availed herself of all the safety which they could yield her.

Angelina next determined upon the inspection of the window, to ascertain if indeed the lattice was an immoveable fixture. To accomplish this, she was obliged to mount a chair, which stood beneath it. This chair, in a decayed condition, tottered under her light form, and, in the first impulse of apprehension to save herself from an expected fall, she threw out her hand against the adjoining wall of the angle the window was placed by, to catch at something for assistance, and grasped at one of the pictures. The force with which she seised it, drew one of the nails (before loosened in it's station) by which it was hung. Angelina now finding the chair only tottered, but did not give way, relinquished her hold, when the picture, suspended only by one nail, slipped obliquely from it's horizontal station, and discovered an aperture in the wall, through which a small ray of light emanated. Evidently this chasm had been made for the gratification of curiosity, or perhaps for some purpose of moment, through a thin lath and plaster partition; and Angelina felt stimulated instantly to explore the crevice, to learn was it in the nature of possibility to discover, through that, any passage or means likely to lead to her escape, in the wild fancy of a forlorn hope that she might, by aid of her pocket-book instruments, widen the breach suffi-ciently to admit her; and now placing a chair beneath the aperture, she again mounted, and through the chasm, to her infinite surprise, beheld the Bacchanalian party she had just separated from, and in the same apartment she had left them in; for the parlour, she now found, ran parallel with her chamber.

Much chagrined at this termination to her faintly-cherished hope of escape, Angelina was turning away in disappointment, when the sound of a bugle-horn arrested her further stay, by transfixing her with painful expectation, through the exclamations of the party she there beheld.

" By the torch of Hymen! here comes the priest, to noose you, my enamoured boy," exclaimed Salimbini.

" Or, more likely, the goodly conte, come to learn the success of our trusty mission," said Scaltro.

Instantly Orsino started from his seat, in evident alarm — " Then, signóri, I must retire until the guest is ascertained, since the conte yet knows not that I hold intercourse with any of our community but with you, my father; and for worlds I would not let him see me at the social board with Scaltro the renowned," he exclaimed, as with precipitance he departed; and, in a moment more, Lady Angelina heard his hasty footsteps in the room over that she occupied.

Scaltro now staggered out to admit the guest; and soon returned, ushering in a conventual figure, with his cowl so overshadowing his visage, that not a single feature of which could Angelina, from her elevated situation, distinguish; but her shuddering heart, in the soliloquy of thought, exclaimed —

" It is he! the very monk who accompanied Father Ezzelino to Santo Valentino, come, come, alas! to unite me to this wretch's son! but my funeral obsequies shall he perform in gladly-welcomed preference to my mystical ceremony with such a being !"

" It is the conte," Scaltro audibly exclaimed, as he preceded this conventual figure, who, the moment the door was closed upon him, threw off the sacerdotal habit, and discovered the conte indeed, the Conte Fredrico di Alviano!

CHAPTER VIII.

THE heart of Lady Angelina was chilled with horror: " This then," she sighed in anguished sorrow, " is the very Conte Fredrico di Alviano, whose complicated crimes drove the poor Signora Salimbini to insanity : but could he, could he have committed crimes, and smile as he did, before the altar of the Deity ! Impossible, impossible; O, no, no, no! that smile beamed with conviction to my senses, that he is not the man of crimes.

" Salimbini, have you, have you found him, as you gave me hope?" exclaimed the conte, in trembling agitated anxiety.

" Found him! No; how should I? You disposed of him too well for that,": Salimbini savagely replied, irritated at this interruption to his dearly-loved libation.

"Salimbini," said the conte indignantly,— "what means the injustice of this suspicion? Had I not weakly and incautiously intrusted you with many of the dreadful secrets which oppress me, had I not had, alas! a dire occasion for your services, you dare not treat me thus."

"The man who is shunned, who is scouted from society as a homicide, who shortly may stand a public trial for murder, and murder too that shall be proved, unless you give me your full confidence — cannot expect the homage of respect from those who know him," retorted Salimbini insolently.

The flush of indignation, which before had animated the cheeks of the conte, now heightened to a livelier tint, his eyes flashed fire, and the smile of scorn sat on his lips.

"Then the murder must be proved against me," he exclaimed in a voice of firmness ; "for never, never will I reveal the secret to you, which for your own atrocious purposes you pant to be informed of."

"Very well, very well then, conte," re-

plied Salimbini, with a look and in a voice
of malicious determination; " I can take
my vengeance for your want of faith in my
honor without your assistance. I, I know
enough of your secret to rend you heart. —
I know who did give the mortal blow; and,
'fore heaven! I will betray him, will lead
him to the tortures he has earned."

The before intrepid firmness of Conte di
Alviano now fled at once; his countenance
was promptly faded to the hue of death, the
chill of direful terror struck on his heart,
crept o'er the surface of his frame, stood in
cold drops upon his forehead, taught his
knees to smite each other, and only by
sinking into a chair just near him, did he
save himself from falling to the ground, subdued by anguished agitation.

" Salimbini," he falteringly articulated,
" you could not prove such a villain. My
own life I will freely yield to your vindictive enmity, but spare, O! spare my ....."

Fredrico could articulate no further; but
bursting into tears, sobbed in the agony of
an anguished heart.

"All depends upon yourself," replied Salimbini sullenly : " the man whose life is in my keeping is not to talk arrogantly to me, illustrissimo Signóre Conte! No, no, no; when you sought my friendly services, your pride and passions ought to have found an opiate. I am not to be bullied, monsignòre."

" If— if by my conduct I have irritated you to such a direful thought of vengeance as that you have paralized my senses by, tell me, teach me how to make atonement, how to appease your wrath, your terrible threat of fell vindictive enmity," said Fredrico, in a quick, unsteady tone, that told how painful was the supplication urged by necessity to the being we despise.

" Your first step must then be to learn humility," returned Salimbini insolently, " and to look upon me, not as your tool, but your fate."

" The decrees of Fate are arbitrary," said the conte impressively, yet smiling in the sad resignation of despair : " I have outlived my loss of man's prized treasure — fame, of the annihilation of the most fondly-cherished hopes of my heart; and it is therefore very possible I can survive servility even to Salimbini. What wouldst thou then I should do to pay thee homage?"

" Get drunk with me !"

" That you know I will not. When free uncontrolled inclination guided my actions, I never committed excesses to degrade me, and now it would undo me; and you, who know so much, know I dare not hazard even a temporary deprivation of my faculties. Is there then nothing else I can perform to appease your indignation?"

" Unlace my boots — my legs ache and swell confoundedly; — unlace my boots, I say," exclaimed the savage.

" Unlace your boots !" repeated the conte, coloring again with indignant astonishment.

" Unlace my boots; unlace them, mighty conte, illustrious heir of Alviano, upon your humble knee, with your head uncovered, or your secret comes to light, and the guilty shall suffer all the horrors of inquisitorial vengeance," shouted Salimbini imperiously.

Instantly Fredrico dashed off a kind of hunting cap he wore, and, bending to his knee, relaxed the lacing of Salimbini's boots; but, whilst his actions thus bespoke submission, his countenance proclaimed the conflict of mental dignity struggling with the harsh decrees of arbitrary destiny. This degradation ended, he arose, and, with a bow, that told the obedience of a hero, not a slave, demanded " What further service he could render Salimbini?"

" A confounded wind blows down the stair-case; it makes me sneeze. Go, shut it out," said Salimbini.

The conte obeyed with dignified composure, and closed a door which led to the upper apartment, and which Orsino had left open in his retreat, to hear the intruder's name announced.

" That won't do," vociferated Salimbini; " merely latching is insufficient; the wind will suck it to and fro, and deafen us with it's rattling. Come, monsignòre, lock it; there — there; now draw the bolt, illustrissimo! below as well as above. Come, the bottom bolt, the bottom bolt — there; nothing so salutary a lesson to pride as teaching it to stoop: and now, signore conte, come and drink a glass of this delicious lachrymæ Christi to recruit you after such unusual toil. Come, sit, and drink; a glass or two will cheer you. I know the consequence, and will not command you to take more."

Fredrico eagerly complied with this mandate, in the forlorn hope that, while so employed, he might draw out something relative to the anxious business which had drawn him thither; for, by Salimbini's increasing approaches to impeded fluency of articulation, he saw that the subject of caution and reserve were threatened with annihilation by the overthrow of reason.

" Come, monsignòre," said Salimbini, " our first glass shall be to the health of my son's beauteous bride."

" Is your son then married ?" asked the conte, in affected interest, wishing to conciliate the ruffian, whom no force could bend.

" Not yet, but to-morrow will see him *la spòso* of ——. It is a project of mine; it struck me as in ambush I beheld the girl in the convent, where she has been for some months secreted : but how to accomplish it was the question — when, lo! I was employed to conceal this very girl, to give death increasing speed in carrying off a tottering obstacle to mercenaries, who long to revel on the spoils of a duca's revenue."

The interest of Conte Fredrico no longer was affected, it was painfully awakened, and the dawning of a horrible suspicion filled his breast with terrorised alarms.

" All was artfully managed," continued Salimbini, now stammering in inebriation, " to turn suspicion from my employers; and I shall let them rest for a time in their fancied security, until my project is accomplished. The girl is in my power, nay, in my very house — my son's bride she shall irrevocably be to-morrow. My employers, by their manœuvring, shorten the life of the present possessor of certain estates and titles; and, lo! I produce the wife of my son as the indisputable heiress ; for already has a spurious bantling been imposed upon the world; the wench who sold her offspring for this purpose, a favorite sultana of my own; and so I acquired that secret: death took that bantling to feed it's worms; and, though another is announced as shortly to appear, I have my suspicions of it's sterling stamp. One imposture may have only preceded another. I have my spies even in the very house; and, by fair means or foul, I'll prove my beauteous daughter-in-law the heiress of ——. Hum! hum! are you dozing, Scaltro?"

The suspicions of Conte Fredrico now amounted to little short of torturing certainty; but wishing to lead Salimbini further on, who had but narrowly escaped announcing names, now endeavouring, by the carelessness of his tones and manner, to conceal those suspicions which agitated his breast, he said —

"And the lady is tolerably handsome, too; or at least you seem to think her so."

"Tolerably handsome!" repeated Salimbini, contemptuously;—then, with vehemence, he added, "I say she is beautiful; far, far surpassing, in personal loveliness your highly-vaunted Violante."

"That I will take upon me to deny," replied the conte, now affecting vehemence too. " I'll bet you my famed war-horse Rapido, whom you have so long set your heart upon obtaining, that this intended bride of your son's is not to be compared to Lady Violante."

" Done!" returned Salimbini, exultingly. " The charger's mine; for, by ——! she surpasses all, all of beauty the hand of nature ever formed, combined together."

" In your opinion, probably; but your judgement decides not the bet," returned Fredrico. " I must have ocular demonstration of your having won him fairly, ere I resign Rapido to you."

" To-morrow you shall have conviction of the animal's being fairly mine."

" But why not to-night?"

" No, no; thank you, monsignòre; with all due respect to your curiosity, and plausible scheme of outwitting me, no eye shall now behold my prize until she is irrevocably the wife of Orsino Salimbini."

Angelina, an agitated witness of this scene, now convinced that this moment must decide her fate, and that one instant hesitation or delay would annihilate every hope of, rescue for ever, sprang to the ground, rapidly unbarricaded her chamber, and taking her light, winged her way, as swiftly as her trembling frame could bear her thither, to the parlour door, where she extinguished her candle, then unclosing the door, exclaimed, in as steady a voice as her powerful agitation could lend her, and entering as she spoke—

" Signòri, I have accidentally extinguished my candle ; will you permit me to relight it ?"

" Furies ! and vengeance ! how dare you to come hither ?" vociferated Salimbini, attempting to fly towards her to inforce her retreat, ere the conte should obtain a full view of her; but the unlacing of his boots had loosened them about his heels, and the strong cording entangling about his legs, both combined in impeding his way, and the conte gained a full view of her.

" It is then, Lady Angelina di Balermo ! —As I suspected, Lady Angelina." He, with now no longer controllable emotion, exclaimed, as he flew towards her,

" Oh! are you, are you, hesitate not to tell me, detained here of your own concurrence?"

" Oh! why insult me by such a cruel supposition?" she replied; " but I conjure you, if ever indeed you loved my father, to fly to my uncle, and tell him, where I am detained, and he will send sufficient authority, sufficient force to rescue me."

" This moment must you be rescued, or else never, from the snares of Salimbini. — Come then, my lovely friend, and let the consequence prove what it may to me, I will attempt, at least, your rescue."

Angelina sprang forward, Fredrico caught her hand in his tremulous grasp, snatched up the sacerdotal robe he had come disguised in thither, and as he bore her from the parlour into the passage, he hastily threw the monk's habit around himself and her.

" By the infernal powers!" vociferated Salimbini, " I will betray thy secret if thou darest to take her hence."

" You and your employers are now com-

pletely in my power, by your own communications, and I will betray you all if you chal-
lenge my vengeance of retaliation," replied
Fredrico, undauntedly rushing forward.

" Say you so ! then might must vanquish
you, and retain our prize," exclaimed Salimbini, endeavouring to pursue him ; but
might was despoiled of it's powers by intemperance and erring judgement; for the
unsteadiness of Salimbini's head, aided by
the slovenly state his own insolence had
placed his heels in, impeded his way; while
Scaltro in vain strove to open a passage for the
now loudly-called-for Orsino to come and
aid the rescue of his prize; for the very bottom bolt, which arrogance had ordered to
be drawn, o'ershot itself; since each time
Scaltro attempted to stoop, for the purpose
of undrawing it, a vertiginous motion in his
head compelled him to forego his effort;
and so much were they both unfitted for
the alertness of pursuers, and so much time
had elapsed ere they could contrive to li-
berate Orsino, or summon any one to chase
the fugitives, that Fredrico, possessed of all
the secrets of passing through these guarded

premises, safely conducted his trembling charge out of this place of peril, unmolested even by the suspicions of the wary sentinels, of his having any companion concealed beneath the habit of the friendly friar, for whom he passed (under sanction of Salimbini) in his frequent visits to that fortress of banditti; and still unimpeded by pursuit, he conveyed the almost-fainting Angelina, some distance through the forest, to the ruin of a Roman bath, speaking, as they proceeded, in gentlest accents, the kindest words of soothing encouragement, to reanimate the energies of her drooping spirits.—At this ruin he paused, and cautiously looking around—

"We are unobserved, thank heaven!" he softly articulated as he led her to the entrance of this place, where the mantling ivy concealed, from the eye of common observation, a low grated door;—the sombre shades of night now aided that concealment; but to Conte Fredrico it was a familiar object. Eagerly he pulled a ring affixed to it, with a touch acquainted with the secret of it's actuating spring, and slowly it opened upon a dark delving passage. Rapidly now he closed the door, and, entreating Lady Angelina to cherish no fears, he cautiously descended until another door impeded further progress. — At this door Fredrico knocked, and a venerable monk unclosed it, and admitted the fugitives into a stone chamber, where formerly the waters of a bath had run, but was now converted to other uses. — In it a lamp was suspended.

"Is he—is he found, my son?" exclaimed the monk, with trembling impatience, the moment his eyes rested on Fredrico, when the agitated Angelina instantly recognised, by his voice, the still, the well by her remembered, Father Marsilio.

"Alas! no," replied the conte; "Salimbini is in every way a villain; but we will talk of this another opportunity, since you are now called upon to welcome a much-beloved favorite of yours, Lady Angelina di Balermo."

"Alas! alas!" exclaimed Father Marsilio, starting back, whilst his countenance most eloquently proclaimed regret; "why has Fate again thrown this fascinating child in your way, unfortunate young man, to increase the misery of your hapless destiny?"

Angelina shuddered at the painful sound of her augmenting the misery of the preserver of her father's life, the rescuer of herself from wretchedness.

"To the will of heaven it is my task to bow with unmurmuring submission," replied Fredrico with energy, "but reveréndo pádre, if I have griefs, I have my consolations too; for even now, mine has been the happiness, the transport, to rescue this lovely being from the villanous machinations of the miscreant Salimbini."

The hue of death instantly overspread the fine countenance of Father Marsilio; as recoiling in anticipating dismay, he exclaimed:—

"Does Salimbini know you for her rescuer?"

"Assuredly he does; no other means were mine to save her."

"Avenging heaven will have it's retribution!" faintly exclaimed the terror-anguished monk; "all, all is now lost, and that dire fate, we have toiled to avert, inevitable."

The anticipating heart of Angelina felt at once conviction of the destruction she had drawn upon her preserver; for one moment it was stunned by horror at the belief; but in the next, remembering that yet such destruction might be averted, she promptly rallied the forces of her mental faculties, and exerting all the fortitude her anguished feelings told her she must command to pay the demand of gratitude, she firmly said: —

" Conte Fredrico, instantly restore me to Salimbini."

Fredrico, recoiling in horrorised amazement, exclaimed: —

" Restore you to Salimbini! — Why, surely, surely — did not you tell me, Lady Angelina, your detention was compulsatory?"

" Assuredly I did; for alas! thinking only of self, I have drawn destruction upon my preserver; but believe not the grateful Angelina will ever endure that insupportable misery. — Oh! no indeed, I will not. —

Take me then back to this horrible Salimbini; appease by that his terrible wrath,
his threatened vengeance, and leave to
pitying heaven some other means, less
dreadful to my heart, of rescuing me from
becoming the wretched wife of a bigand's
s on."

The conte smiled upon her in rapturous
gratitude, pressed her hand with energy,
and in a voice of respondent feeling, said:

"No, never, never will I lead you to wretchedness: even the most direful vengeance of
Salimbini I would brave, sooner than yield
you to his power. But let the benevolent,
generous heart of Lady Angelina cease to
beat in alarm for me, through that miscreant's vengeance: for so singularly is my
fate, combined with this man's interest, that
although in many instances he may have
power to wound and distress my feelings, he
dares not aim at my existence; and inde-
pendent of this apparently-mysterious security from his sanguinary vengeance, he,
this very night, in the unguarded ebullitions
of inebriation, implicated his vile employers in the ruthless villany of conveying you

to his habitation ; a disclosure, which the
law of bravo honor ever revolts from. On
my promise of secresy, therefore, upon his
having betrayed the inciters of this dire plot
of turpitude to me, I can readily compromise
for suppression of his vindictive retaliation
for the heavenly protectors of innocence, or-
daining me to become your rescuer from
the peril that encompassed you ;—but as the
promise of secresy has not-yet passed my
lips to Salimbini, I can announce to you
who were the diabolical projectors of....

"Oh !" said Angelina, gently interrupting him, " I heard all of their ruthless plot,
for the annihilation of my dear unfortunate
uncle, through their cruelty to me, from a
place of ambush, where I beheld you my
lord, and where I formed the hazardous attempt of presenting myself before you."—
And now with her heart filled with the con-
soling hope that the vengeance of Salimbini
might thus be averted by this compromise,
she attempted to make her acknowlegements to her preserver, in which she betrayed that her joy at deliverance was

equaled, if not surpassed, by her happiness in finding her rescue was not to be attended by any evil consequence to him.

" And is it, can it be possible," Fredrico replied in a voice of affecting sadness, " that Lady Angelina, herself so pure, so spotless, retains one particle of interest for me, the outcast of society, a being contemned by all mankind ?"

Angelina was powerfully affected by the subduing pathos of his thrilling voice; and the spontaneous tears of sensibility, straying from beneath the silken fringe of her downcast eyes, fell from her blushing cheeks upon her throbbing bosom, now painfully agitated for the sorrows of him she regarded.

" Ah! Lady Angelina," exclaimed Fredrico, in the faltering voice of varied emotion, " this kindness of compassion, so touchingly evinced, assures me, you only know that I have been unfortunate; not—not that I stand arraigned for direful crimes."

" Alas! I do know you are suspected of them," said Angelina, in the

lowly tremulous tone of agitated kindness,
" since the voice of calumny reached even
me, recluse as I have been."

" The voice of calumny!!!—you, you
call it calumny!!—oh! how my sorrow-laden
heart thanks you, my sweetly, merciful
friend!" exclaimed Fredrico, convulsively
grasping her hand in overpowering gratitude; and trembling in agitation almost too
mighty for subjugation, sunk, vanquished by
excess of feeling, upon a bench beside her,
unable to articulate how his heart thanked
her.

" My poor son forgets," said the holy
father, " that neither Lady Angelina or
himself can tarry here all night; the hour
for prayer approaches, when the monks all
hastening to devotion, some one may wander hither to perform the inflictions of a
tortured conscience."

Lady Angelina, starting from a painful
reverie, exclaimed, " Alas! holy father, and
I have reprehensibly forgotten that all this
time, my dying uncle is tortured by the
affliction of believing I have fallen into the
hands of banditti, or, still more direful, that I

am the voluntary companion in an elopement with one of the attendants,—sent to
convey me to him."

"Reverend father!" said Fredrico, "you
will permit us, I doubt not, to proceed
through the convent vaults to the castle of
Rossarno; from thence, under the auspices
of la contessa, Lady Angelina can safely be
conducted to Montalbano Castle."

"Assuredly; for I would venture even a
greater hazard for the kind preserver of my
life, whom, in my anxiety for your safety,
I have seemed to forget my debt of gratitude to"—replied the good pádre, taking
the suspended lamp from it's station:
"come, my son, assist Lady Angelina to
closely enfold herself in the monk's habit
that concealed her from the sentinels of Salimbini's fort, for here, too, we must hide
her from observation."

And now Father Marsilio, preceding
Conte Frédrico, who tenderly supported the
trembling Angelina, led the way through a
long extent of subterranean passages, which
ran beneath the convent's time-worn cloister, until their further progress seemed ar-

rested by a grated door, but for this the good monk was provided with a key; and taking an already trimmed lamp from a nitch in the wall, he lit it and presented it to Fredrico; and while unclosing the door for the fugitives to proceed, impressively he spoke:

" My conventual duties call me hence, and I can accompany you no further; but you know the way too well, my son, to err in the safe convoy of your sacred charge.— Farewell, my children, and may the blessing of heaven rest upon you, only as long as you shall merit it's favor."

The holy man now returned to attend his devotion, and the trembling Angelina proceeded with Fredrico along the damp and chilling vaults of the monastery of Santo Stefano.

CHAPTER IX.

A GLOOMY silence reigned, whilst our fugitives trod many paces of their sombre route; for Fredrico had many perplexities to engage his meditations, and the pensive Angelina had no longer a wish for conversation; the pang the sound of the contessa had given to her bosom, ere reflection had told her what contessa was most probably meant by Fredrico, had conveyed to her trembling heart the sad and firm conviction, that she loved the long betrothed of Lady Violante St. Seviero, the man accused of direful crimes.

At length, having reached the termination of the convent vaults, they entered those of Rossarno Castle, when Fredrico broke the gloomy silence in the plaintive voice of sadness.

" Alas! Lady Angelina," he said, "our mutual enemies have caused for you a widely different entrance to, and reception in, the Castle of Rossarno to that I once fondly-cherished the delightful hope of Fate's permitting.—Then I portrayed in Fancy's rapturous visions, all—all of homage, the heart of ardent—friendship and esteem could devise; to give to you smiling wel-come would have greeted your approach to the castle of my father; but now, alas! taught by the contemning world to feel shame at your conductor, you come a fu-gitive, led hither by a proscribed being, who dares not himself present you to even his once kind, his once-adoring mother."

The vibration of Angelina's frame felt by Fredrico, as she leaned upon his arm, informed him how much he had affected her, for she had not power to answer him.

Silence again prevailed, until they reach-ed the last of the subterraneous arcades of the castle, when Fredrico requested Angelina to dismantle from the monk's ha-bit, that he might leave it in it's accustomed place, to be in readiness to form his disguise,

when necessary, for his mysterious visits to
the fortress of Salimbini. Instantly she
complied, and immediately after they entered from this range of vaults into the
chapel of the castle, at the rear of a magni--
ficent monument of the finest sculpture;
and as emerging from .behind it's, shade,
Angelina perceived the quickly-affecting
influence of a sudden shock agitate the sensitive frame of Fredrico, who started with
recoiling emotion, and would promptly have
retreated to the vaults, had it not been too
late, since the object he would have retreated from had beheld him; and for Lady Angelina's sake he braved the torturing conflict,
which he was well aware must await him,
in an interview with his mother, who, clad
in the mournful weeds of Sorrow's most afflicting state, had been devoutly kneeling
before the sarcophagus of the superb sepul-
chral structure, raised to the memory of her
husband, until disturbed by Fredrico's entrance with his lovely charge; and when
with whom he attempted to advance, the
contessa, with recoiling horror depicted on
every line of a countenance faded and at-

tenuated from extraordinary beauty, by the pangs of 'mighty woes, started from her knees, when the majestic grandeur of her mien seemed to acquire still more commanding powers; as in the piercing tones of indignation, blended with the thrilling ones of anguished despair, she exclaimed:—

" Monster of unnatural cruelty! how dare you thus appear before me? Can—can your callous heart, now black in turpitude, forget that, when your impious hand despoiled me of my husband, I tore my diabolical son from my heart, and forbade him my presence for ever?"

" Oh! no, madam, I have not, I cannot cease to remember the hatred, the prejudiced injustice of my mother," replied the conte, in a tone of the most affecting despondence: then with an air of the firmly conscious dignity of innocence, he continued, — " nor is my disobedience to my mother's afflicting mandate voluntary; nor at the tomb, him you believe my impious hands have immolated, could I, however black in turpitude you deem my heart, have dared to present myself before the widow of the man I murdered ?"

"Murdered !" the Contessa di Alviano shrieked—"murdered! and by his own child!—by my own child!—by mine! oh Fredrico!" and subdued by horror and despair, she sunk upon the ground.—In an agony of alarm and grief, her agitated son flew to raise her.

"Approach me not! touch me not!" she wildly cried, "lest in my horror, at the contact, I learn to curse my child as often in the ravings of my phrenzied grief I have the hour which gave him birth."

Trembling in the agony of his wounded feelings, Fredrico retreated several paces from the contessa; his fine and fascinating countenance, clad in the hue of death, and whilst his heart writhed in anguish, he falteringly articulated—

"Could my mother curse me?"

"If mercy yet has influence over you," exclaimed the contessa, raising her hands in a suppliant position, "sound not such tones as these in my ears, nor look thus on me, sending your melting eyes, beaming with heaven-borrowed innocence into my very heart, to teach me forgetfulness of your crimes, and infatuate me into becoming an accomplice in your direful sins, by taking to my love again the fell murderer of my husband."

" Oh! my mother! how you torture me! supplicate not me, I implore you, I conjure you," Fredrico replied, in all the softened pathos of wounded affection; " yes, yes, I will obey my mother, who forbids her heart-rived child to look upon her; — yet, that mandate is merciful, for to see you thus, must rend my very soul!"

-" Soul! soul! Fredrico," exclaimed his mother, wildly starting from the ground, "where is now your father's troubled soul? where his unquiet spirit, sent to an unhallowed tomb by him, his loved Zarina bore him? Oh! Fredrico! once, once the precious treasure of an adoring mother's heart, how could you sink to infamy like this, and teach that mother, to preserve the favor of her Creator, she must learn the afflicting lesson — to abhor you?"

"Oh! heaven Omnipotent! in mercy spare me such heart-torturing conflicts, lest I should be led by them to shrink from that great duty, which thou, in thy wisdom, hast assigned me to perform!" Fredrico ejaculated, with all the fervor of animated devotion; but while his spirit caught from piety the sublimated fire of energy to support his mental trials, his frame was subjugated by mortal weakness; and vanquished by the convulsive tremor of agitation, he seemed no longer able to stand beneath his weight of sorrows; when Angelina, starting from the steps of the monument upon which she had sunk, subdued by horror, amaze, and sympathy, caught one of his grief-chilled hands in hers, and gently drew him towards an adjoining pillar, upon the base of which he found a seat.

"Heaven does grant it's mercy to me," he feelingly exclaimed, pressing with fervor the hand which led him, as he gazed on Angelina, with an expression of grateful tenderness that no language could delineate: "heaven does grant it's mercy to me, in teaching you to pity my afflictions."

"Oh! holy saints! who is this?" exclaimed the contessa, first observing the presence of a stranger, and now with all the awakened terrors of a mother, for the safety of a child trembling in her heart, she said:

" Who, who," infatuated young man, have you conducted hither to witness my sacred sorrows, and hear the wild ravings of distracted grief accuse the innocent of crimes they never, never perpetrated ?"

The long-tortured heart of Fredrico throbbed with sudden, unexpected joy; he started from his seat with every nerve new strung, and darted towards his mother, but paused at a respectful distance from her; and sinking on one knee before her, bowed his grateful acknowlegements for this spontaneous proof of still existing interest for him; and with such expressive eloquence he performed the action, it's import could not be mistaken, while the affecting, reverential homage it portrayed, subdued poor Angelina to the sobbing weakness of a child; but quickly starting from this overpowering sympathy, she hastily, yet resolutely, remanded her fleeting firmness to her bosom, and gracefully advancing towards the contessa, as Fredrico, arisen from his knees, had retreated to a greater distance from his agitated mother.

" Believe, madam, that il Conte Fredrico brought not in me an invidious witness of your sacred sorrows," Angelina said in the soft thrilling tones of sensibility, and with the beautifully blushing countenance of interesting timidity. " O! no; he led me hither to find a safe asylum in your honorable protection, from the most pitiless scheme of treachery humanity and valor ever rescued a helpless woman from."

While Angelina spoke, the eyes of the contessa were riveted upon her, expressing in that gaze the strongest emotions of admiration and interest, until perceiving the dress which Angelina wore as a boarder in the convent of Santo Valentino, and believing her to be a noviciate of a religious order, the moment she ceased, the contessa exclaimed, in terror, to her son : —

" O, wretched young man ! how do your crimes accumulate ! Again, then, has your sacrilegious hand stolen a votary from the profaned altar of your Creator. O, Fredrico! Fredrico! in mercy stab my heart too, and give me not the rack of your increasing errors to writhe upon, in lingering torture, thus!"

The wounded feelings of Fredrico were too powerfully agonised to yield him utterance, but he beamed the desponding smile of conscious innocence, aggrieved by the cruel suspicions of injustice, as mournfully he bent his eyes to the ground, in obedience to the wishes of his mother not to look upon her: but the grateful heart of Angelina, now painfully throbbing with indignation at such unfounded censure, led her on to speak in vindication of her oppressed deliverer; and, with all the glow of animated enthusiasm in the cause, she again addressed the Contessa di Alviano.

"I am no votary of conventual vows, stolen profanely from the altar of my Creator, madam. O! no; the persecuted orphan of a noble house, I was stolen by villany from the bosom of protection, and was consigned to infamy and wretchedness; from which the hand of compassion, braving all danger, set me free; and that hand, madam, was the Conte Fredrico di Alviano's — Conte Fredrico, whom long I have known as my shield in the moment of peril, known only to learn how humanity could vary it's form, and by each new and surpassing appearance evince more surely the celestial source from which it sprung." Then turning to Fredrico, with cheeks mantled by the indignation her pained gratitude inspired, and giving her hand to him to lead her, she firmly added : —

" From the unjust mother of my gallant preserver I will not ask protection. Where then, my friend, can you lead me to seek a safe and honorable asylum?"

Fredrico pressed the hand of Angelina with reverential, trembling, ardent gratitude ; but ere his agitated feelings permitted his reply, the contessa, in grief, exclaimed : —

" Alas! alas! my profligate son has corrupted the principles of this lovely, this fascinating, innocent-looking, young unfortunate, and has taught her to become his avowed, his approving friend."

" No, madam!" haughtily and emphati-

cally Fredrico replied, sensibly pained that
even a moment's suspicion should be drawn
by her pitying kindness to him to rest upon
the spotless purity of Lady Angelina: "No;
whatever my inclination, I could not corrupt that which is incorruptible. In every
instance which it pleases the sadly-changed
opinion of my mother to judge me harshly,
let her believe me culpable, so she acquits
me in this. O! could heaven thus set it's
own celestial stamp upon a countenance, to
index a mind that could be taught depravity? O! surely not, my mother. Then
hasten, in atonement for unmerited suspicion, to admire, to love, and estimate, in
Lady Angelina di Balermo, those transcendent virtues you discovered and paid homage to in both her sainted parents."

Zarina started at the name with no common share of actuating emotion, and with a
look of mournfully expressive meaning at
her son (which his heart acknowleged it's
perfect comprehension of by an anguished
sigh), she clasped her hands in agony of
grief, as falteringly she articulated: —

" O, Fredrico!" then after a pause, in which she seemed oppressed by direful regrets, she tremulously added : " This, then, is the interesting child of my beloved, lamented friends, whom I was delusively led to hope I should have welcomed to my arms with a mother's sanctioned tenderness."

At this moment a door from the inhabited parts of the castle suddenly burst open, and a man, attired in pontifical canonicals, entered the chapel.

Uncommon manly beauty marked this man's countenance, which, still untouched by the harsh traces of past years, announced him yet in the meridian of his days, while his ungracious deportment proclaimed the unbending loftiness of strongly felt episcopal magnificence ; repellent austerity marked his manners, and stamped them with the harsh counterfeit which ambition, to be deemed a miracle of piety, had borrowed from dissimulating sanctity, to deform the meek and lovely aspect of religion by.

On beholding Fredrico, he started back

several paces in apparently recoiling horror, and, with indignant scowl, turning to the contessa, imperiously exclaimed:

" Sinful, degenerate woman! what infatuating powers of darkness have acquired dominion thus over you, to lead you into communication with that vile unnatural scorpion, who preyed upon the vitals of his inestimable sire!"

The eloquent eyes of Fredrico now flashed with the fire of indignation, his cheeks glowed to a painful heat, whilst his heart swelled and bounded with feelings almost too mighty to sustain, until the promptly-rising dictates of those principles which led him on to bear with unfaltering firmness the heart-rending humiliations, which almost every where assailed him, spread their magical influence through his frame, and tranquillised at once the innovating turbulence of angry passions into the sweet aspect of the dignified calm of fortitude, when looking with the mild eye of patient Christian suffering upon the infuriated prelate, spoke with the unruffled serenity of conscious innocence:

" I would recommend your lordship to suspend your pious indignation until the transgressions of the Contessa di Alviano may sanction so firm a display of it's sublimity. At present, she is perfectly innocent of maternal weakness; for her reception of her son was not more kind than the probationary Arcivèscovo di Mazzarino could have wished it. Believe me, my ever tenderly beloved mother, I mean not to upbraid you, since well do I know the toils of my pitiless foes have spun their web of arts so nicely around me, as to exclude even from the view of partiality itself every belief of my innocence. But, though now even thus encompassed by the snares of villany, a time may yet arrive when the susceptibility of your heart will feel the pangs of self-reproach, for so rigidly performing what you now consider the arbitrary dictates of an imperious duty. But not longer to protract an interview, torturing to us both, my beloved mother, I shall hasten to inform monsignòre arcivéscovo why I am here, and solicit his protecting aid, not for the proscribed culprit he denounces, but for the pure, unsullied child of innocence; and to assist such, his immaculate virtue cannot feel a scruple."

And now, with all the impressive animation of a feeling heart, Fredrico related the snares of villany (as far as his intended compromise with Salimbini would admit of) from which he had rescued Lady Angelina; and the anxiety he experienced for her being safely and expeditiously conveyed to the Castle di Montalbano, before alarm for her disappearance should have any serious effect upon the invalid duca.

" Alas! alas! my son," exclaimed the contessa," melting into an agony of tears, " how came you acquainted with the haunts of banditti? How gained you unmolested admission to the habitation of those sanguinary brigands? O, Fredrico!"

" Woman!" vociferated the archbishop haughtily, " pollute not your breath by holding converse with this devoted sinner. Our present duty is, to provide for the safety of a daughter of the illustrious house of Montalbano, who, to deserve the protec-

tion of the virtuous, must first, ere we grant
her ours, solemnly promise before the altar of
high heaven, to abjure all further communication with Fredrico di Alviano, and to
forswear now, and for ever, all friendship
for, and every grateful remembrance of."

" What!" exclaimed the astonished and
recoiling girl; " what, monsignòre, vow at
the altar of my Creator to become a wretch
undeserving of the future mercy of pitying
Heaven! Forswear the preserver of my parent's life, the protector of my own from
wretchedness! Forget my gratitude to Conte
Fredrico di Alviano! Never, no, never.
And if on terms of infamy like these only I
acquire the Reverendissimo Arcivèscovo di
Mazzarino's protection, proudly, exultingly,
in the purer spirit of superior virtue, I re-
nounce it with abhorrence."

" Indeed!" ejaculated the mortified prelate, reddening with chagrin : " then,
sister, come away; quit such degrading
society, and leave this wilfully wicked
girl to the real infamy of your son's protection."

" Stay, I conjure you, stay," exclaimed the highly-agitated Fredrico, " nor thus indiscriminately denounce your wrath against all; let not indignation against me render you cruel and unjust to innocence, that claims protection. If only on those who never erred you bestow your benefits, limited indeed would be the exercise of the Archbishop di Mazzarino's benevolence. If the prejudices of Lady Angelina in my favor offend your reverenza, recollect, she believes her gratitude is my debtor, and, remembering the source from which her offences spring, is, in the general opinion of mankind, an exalted virtue, you cannot surely condemn her for it, although it may unfortunately be awakened for an unworthy object."

" Plead not for me, I entreat you, my most amiable friend," said Lady Angelina haughtily: " I will not owe an obligation to the unchristian being who would teach me diabolical sin in the form of base Ingratitude. Protection, thus supplicated for, would indeed mortify me to accept; whilst your guardianship, the prompt offering of humanity to helplessness, it will be my pride to avail myself of and to acknowlege. Send me then, my friend, with even the meanest of your vassals to the castle of my uncle, and I shall feel more exalted by my escort, given in kindness to me by benevolence, than if guarded thither by the pompous retinue of those who believe me undeserving of their favor."

The Archbishop di Mazzarino had angrily taken the contessa's hand to hurry her away, but she now, with a struggling effort to remain, eagerly exclaimed —

O! stay one moment, I entreat you, Giuseppe, stay; this lovely child possesses the inflexibility in virtue of both her sainted parents; and, O! how can you but admire and applaud that firmness which her feelings of rectitude inspire, even though exerted in a cause you approve not of? and, besides, she is the child of my earliest, my dearest friend, and I must — I will yield her my protection!"

But the contessa pleaded in vain; the bosom of the probationary prelate knew not how to relent. An opinion, once formed in his mind, could only by interest be ever taught to change; and a determined bigot to his lately assumed appearance of rigid, unbending virtue, he haughtily and arbitrarily forced Zarina from the chapel.

CHAPTER X

" ALAS!" exclaimed Fredrico, in a tone of mournful despondence, the moment succeeding the unfeeling Giuseppe's departure, " what can I now do to secure your safety, my lovely, my precious charge, compatible with the preservation of your spotless fame?"

" Have you, my best friend," said Angelina, in sad disconsolation, " no domestic, no vassal, whom you could intrust to accompany me to Montalbano Castle? The banditti, believing your mother would grant me protection for this night, will not be abroad to seek me."

" In my own carriage would I instantly and safely convey you thither, could my protection and convoy be considered any thing but inevitable disgrace," replied the conte, in mournful conviction of the contageous infamy of his reputation: "or, even should I, in defiance of that ruthless man, my uncle, order an equipage of my mother's to take you to Montalbano, could we insure your admission — your secure restoration to the presence of the duca! but, ah! I fear, those whose interest it was to plan that pitiless scheme of villany against your peace and his life, would still devise means to banish you again without the knowlege of the Duca di Montalbano."

"Through the auspices of my mother and Conte Giuseppe, I had hoped to effect your safe return. The archbishop's influence would have unbarred the gate, and, accompanied by my mother's chaplain, your way would have been unimpeded to the sheltering arms of your uncle; but, without the sanction of Count Giuseppe's approbation, the security of his power, I dare not venture your return, even with the venerable priest Tommaso, lest without protecting influence, I should consign you only to a repetition of ruthless treachery.

Lady Angelina now felt most sensibly the imprudence of her own impetuosity in leading her to listen only to the voice of indig-nantly wounded gratitude, since it thus un-fortunately caused destruction to the conte's hope of her security, and had thus involved him in a labyrinth of perplexity upon her account, which she, alas! knew not how to aid in extricating him from.

Mutual consultations now took place up-on the most expedient method to pursue in this dilemma. Fredrico's solicitude for her safety, still more powerfully augmented by the heart-soothing recollection of how she forfeited the protection of the Archbishop di Mazzarino; but no scheme of promising aspect appeared until Angelina suggested that probably though the Monk Jeronimo, if such a monk there absolutely was at the convent of San Stefano, and that he had really been summoned to attend her uncle, the duca might be made acquainted with her rescue from destruction, and of her asy-lum in the chapel of Rossarno Castle, from whence she then doubted not her uncle would send safe escort to conduct her to him.

Fredrico knew there was such a monk,

famed amongst the sons of Æsculapius, attached to the monastery of San Stefano ;
and not doubting the probability of his having been summoned to attend the duca, to
give plausibility to the innocence of Ezzelino relative to the disappearance of Lady
Angelina, it promptly was determined by
them, that Fredrico should immediately seek
Father Marsilio (by this time returned to his
cell from prayers), and under his auspices to
obtain the services of Father Jeronimo.

But how to dispose of Lady Angelina in
the intervening moments of his absence,
was a difficulty not to be vanquished in the
mind of Fredrico. To conduct her again
unlicensed through the convent of monks,
was not to be hazarded, although the disguise she had worn was in their power to
obtain. Her objections to entering the
castle without the express sanction of the
contessa, he saw, could not be overcome
without pain, which he was unwilling to inflict; and should he enter the castle alone,
to summon Father Tommazo to remain with
her during his embassy to San Stefano, he
must leave her by herself in the lorn darkness

of the chapel, for he must take the lamp to guide him to the apartment of the good Tommaso, the only light they had left; for Giuseppe, as if possessed of the power of divining, had maliciously taken both his own and the contessa's with him; and although there surrounded by candles, they were consecrated ones, and they dare not light them for any thing but sacred purposes; and although Angelina betrayed no fear of solitude and darkness, Fredrico could not brook the idea of dooming her to endure it.

"For although," he said, " I see you possessed of no common share of firmness, yet who can tell the painful apprehensions which, in this sombre place, may assail you, after the direful shocks you have in the last few hours sustained, when left here unprotected in solitude and darkness."

" But in that moment, when we are called upon to make exertions for our own preservation from impending evil, we must not shrink from the performance of them, because they may give us some suffering of inconvenience," replied Angelina cheer-

ingly.;.." but, although I ought to suffer a
much greater punishment for that erring,
impetuosity..which led to this perplexity,
than your seeking the reverend Tommaso
will inflict, I know you will not doom me
to a long continuance of this slight one,
since I am sure you will return to my relief
as soon as possibility will permit you."

"Return to your relief! yes, yes, I would
return to you with that anxious speed in
which the miser would re-visit his most valued treasure; but, most heroic Angelina,
what in my absence shall lull my fears of
harm betiding you? What......"

At this moment, the anxiously-agitated
Fredrico was interrupted by the unclosing
of the door through which the archbishop
had hurried away the reluctant Zarina;
when a venerable looking woman, in the
garb of a domestic, cautiously entered, and,
with the half-unwilling step and alarmed
aspect of terror struggling against duty in
the performance of a task assigned her, she
advanced into the chapel, gazing wistfully
around.

The countenance of Fredrico brightened

with the joy of hope on her appearance, and hastily approaching her, she soon beheld him, and, in the tone of gladness, exclaimed —

" O! monsignòre, I rejoice I have so soon found you, for I sadly feared you were gone hence."

" And I rejoice to see you, my ever good and kind Claudia," he replied ; " for, if you love me, you will not refuse to perform an essential service for me."

" If I love you!" returned Claudia ; " how can you suppose I do, when you refuse to let me into all that dismal load of secrets you have hanging so heavily about your once gay heart, that I might then judge for myself whether I must indeed learn to hate you; or as heretofore doat upon you like an old fool, that set up an idol to worship ; and you ought, you know you ought, to tell me all, that I might be able to defend you, and have the last word when Andreo —for upon your account we have become a wrangling couple in our old days — shakes his head at me, and tells me ' all the evil stories of you are too, too true."

" Well, well, but my dear, good Claudia,
we must leave the last word, in fancied tri--
umph, a little longer to honest Andreo,"
said the conte, smiling gratefully and kindly; " but now a matter of the greatest anxiety to me engrosses every thought of mine,
and leads me to entreat your ever friendly
assistance.   You see this lady, Claudia,
and ....."

" To be sure I do, and right glad I am
so soon to see her," replied Claudia, inter--
rupting him; " since it is for her I came
wandering into this now dismal chapel at
this fear-inspiring hour; for the contessa
sent me to conduct the young lady to her."

" My mother sent you for Lady Angelina! my dear and amiable mother sent you
for her," repeated Fredrico, with tears of
fast-renovating filial tenderness glistening in
his expressive eyes.

" Yes; the contessa, dear young lady,
sent me for you," replied Claudia, now par-
ticularly addressing Angelina, " and glad I
am to see you again; and grown into what
you promised to be; for I never danced in
my arms a lovelier girl than you were al-

most seventeen years ago; when many, and many a time, I have dandled you in my arms in the villa di Alviano. — Why, it was I who discovered the very first tooth you ever cut, and it was, too, on the identical day Fredrico completed his sixth year — O!· lack-a-day! how fond Fredrico was of you then, fancying you were his wife, poor innocent soul, because we told him so."

It would be a difficult attempt to determine which, Angelina or Fredrico, blushed most deeply at this nursery legend; but Angelina, alarmed at her own betraying consciousness, made an anxious endeavour, though with a tremulous voice she did so, to turn the good dame's thoughts from such embarrassing reminiscence.

"I am happy in an opportunity of thanking you for the kindness you bestowed upon me in my infant days, she said, holding out her hand in gratitude to Claudia. "But you say the contessa di Alviano wishes to see me: Can you tell me for what purpose she intends me that honor?"

"Why, to give you that respectable protection, dear young lady, which the child of your parents claims from her," replied Claudia; " but she must give it to you under the mortifying circumstance of doing it secretly, since our intended archbishop has peremptorily commanded her to leave you to your fate; for he is as hard-hearted, and as much set against all who will not shun and abominate my Lord Fredrico as, if he himself had never done a wrong deed; although, if Fame says true of him, the will not be an arch—bishop in another world, if rank goes there by merit."

" Does the contessa kindly mean to send me immediately to Montalbano, to remove my dear uncle's fears for my safety?" asked Angelina anxiously.

" No; that could not be accomplished without Conte Giuseppe's knowlege," said Claudia; " so she means that you should occupy an apartment in this castle to-night."

Fredrico was infinitely happy at the idea of this arrangement, since he could now, without any painful anxiety upon Angelina's account, proceed in his intention of immediately sending intelligence, through

Father Jeronimo, to the Duca di Montalbano, of Lady Angelina's safety : and now,
after promising to see her early on the morrow with every information he could obtain
of her uncle from Father Jeronimo, and after repeated adieus, and sudden recollections of something more, and still more, of
importance to say to her, or some further
charge for her security to give to Claudia,
Fredrico departed for Santo Stefano; and
Lady Angelina, with a heart agitated by
many conflicting emotions, attended the
good Claudia into the inhabited part of the
magnificent castle of Rossarno.

"You need not, my dear compassionate
young lady," said the loquacious Claudia,
as they proceeded towards the contessa's
apartments, " you need not have expressed
so much concern at the idea of detaining
my young lord, or, alas! now our only
lord, from his pillow, by going on this embassy for you, as he now never sleeps, never seeks a pillow, unless he finds one upon the cold earth, when, overpowered by
fatigue, he drops into a slumber in his mysterious rambles through the woods and fo-

rest, where he often wanders now all day long; and then all night he sits up in my late lord's library, locked and barricaded up from the possibility of any intruder, where his enemies say ' his wicked companions assemble,. to plot new crimes with him;' but I say, ' how do they get in, unseen by any one?' and then I am told, ' that those who consign themselves to, the powers of darkness can become invisible at pleasure.'

"Then there is the arcivescovo, as he chooses to be called, although he has not taken holy orders yet, no, nor has commenced any of the rules of priesthood, that I know of; he is fond of nocturnal meetings too, not always liking to remain in his own chamber either; but then his associates have not consigned themselves to the fiends of darkness, for they are not, like my young lord's, always invisible."

At this moment, a door they were passing in a long gallery suddenly opened, and the archbishop stood before them.

"Whither, woman," he sternly said,

" are you daring to lead this stubborn apostate from all decorum, from all propriety?"

" O, no, most reverend signore! I am not leading her from either, I assure you; since it is from my young lord I am leading her to my own apartment," replied the half-alarmed Claudia, with an air of the most genuine simplicity; " for as I heard you, colendissimo Signore Giuseppe, tell my lady such things of Conte Fredrico but just this moment, when you ordered her, ' on her peril, not to protect the young lady,' I thought it would be a heinous sin, which his Reverenza Tommaso might make me repent full sorely, should I leave her in the power of such fell wickedness."

The stern brow of Giuseppe contracted to a darkened expression, and, after muttering something diametrically opposite to a blessing for such officiousness, he demanded from Angelina " where the unexceptionable protector she had so prudently chosen was gone, that he had so readily yielded up his charge?"

" Gone, my lord," replied Angelina,

with dignified composure, " to effect the benevolent purpose of informing the Duca di Montalbano of my safety."

" Gone!" repeated Giuseppe with more eagerness than was quite consistent with his determined stateliness; " gone! Fredrico gone from the castle?" For a moment he paused; something of the nature of a smile betrayed an effort to diffuse itself over his inflexible features; and as, with relaxing courtesy, he fixed his attention upon the agitated Angelina, he continued —

"" Then, since you are left by your chosen protector to your fate, Lady Angelina, I may, without deviating from the arbitrary precepts of conscience, take you under my immediate care."

" I am nearly subdued by fatigue, and requiring rest, my lord, this good woman's projected kindness would prove more congenial to my feelings, more appropriate to the hour, than your reverenza's meditated benevolence," Angelina replied, with impressively repelling dignity.

" Certainly, most certainly;" said Claudia, something officiously; " so now, reverendissmo signore, with your permission, I can take the Lady Angelina to more comfortable apartments than mine could have proved."

" Silence, officious babbler!" exclaimed Giuseppe angrily; " when your opinions and assistance are required, I shall issue my mandate for them. I think it necessary to conduct the Lady Angelina to the apartments of the contessa, before I conceive it expedient for her to retire to rest. Allow me, disdainful young lady, to give you the consolation of an interview with my good sister;" and he took the unwilling hand of the recoiling Angelina.

The wary Claudia, promptly perceiving that he purposed taking the light from her, and conjecturing, from that meditated manœuvre, that he intended to command her absence, she became at once stupidly inapprehensive of his obvious meaning, grasped her light with more determined hold, dropped her acquiescent curtesy, as if she had received an order to proceed, mended her pace, and, as she seemed respectfully intent upon lighting them on their way, au-

dibly exclaimed, although as if merely arti-
culating her anxious thoughts —

"Dear me, I hope my lady may not yet
have retired to rest; for, not expecting us
(unless her devotions are extended, as they
sometimes are), it is scarcely probable that
we shall find her up."

"Leave that light with me, and depart,"
said the archbishop, now finding he must
speak his wishes; "we shall not require
your attendance, most officious dame, to
the apartments of the contessa."

"O, colendissimo!" exclaimed Claudia,
in affected amazement and veneration of
simplicity, "What! and leave your holy
hand to the irreverence of carrying a menial's
light! O, no, illustrissimo signore, I know
my duty to the mother church, my respect
to the Reverendissimo Arcivescovo di Mazzarino too well, not humbly and obsequi-
ously to wait upon you," and, curtesying
profoundly, she still hurried on."

"Leave the light, and depart, as I command you," said Giuseppe peevishly:

"Dear now, your reverenza's holiness,
I pray you command no such imprudent

thing; for — for (pardon me, colendissimo signore), but my mind misgives me for your safety; 'you painted so horribly the profligacy and cruel turpitude of Monsignòre Fredrico 'so short a time since, that you cannot wonder I should still tremble at the very thoughts of him; or that I should fear, was 'he to return as speedily as I expect him, and find your reverenza protecting the young lady, that he might not with his terrible stiletto, which you told my lady ' was still reeking with his father's gore,' and give your holy merit a sly stab too; and indeed, may the saints protect your worship! but I have lately had a very portentous dream about you; fancying that I beheld your reverenza, in the very dead of night, enter *that very chamber there* (and Claudia pointed to a door), with (Heaven preserve us!) the *diavolo* before you, leading you in chains, which he seemed to have thrown around you; and who knows but, as dreams come always by the rule of contrarieties, that the *diavolo* may come after you in the form of Monsignòre Fredrico: and, being so forewarned by my vision of some impend-

ing evil threatening your holy reverence, **I**
dare not in conscience, I dare not in humanity, quit my post of guarding you!"

Lady Angelina had perceived, the moment Claudia pointed to the door where
the *diavolo,* in her dream, had led his reverenza to enter, it operated like an electric
shock upon the sensitive frame of Giuseppe,
felt the subsequent tremor of his hand, and
observed he no longer commanded the departure of dame Claudia — when promptly
she conjectured, that the apparently simple
superstition of this dream had it's meaning,
which the conscious prelate understood.

Giuseppe now, in thoughtful musing, led
his lovely companion after the sagacious
Claudia, his plans, from his ruminations,
seeming to undergo some decided changes,
for his complacency of countenance gra-
dually resumed the stern austerity it had
put on with his prelate's robes; and, on the
first opportunity, he dropped t'e hand of
Lady Angelina, which he had taken in innovating condescension.

At length they reached the contessa's
apartments, and, upon entering the anti-

chamber, Claudia darted forward, and, throwing open the door of an interior room, audibly announced —

" Monsignòre archbishop and Lady Angelina."

The haughty Giuseppé now preceded Lady Angelina into the last opened room, where the afflicted Zarina sat, anxiously expecting the child of her tenderly lamented friends, and who, upon finding by whom she was so unexpectedly accompanied, felt the most painful fears take possession of her bosom, in the alarming belief that her having dared to send for Lady Angelina, against his positive command, had been discovered by him.

" Your profligate son, Zarina," said the archbishop, when he had commodiously seated himself, " has left the castle, under the plausible pretence of further serving this infatuated girl. On my intended way to perform my last duties in the chapel for the night, I found this imprudent child under the auspices of your woman Claudia. Now, as this very degenerate daughter, of inestimable parents, is not, at this identical mo-

ment, under the guardianship of your diabolical offspring, I think we may, even con-
sistently with every conscientious scruple,
venture to give her temporary protection;
and therefore I have condescended to pardon her irreverence to me, and have brought
her to you, with my permission for your af-
fording her shelter for this night."

Lady Angelina would have only proudly
bowed her thanks, for protection so ungra-
ciously bestowed upon her, had not her recollection of the perplexity she had occasioned to Conte Fredrico, by that line of
conduct, subdued her rising indignation,
and now taught her, in a voice and with a
look of gentle conciliation, to say —

" I shall indeed be most grateful to the
Contessa di Alviano for permission to remain under her auspices until my dear uncle
sends a proper escort for me. I should not
be thus compelled to 'the hard necessity of
intruding upon any one for protection, had
time been allowed me, ere I was taken from
Santo Valentino, to apprise the Cardinal Gulielmo, that I was again exposed

to the dangers of the Tolmezos' enmity to
me."

Angelina had learned, in her long consultation with Fredrico upon the subject of
her safety, that the closest compact, under
the profaned name of friendship, subsisted
between Conte Giuseppe and almost all the
individuals of the Tolmezo family resident
at Montalbano castle: from this knowlege,
she had learned to tremble at Giuseppe's conduct in the corridor, fearing that it unequi-
vocally portended his meditating the project of aiding in their vile plots; and firmly
believing nothing could more effectually
secure her from the machinations of himself
and allies, than the intimation of her pos-
sessing a great man's favor, she was thus
induced (though shrinking from the idea of
a libertine's friendship) to announce, as a
friend interested for her, the powerful name
of Gulielmo.

The archbishop was electrified by no very
gentle shock at this high name. A crimson
tint diffused itself over his eloquently amazed countenance, and eagerly he reiterated

—" The Cardinal Gulielmo! the Cardinal Gulielmo! and is the Cardinal Gulielmo then interested for you, Lady Angelina?"-

" So kindly interested," she replied calmly, " that I have only to apply to his eminenza to have my safety most permanently secured."

" It has been unfortunately, infinitely unfortunate," returned Giuseppe, most evidently embarrassed and disconcerted, yet, with a powerful effort, again relaxing into the semblance of complacency, ' that I was not earlier apprised of this circumstance; for very widely different would then have been the reception the Contessa di Alviano and myself would have had the honor of giving you; for since his most illustrious eminence, my Lord Cardinal Gulielmo, is interested for the safety and happiness of Lady Angelina di Balermo, she must incontestibly merit the respect and services of all the estimable and discerning."

" Indeed," returned the grateful Angelina, something sarcastically, " the Cardinal Gulielmo stopped not to inquire my merits, when I awakened his interest. He learned I was a persecuted orphan, and he believed it no disgrace to a Christian prelate to befriend me."

Giuseppe keenly felt the sarcasm, but, endeavouring to conceal the mortification he experienced, hastily and pompously commenced a long and elaborate succession of offers of hearty services, and then entered with the sincere contessa upon the plan most prudently to be adopted on the present occasion for Lady Angelina's comfort and accommodation, when it was at length finally determined that an express should be instantly sent off by Giuseppe to the Duca di Montalbano, to accounce the perfect safety of Lady Angelina, who, from her recent alarms and fatigue, and from the duca's alarm too, they judged it expedient should take her répose that night at Rossarno castle, to spare her uncle and herself the agitation of their naturally affecting interview, until they were both better able to sustain it, by some hours at least of composure, if not of sleep."

All these matters being finally, and on

the part of the contessa kindly arranged, the dreadfully fatigued Angelina (who declined all refreshment from food, although ostentatiously pressed to it by the arch-bishop, and with maternal tenderness by the contessa), was consigned to the care of Claudia, who safely conducted her to an elegant and comfortable suit of apartments, to take her much required repose in.

"Ah, well!" exclaimed Claudia, the moment they had entered the dressing-room of those apartments, " here you would not have been to-night, let me tell you, had it not been for my ready dream, that promptly conveyed the knowlege of my being acquainted with more of his hy-pocrisy than he suspected. Marry, hang his mock reverence! how he scared me when he so unexpectedly popped out upon us. Going to his last chapel duties indeed! I wonder where was his light to guide him thither? Ah! no, no, the Deity who pre-sides there is not the one he wanders in darkness to worship. But, indeed, my dear young lady, had it not been for my fully awakened suspicion of his cloven feet, heaven knows what might have befallen you; for he is on too perfect an understanding with the folks at Montalbano castle, to have proved a faithful guard to you; and now solely to the Cardinal Gulielmo's great favor with the pope, and other motives for Giuseppe wishing to be in the good graces of his eminence, are you indebted for your present security."

Angèlina was again hastening to make her grateful acknowlegements to this shrewd and worthy woman, for all her kindness to her, when Claudia hastily interrupted her.

" It was not to lay your thanks under such heavy contributions, that I mentioned what I had done," she said; " it was only to gratify a propensity I have for talking; for, should you come to know me better, you will readily discover that Nature intended me for an old maid, though Fate played her a trick, and made me a wife; for never was antiquated spinster so incurably diseased with agonising curiosity as I am, never one so infatuatedly in love with other people's concerns than I am; and to

talk of them, good heaven! what a luxury
it is to talk of them! But come, dear
young lady, hasten to bed, that I may
go and give comfort to my poor dear child
Fredrico (whose principal nurse-maid I
was : I had him from the month, and
loved him from that hour), should he be
yet returned, with assurances of your perfect
safety.

Anxiety to spare her gallant preserver
every alarm upon her account, induced
Angelina to make more than usual expedition in her preparation for her pillow; and,
after devoutly returning her pious thanks-
givings to merciful heaven, for her late mi-
raculous escape from destruction, and for
her present promise of safety, she charged
the good Claudia not to delay seeking Conte.
Fredrico, to tell him, with her grateful re-
membrances, all that had befallen her since
they parted; and to hope she might see
him on the morrow.

Claudia, promising her all that she required, departed; and Angelina, again
invoking the protection of heaven, retired

to her pillow, cherishing but faint hopes
of finding her necessary repose there, while
it was thus strewed with those thorns she
'had now only to look for in her walk of
life.

CHAPTER XI.

CONTRARY to the cherished expectations of Angelina, the weariness of fatigue so successfully overpowered her with drowsiness, that, in defiance of all her sorrow's sad themes, she had benefited by some hours of sweet refreshing sleep, ere she awoke on the morrow, and found the good Claudia seated by her bed, patiently awaiting the dissipation of her tranquil slumber.

Angelina, blushing at finding it was late, sprang from her bed; and while Claudia was assisting her in her toilet, that good dame fully gratified her acknowleged propensity for talking.

" We have all been dormice this morning," said she, " as it was so much later, even than usual, when we retired : for my part, I scarcely think I should have been up by this time, only Conte Fredrico (I can never bring myself to call him by his unfortunate title of Alviano) roused me by tapping at my door, two hours ago, so anxious was he that I should be in readiness to serve you, and to deliver his messages to you."

"How good he is," said Angelina, brightly blushing; "you saw him, I hope, last night, Signora, before you retired."

"Indeed I did; and, holy virgin! what an agony he was in, when I told him, ' that pretended Arcivéscovo wanted to take you from my protection.'—Bless my sagacity, but I hope he has not got the freak of love into his head again; he has had enough of that folly I should think, to steel his heart against even the beautiful face he seems now ready to fall down and worship."

"Not but that this second choice, I have my suspicions of, is much more likely to make him happy than Lady Violante ever could have done; for amiable and lovely as she is, in mind and form, she has her faults; faults most likely to make a feeling husband wretched. Her vanity is even greater than her beauty, and she thirsts intemporately for universal admiration, as if that is all that is worth living for: it was her terrible propensity to coquetry, that aided the enemies of the family in the destruction of it's once most enviable happiness."

" But," said Angelina eagerly, most powerfully actuated by gratitude to her beloved Lady Constantia, whom many a suspicion in her mind identified as Violante. St. Seviero;—" but that propensity to coquetry may be, nay I am sure is, quite, quite subdued by sorrow and misfortunes; and fervently I hope, (if it is for their mutual happiness), that they may be yet united."

" Ah! no, from all that has happened, they never—never could be happy together, therefore do not wish them united, dear young lady," replied Claudia; " but surely you do not know all that has come to light in this sad business, or you could not, even for a moment, suppose they could ever be united."

" Indeed," said Angelina, sympathisingly, " I only know they loved, were to have been united, and that some direful calamities prevented that union, and consigned them both to misery."

"Ah!" returned Claudia, "there was not a livelier youth upon the surface of the earth, than Conte Fredrico was, only knowing sadness when others sorrowed; even gay as a guileless heart, the favors of fortune, and the affection of fond, indulgent parents could make him, until aided by his elder brother Conte Rolando, he unfortunately carried off Lady Violante, from the convent of Santo Rosolia in Rome, where she had just completed her noviciate.

"Well, this ill-omened step caused terrible consternation amongst us all, for she was the cardinal Gulielmo's own niece, and the most dreadful anathemas were denounced, by the whole conclave assembled upon the occasion, against the sacrilegious Fredrico. My lord and lady went off immediately from the villa di Alviano to Rome, where there was nothing but meetings between them and the cardinal Gulielmo; and at last it was settled, that the young lady should live with my lady, and marry the young conte as soon as he became of age.

" The Lady Violante was as much as
five years older than Fredrico, who seemed
at first, as if a mere youthful frolic had led
him to steal her from the convent, for love
did not appear to come voluntarily to his
heart ; but at last, gratitude for her partiality, and a sense of what honor obliged
him to perform for one who had risqued so
much through love for him, led him to return her affection ; and at length he appeared to become very much attached to her;
but as his love seemed to increase, hers as
apparently diminished; for she used to
plague him shamefully with all sorts of ca-
prices, to display to every one her unlimited power over this universally-admired
young man; and she would flirt too, and
sometimes to an almost unpardonable excess, with all the handsome young men who
flocked around her, on purpose, as it seemed, to make Fredrico jealous : but soon that
baneful passion recoiled upon herself; for
upon his return from the Morea, she strongly
suspected his passion was weakened, if not
destroyed, and she did nothing but pout, and
rage, and upbraid him.

" Soon after this period of Fredrico's return, Conte Rolando unfortunately came home from the wars too, and repaired to this castle, whither we had but just removed to, and for the first time of visiting his father's house, since Lady Violante had become an inmate in our family.

" Conte Rolando was, but perhaps you already know it, the only offspring of my lord's first marriage; and although my present lady is a woman of a strong, as well as an amiable mind, she never could divest herself of the fear; ' that as her lord's first wife had been like herself, the chosen of his heart, and that; it is said, first love is always the most tender, his attachment to even the memory of his first contessa must be more powerful than that he felt for her, and therefore her child Fredrico could only claim an inferior place in the paternal heart.'

" My late lord was a most acute observer, and he soon developed this secret, although so carefully guarded by my lady. In respect to herself, this belief was totally unfounded. I, among many of the household, had lived in the family during the first contessa's time, and we all saw he was more tenderly attached to his second wife, more truly happy with her, and that we all, too, thought most natural, since the second lady was infinitely more attractive, both in form and mind than the first: but relative to her child, my dear lady was not mistaken; — not that my lord did not tenderly love Fredrico, but Conte Rolando was his first born, had first awakened his paternal pride and affection in his father's heart, and pity mingling with it for his having so early lost his adoring mother: this sentiment gave more tenderness to his attachment for Rolando, than to that he bore Fredrico, who had known no sorrow or misfortune; but with consciousness of this partiality in his breast, he unluckily strove to conceal it, with the laudable view of sparing his adored wife a grief; but, alas! in doing which, he impress-ed upon the susceptible mind of his elder son, the painful certainty of being less dear to his father's heart, than his more univer-sally-beloved brother.

"Conte Rolando, six years older than his brother, was like that brother, one of

the noble youths the world had to boast of;
but although alike in mental and personal
endowments, in many of the dispositions of
their minds, the resemblance failed. — Fredrico was open, spirited, full of whim and
vivacity, making friends by the fascinations
of his manners, where the rank and expectations of the heir could command them,
but Conte Rolando was meek of spirit,
though still brave in battle : of trembling
sensibility, and not justly appreciating his
own intellectual stores, his manners wore
the restraint of invincible reserve, and believing all, I doubt not, his uncle Giuseppe
instilled into his mind, he imbibed the misery of thinking, that with his mother he
had lost the only being who tenderly regarded him; and from this conviction torturing to an affectionate disposition, his
heart became the abode of melancholy; and
his deportment was infected with that sadness.

" But soon after his last calamitous return to the castle of his father, his habitual
melancholy assumed the appearance of despondence. — Lady Violante seemed wretch-

ed, and Fredrico became restless, and thoughtful, and at length set out post for Rome, and scarcely was he gone, when Conte Rolando fell dangerously ill: Lady Violante was his principal nurse, and from the whole of her conduct then, and upon his recovery, it became evident in all around her, that she had transferred her love from Conte Fredrico to his brother.

" At length Conte Fredrico returned, more melancholy than he departed, and had a long conference the day of his arrival with each of his parents; with his brother and Lady Violante; and then they all, afterwards with each other; and after these separate conferences, each individual seemed to part dissatisfied with the other.—Oh! it was indeed a mournful day; the family met not at table; and all was gloomy sadness, foreboding the calamities of the night.

" At midnight it was discovered that Conte Rolando and Lady Violante had eloped together.—My lord too was absent, and Fredrico no where to be found; and from all that has been collected from presumptive evidence, thus appears the horrid aspect of affairs.

" My lord, favoring the cause of his eldest son, had planned the elopement, and had himself gone off with the young couple to see them united. Fredrico, apprised of the plan, in jealousy and indignation, was in wait to frustrate it — but how the direful catastrophe was perpetrated, no witness appears to tell. Lady Violante refuses to make any communications, except in announcing ' her firm belief of Fredrico's guilt.'

" But, alas! my lord and Conte Rolando disappeared ; the attendants described ' their being surrounded by an armed troop, who dragged their lord from the carriage, whom they saw no more.' However, from the search which was made afterwards, a track of blood was discovered from a spot near where the carriage was stopped to an obscure coppice on the banks of the Arno, where Rolando's hat, some of his clothes, and part of the insignia of the military order of St. Marc, which he wore, were found. Of his assassination there is

certainly no doubt, although the Arno ne-
-ver returned his body, for into that it was
surely precipitated: and in sad, sad confirmation of the further direful catastrophe of
the night, the emissaries of Giuseppe found
the body of my poor lord, clad as he left
home, with the well-known dagger of Fredrico (which he had taken in battle from a
Mahometan janizary in the Morea) stuck in
his heart, hid under a heap of stones; but
in such a state of putridity, that, only for
his clothes, he could never, I think, have
been recognised.

"You can easily imagine, my dear young
lady, what a distracted family we since
have been. Conte Fredrico, although arraigned for murder, would not fly, but voluntarily delivering himself into the hands of
justice, has been, through powerful interest, granted the pontiff's protection to remain at large, to seek some witness of his
innocence, who, it seems, has fled, bribed,
no doubt, by the enemies of Fredrico; yet
further than the neighbourhood of this castle
he has never but once wandered in that
search; and, by that mysterious conduct,

makes almost all believe there is no witness to find, and that he is absolutely guilty.

" Then, although no longer enduring the presence of her universally-condemned son, the distracted contessa would not remove from this castle, where the body of her murdered husband is interred, and to whose memory the hypocritical Giuseppe erected that magnificent monument you beheld in the chapel, solely at his own expence; and remains here to irritate the contessa still further against her unfortunate son, to be a spy upon poor Fredrico, and to carry on still further his co-operations with the enemies of that unhappy young man."

Most powerful was the effect this dreadful narrative had upon the susceptible feelings of Lady Angelina; but still, like Claudia, her mind clung to the firm conviction of Conte Fredrico's innocence; while the long-cherished belief of Lady Violante, and the abadessa of Santo Valentino, being the same individual, was almost annihilated. "No," Angelina thought, in grateful, affectionate partiality, " no, the sweet, mild,

lovely excellence Lady Constantia ever
evinced, proclaimed at once that she could
never have been the capricious, flirting, perfidious Violante: yet, if she was not, how
came she so deeply in the secrets of Fredrico? how came she to learn such detestation of him? O! she could not well tell!"
and the more poor Angelina meditated upon the subject, the more perplexed she became, until her anxiety to learn, if possible,
the fact, overcoming her disinclination to
prolong, by even a single question, the sad
theme of those direful calamities, which she
considered it almost reprehensible in any
one not connected with the family even to
listen to, she ventured, in the least unpardonable method she could devise for the gratification of a curiosity, prompted chiefly
by her affection and interest for Lady Constantia, to inquire " if there was any portrait of Lady Violante in the castle?"
" Not one that you can see, dear young
lady, although, I believe, there is one, but
it is in monsignore's closet, locked up there
as carefully as the dreadful secret, which
will at last destroy him, is within his bosom.

I never saw the portrait; but I fancy it was displeasing to Lady Violante's vanity, in not being beautiful enough for her, as she was heard to say, ' she saw nothing to admire in it but the motive which caused it to be drawn.' That motive was Fredrico's affection for her, which she then severely wounded; for he, dear young gentleman, answered, in an unusual tone of pique for him, ' that, although he saw every thing to admire in it, yet she should never more be displeased by viewing it;' and with a countenance flushed to the tint of a damask rose, he ordered Fernando, his own attached *camerière*, to take it instantly to his own (Fredrico) private *gabinètto*, where it has since remained."

"I wish," said Angelina sighing, " I had some description of Lady Violante; because I—I think I have seen her."

" I'll describe her for you," replied Claudia; " yet, if I do so, I may get into one of my long stories again, and you will stand no chance of hearing the young conte's messages to you."

" O! signora, and have you messages

from Conte di Alviano to me, and forbore all this time to declare them?" exclaimed Angelina upbraidingly.

" Why, bless your little impatient heart, that I am sure is as pure and as clear as your complexion; I intimated something of the kind, just after you opened these dazzling orbs of yours, but you did not seem to care about it."

" O! I must have been still in my heavy sleep then; for surely any message Conte di Alviano is so good to send me, must be received with attentive gratitude by me, who am under such an incalculable debt of obligation to him."

" Well, it cannot now be demanded with more eagerness than the first order I received this morning was given : for me to arise, that I might hasten to your chamber, with an entreaty ' for your granting him an interview,' but in my presence, mark you! so thoughtful was he of propriety,—' as soon as it was possible for you, in my late lord's library.'"

" Well! I—I am ready, quite ready to attend him now," said Angelina, brightly blushing.

" And now he does not wish to see you, so capricious a thing is man, young lady; for I was scarcely dressed, with all my expedition to oblige him, when back monsignòre comes, his eyes having lost all that short-lived animation the thought of seeing you, who did him justice, had inspired; and in the sad tones I hate to hear him speak in, he tells me, poor dear soul —

' That, upon reflection, he was painfully convinced of the absolute necessity he was under of foregoing the happiness of seeing you, ere your departure from Rossarno; since he feared the breath of calumny might dare to rest upon your spotless fame, were you known to hold a moment's conference with a proscribed being like him, after the dire necessity you found yourself in of accepting his services to protect you from an imminent peril had subsided. He had few in the world now but foes, and some of their invidious enmity would unquestionably revert to you, did your compassionating feelings lead you to appear his friend; and, therefore, for your sake, he must henceforth — unless you should again calamitously require a protector — shun the gratification of conversing with, or even of beholding you, until the period should arrive when even the most fastidious could deem it no degradation to the immaculate fame of Lady Angelina di Balermo, should she own she believed him not unworthy of esteem.' "

" Alas!" exclaimed Angelina in grief of heart, " and am I no more to behold my preserver until the world learns to be just to innocence ?"

" Why, so monsignòre has determined, and very nobly determined, I see you think," replied Claudia archly; " but, although he is adamant in keeping $resolutions$ inspired by his sense of duty, yet it comes into my head, I cannot tell why, that some little untoward, teasing, unforeseen circumstances will be continually arising to frustrate this very judicious resolution of his; but, in the mean time, let me not omit to give you another message.

" Monsignòre desired me to tell you, ' that Father Marsilio has promised faithfully to engage his Fratello Jeronimo in your interest, who was certainly summoned to attend the duca by Father Ezzelino (the time he quitted you to proceed to San Stefano for that purpose), that he sat up with il signó dúca, and was not therefore at the monastery when Fredrico saw Father Marsilio upon that subject.'

" But, although Monsignòre Fredrico was sadly grieved at the idea of not being able to inform you of all this himself, yet I gave gladness to his heart when I told him how judiciously you had managed to secure your safety, and the civility of Giuseppe by the intimation of the Cardinal Gulielmo's interest in your concerns. Indeed, my intelligence seemed to inspire him all at once with new life; ' as it hushed,' he said, ' all the alarming apprehensions he had sustained relative to your return to Montalbano Castle.' "

" O! how benevolent Conte di Alviano is," said Angelina feelingly; " with a heart rived by such direful afflictions, so kindly to turn his thoughts upon my interest and safety."

" Ah! it will be well if the knight errantry of his benevolence does not lead his thoughts too frequently upon your interests, until he ceases to remember his own," returned Claudia.

A loud and lengthened peal at the great portal bell now announcing an importunate candidate for admittance into the castle; Claudia abruptly quitted Angelina, to learn who was arrived, not quite devoid of apprehension of it's proving some hostile harbinger of fearful justice to her beloved Fredrico: however, she soon returned with a brightened countenance, to announce to Lady Angelina, " the arrival of the courier who preceded the Duca di Montalbano's physician and la duchessa's confessor, who were on their way to Rossarno, to conduct Lady Angelina to the castle of her uncle.

" Giuseppe, I have found out," continued Claudia, " sent a private letter to that bird of his feather, Ezzelino, when he dispatched the messenger to announce your safety to il signore duca; so I warrant me, you may thank his Eminence Gulielmo for this speedy and respectful escort home, as well as for our probationary archbishop's civility; for he has himself ordered your breakfast to be served with all possible elegance and attention, but in these apartments; as he has expressly forbidden my lady's intention of receiving you at her breakfast table, and, indeed, has prohibited all further intercourse between you and her at present; I suppose, because you are so stedfast to your gratitude for Fredrico; and he fears you might soften the mother's heart from that harshness and abhorrence he has toiled so hard to steel it with against her unfortunate son; and my lady's griefs have so unhinged her once strong mind, that she no longer seems to act from her own judgement, but rests implicitly upon this man's advice, because he is the brother of her lamented husband; and that, with all my endeavours, she has yet imbibed no suspicion of the hypocrisy of his heart."

Another loud peal of the portal bell proclaimed the arrival of Fathers Jeronimo and Ezzelino, when Claudia would have hurried away, to yield further gratification to her insatiable curiosity, had not the entrance of Lady Angelina's breakfast pre-

vented her departure; as she considered it
her duty to remain and assist in attendance
upon her—'a duty which, she felt assured,
would oblige both the contessa and her
son by her voluntary performance of.

AT length Father Jeronimo, having a numerous list of patients to visit, became impatient at the protracted consultations of Ezzelino and Giuseppe, which they held in earnest and private conference, when announcing that he could no longer delay the performance of the duties of his medical profession, the congress unwillingly broke up, and Lady Angelina was summoned to depart; but, ere she quitted the apartments she had reposed in, she received a message from the Contessa di Alviano, by her chaplain, Father Tommaso di Sanfermo, expressive of " her infinite concern that the domestic calamities, by which she was overwhelmed, had prevented her giving, to the child of her once dearest friends, the reception her heart would have dictated under happier auspices."

To this politely kind remembrance of her,
Lady Angelina returned a courteous reply;
and, after making her acknowlegements to
Claudia, for all her goodness and attention
to her, she obeyed the summons of the archbishop.

In the grand saloon of the castle Lady
Angelina was most graciously received, by
the probationary archbishop, where every
bow of homage he met her with, she placed
to the account of the cardinal patron, whose
gratitude alone was debtor for such an innovation of revenue and courtesy; but Angelina soon perceiving a stranger monk present, and concluding him to be the physician Jeronimo, she hastened to make her
anxious inquiries relative to her uncle's
health from him.

Her belief was just; and Father Jeronimo conveyed to her affectionate heart the
unexpected gratification of a promising account of the Duca di Montalbano's health,
since the dreadful alarm he had been un-
guardedly thrown into upon her account
the preceding night, had been productive
of the most happy consequences; having

aroused him from a nervous apathy, or lethargic languor, which it might have proved difficult, even by medicine, to overcome; and, from all the energies of his mind being thus awakened to the acutest sense of feeling, the ultimate consequence might be hoped for in the most auspicious form.

The joy of Angelina at this most happy and soothing intelligence was lively and sincere; and she felt almost reconciled to the terror she had been doomed to endure, since it had led to so fortunate a change in the alarming indisposition of her uncle.

The wary Ezzelino, perceiving that Lady Angelina had not bestowed upon him even the common place civility of a meeting compliment, and tremblingly alive to the apprehension of any suspicion, combined with her alarming adventures of the preceding night, resting upon him, resolved to assume the aspect of indignant feeling at unmerited slight; and, with a sarcastic smile of highly-offended dignity, he addressed her: —

.. " I should have thought — should have expected, that the exquisite humanity, and pre-eminently refined urbanity of Lady Angelina di Balermo, would have led that most renownedly amiable young lady to the inquiry, at least, of how I found myself, after the very direful degree of alarm her mysterious appearance occasioned to me?"

"Could I have supposed it, in possibility, for Father Ezzelino to have felt the surprise of an alarm for my fate," replied Angelina, calmly, " I should most certainly have gone through the ceremony I omitted; but as I saw that most reverend father had survived the greater trial of hearing of my safety in honorable protection, I perceived all inquiries for the state of his nerves were totally unnecessary."

The voluptuous purple of Father Ezzelino's cheeks changed to the pale shade of death; and, while his lips quivered with spiteful passion, his rage and mortification stifled his reply, in each attempt he made to utter it; and Angelina, no longer condescending to bestow her attention upon him, requested the archbishop's permission to depart; when Father Jeronimo anxiously seconding the request, the wily Giuseppe graciously granted permission, and Angelina set out, without further delay, to the castle di Montalbano.

The mellow tones of the portal bell, announcing her arrival, vibrated with melancholy thrill through the heart of Angelina. It seemed to toll the knell of her lost parents, of her devoted uncle, and of the fell blight of all her own individual happiness.

To this castle, and all the possessions of her illustrious ancestors, she had now conviction that she still might prove the only lawful heir; yet now she was about to enter as a poor persecuted dependent, despoiled of the favor and courtesy of all; where once every sweet smile of affection, kindness, and respect, most fondly greeted her. She sighed; tears trembled in her eyes. "But, are not these trials," whispered pious reflection, "which you are thus doomed to endue, inflicted by the all-wise and unerring Ruler of the universe?"—Angelina blushed, in penitent acquiescence. "Assuredly they are," she firmly, but mentally ejaculated— "and, Oh! may I never, never, falter in the task of submissive duty; never murmur at the thorns which strew my path of life, but still cherish, in the memory of my heart's veneration, a lively recollection of the sacred hand which sheds them there."

These were the thoughts, and such the aspirations, that gave fortitude to the heart, firmness to the steps, and serenity to the fascinating countenance of Lady Angelina, as she once more entered that castle, where pained reminiscence told her, "how she had been loved, and how severely tortured."

The last venerable porter, whose hoary head proclaimed the past years of faithful service, was now replaced by a youthful voluptuary, reared by sloth and dissipation. Nothing familiar to the fondly-cherished remembrance of local attachment met the wistful eyes of Lady Angelina, but the antient walls of the palace of her ancestors. All those living objects were removed, which still retained a lively image in the memory of an affectionate heart; and sighs only of regret were now left to fill the void so painfully made, by being so lost, and so regarded.

The domestic, stationed to watch for the

arrival of Lady Angelina, instantly, (according to the orders he had received,) announced this event to Father Patrick O'Carrol, who promptly appeared to receive her.

This Catholic Priest had a face that, while it refused to answer the inquiring eye, relative to the store of intellectual endowments he possessed, most promptly and irresistibly prepossessed every beholder in his favor, by the invincible good humor it betrayed, and the stamp of a guileless heart it guaranteed.

He was a native of Ireland, born of parents who, although tenaciously impressed with a visionary belief of their claim to antient high descent, classed with the most indigent of their fellow beings. At an early age he evinced a strong propensity for the achievement of learning to read; which none of his then-living kindred had ever discovered. The priest of the parish he resided in, pleased with this little fibre of genius, became his instructor, and, in the course of a few years, accomplished him for the practice of an itinerant professor of knowlege; a sort of occupation followed in that coun-

try; under the denomination of a " poor
scholar ;" and never, perhaps, was appellation more appropriately bestowed, than it
then was upon the hero of our present di-
gressive tale. But, although humble his
pretensions to knowlege, some pious Ca-
tholics thought otherwise; and, believing
him a saint in embryo, who would, if pro-
perly nurtured, mature into an ornament to
learning and the church, they commenced
a subscription for his benefit, which enabled
them to send him, for the completion of his
education, to the convent of St. Bertam's,
at St. Omer's; and when that great task
was performed, and that he had entered into
holy orders, the principal of his partially-
kind Hibernian patrons exported an only
son from Ireland, consigned to the care of
Father Patrick O'Carrol; under whose auspices he was to make the then grand conti-
nental tour of Europe.

This task being at length most conscien-
tiously accomplished by the worthy Patrick, he, with his pupil, were about to em-
bark at Naples, on their return to their native country, when, to the unfortunate

priest's infinite dismay, his sacred charge performed a most unexpected frolic, by eloping with a beautiful opera-dancer, with whom, totally unknown to the unsuspecting Patrick, he had united his fate; not only to his own complete ruin, but to the eternal disgrace of poor Father O'Carrol, who, implicated as a coadjutor, was utterly, and for ever, discarded by his Hibernian friends.

After the elopement of his pupil, whose valet contrived to rob poor Patrick of all his cash, and every valuable he possessed, ere he departed with his master, the now destitute priest wandered about Naples, encountering a diversity of fortunes, but chiefly of ungenial aspect, until the lately ennobled Lorenzago, elder brother to the Duchessa di Montalbano, to the poor priest's infinite amazement, as well as joy, appointed him domestic chaplain and confessor to the hypochondriac Duca di Montalbano.

Although nearly thirteen years had elapsed since Father Patrick had quitted his native country, he still retained his national brogue; every peculiar idiom of speech, with each endemial expression, as

powerfully as the language he now spoke in
would admit of, as if he still scrupulously
cherished them with religious veneration;
indeed so cherishing them, that, if he found
no Italian word ready to assist his meaning,
he unhesitatingly made use of those he had
been accustomed to in his own country; so
that those, who associated with him, soon
learned to understand the definition of
" *kilt ! palaver ! botheration ! spalpeen !*
&c. &c.'' as well as he did himself ; and in
whom the wary Lorenzago having developed a simplicity of heart, and an unsuspecting, open, unreservedness of mind,
which led him to perpetually to repeat, in
his blundering ingenuousness, all he heard,
or all he knew ; not even making his own
concerns an exemption from this unbridled
flow of communicative propensity, which so
exactly suited him for Conte Lorenzago's
purpose, that he gladly gave him that already-mentioned lucrative and honorable
situation, in which the guileless Father
O'Carrol was often unconsciously a powerful agent in the promotion of plots, from

which, had he been aware of, his integrity. would have led him to recoil in horror.

The moment Father Patrick beheld Lady Angelina advancing towards him, a smile of animated pleasure beamed promptly over his ever-placid countenance; and, hastening to meet her, he seised her hand, more with the air of honest plebeian cordiality, than with any thing like a tincture of courtly polish.

"Och! welcome as the flowers, in May! —welcome, as a beautiful, drizzling shower, to the parched up traveller, in the desert, are you to my two looking eyes, jewel of the world!" he exclaimed—"for sure it was myself (and more grief to me for it) who *kilt* the Duca (and good luck to him) with the black tidings, of the banditti, having brought you away, with all the other rubbish, which brother Ezzelino, made such a botheration about;—but success, to my own big blunder! for after the duca was *kilt*, with my news, his faculties suddenly started from the knap, we thought was upon them, for life; and from their bed ridden sloth, began to be making such a *hulabaloo*, of feeling; that myself thought, he never would, any how, survive this sure, and certain, road to dying, but when the gay news came, that you were found my honey! Oh to be sure, he was not glad! Och the fates! and sudden dissolutions! but it was I, who thought, it was all over with us; and that joy, would be, our mutual executioner; for there was the poor duca, chattering his glee, in an ague fit; and myself struck dumb, with the choking quinsy, of sympathy."

Angelina was sensibly affected at this account of the distress her affectionate uncle had been overwhelmed with, by that direful plot of villany, from which she had so miraculously escaped; and Father Jeronimo, apprehending some evil consequences to the invalid duca, from the guileless Patrick's acknowleged propensity to blundering, was he intrusted to announce the arrival of Lady Angelina, undertook to be himself the herald of that pleasing intelligence.

While waiting in the antichamber to the duca's apartment, anxiously expecting her summons to attend her uncle, Angelina learned, from the communicative Father Patrick, some particulars of the scene of consternation her disappearance, the preceding evening, had occasioned in the castle.

"'The hours, seemed to have got, mill-stones round their necks;'" said he; "'and the minutes, to be having leaden wings, to their heels;'" from the instant, the poor duca, and myself, sat, with the time-length-ening cap, of expectation on us ; he with his watch, in his trembling hand, eying it eagerly, with reproachful glances, for the tardiness of it's motion.

"'Alas! holy father!'" he says—says he. "'Time lags even more than ever, I think; and it has gone, but heavily with me, since my beloved Angelina, forsook me. This slothful progress, of time, tells me, in anti-cipating despondence, she will never, never, return to me.'"

"'Ah! then, can't you be easy, you crea-ture you?'" says I, "'and don't be mind-ing, what any of the tribes of sloth, will whisper to you; for they are but a *spalpeen*

race:—'tho indeed, indeed, myself is tired
too; and thats a sure thing, in this gloomy
waiting room, of expectation; for sorrow
thing, exhausts the patience, of an Irishman sooner; than to be waiting, to give
the kind, and cordial welcome, of hospitality, to any one.'"

" Just at this moment, tatter away, went
the portal bell, ready to bother the deaf.

" 'My niece! my child! my darling!' "
exclaimed the duca, in the shaking palsy,
of joy. " 'Oh! run, fly holy father, and
bring her, to her parent's arm.'"

" 'Faith jewel!' " says I, " 'I'll run for the
bare life; but as for flying, thats out of my
element; altho my wild Irish wings, were
never clipt, even by that careful housewife,
adversity.' "

" So with that, down I went to the big
hall; where who should I meet, but my
brothers, Jeronimo, and Ezzelino; the latter, thumping his breast, for all the world, as
if death was come without a moment's
warning, to bring him away; and that he
wanted to belabor, every sin out of him, before the leveller of all, should lay him mo-

tionless ; but as soon as he set eyes, upon myself, he began to chaunt out, his Italian howl of lamentation, ' about Lady Angelina, being brought away, in the forest, by theives of a banditti ; with his own strong box' (—" henn myself is mighty apt, to suppose, out of the same stone, with his heart")—' in which, was contained, the title deeds of an estate, just dropped from the moon; to him ; and the manuscript of a work'—(" written as, I take it, by the light of that same, convenient moon")—' for which he expected a cardinalate.'

" On my safe conscience, and you *may expect*, to the end, of every chapter, in your last labor, thinks I, to myself; for I was so stagnated, with all this tribulation, that sorrow speak, could I, speak.

" Then comes Conte Lorenzago, picceering into the hall, to add to the *hulabaloo*; and there he kept singing out, about your loss; which would inevitably kill, your poor uncle; while Ezzelina, whined out his recitativo lamentation, for the loss of his estate, and cardinalate; which those more fortunate rogues, had invested themselves with ;

and at last, they both chimed into a duet, of botheration to me; ' not, to let the duca be knowing a morsel, about the loss of his niece; until every thing would be attempted, to discover, and regain her;' and then, bid me, ' hurry back to my patron, and invent, some plausible excuse, for Lady Angelina's nonappearance,' but somehow, sorrow worse hand, at invention any where, than Father Pat.—I never could be getting a lie, to rise out of my throat, in all my born days; and even a sermon, myself could never invent, for the edification of our congregation, at St. Bertam's; so that it was I, was the fine fellow, to be sent, as the mother of invention, and by dad ! so overcharged was I, with this secret; that in hiding it, it was so big for my bosom, that I betrayed it all; every word of it!' and if it was not lucky, that Father Jeronimo, was within call, I wonder at it !"

At this moment the medical monk appeared, to announce the Duca di Montalbano being ready and anxious to embrace his niece, when the lovely and affectionate Angelina, summoning at once all the firmness she could command, to sustain her, without subduing the sensitive invalid, through their affecting interview, promptly followed Father Jeronimo to the chamber of her uncle.

CHAPTER XIII.

SIGISMUND, Duca di Montalbano, was at this period in his thirty-ninth year; his brother ('Theadore, the father of Angelina), and himself, had been the only children of their illustrious parents. Theadore, three years older than Sigismund, was endowed with every personal attraction, every mental excellence and treasure of the heart. Sigismund, equally gifted by nature with intellectual stores and goodness, had, from his earliest days, drooped beneath a weakliness of constitution, which unfitted him for any of the active, health-inspiring pursuits, his brother found delight in; neither in their mode of education could they tread the same path.

Strong in genius, as robust in frame, Theadore seised at once all knowlege pre-

VOL. I. M

sented by his preceptors to him; and endured every deprivation and toil of education, at a public school, without feeling them as such, or regretting the pleasures his absence from home debarred him of. Learning to him was no exertion, yet it was no delight, since his pleasures he found in á more active field; exercise was his loved pastime; and tilts and tournaments, campaigns and battles, the idols of his bosom; and he was, in consequence, the pride and treasure of his father's heart; who, himself, a renowned general, estimated only in mankind the heroic hardy soldier.

Sigismund, in helpless weakness, clung to his mother, and upon him her tenderest maternal affection rested; although pride still taught her to glory in the beauty, talents, and valor of her elder boy. Under the auspices, therefore, of his fond indulgent mother, poor Sigismund received his education from private preceptors, whose principal charge was, to exact no diligence from him inimical to health. But while she considered almost every species of exercise too powerful for his delicate frame to sus-

tain, she injudiciously, by promoting sedentary pursuits, awakened in his mind a love
of deep and intense study, injurious to that
health, her anxious wishes panted to promote.

In vain did his father remonstrate against
the evident errors of her plan; in vain did
Theadore, disapproving of what he saw was
rapidly increasing the weakness of his brother's frame, seduce him from his studies,
and place him on the least spirited horse of
his own stud, and carefully lead him round
the demesne; in vain teach him the use of
the gun—place a bow and arrow in his
hand—or give him the lightest bar he could
procure to fling. The anxious duchessa,
missing her tender charge, would promptly
seek him; lecture Theadore for cruelty,
and lay her nursling up again in inactivity,
to polish his mind more brilliantly, and to
find his amusements in the varied attain-
ments and accomplishments of the arts and
sciences.

The result of this different mode of education and indulgence to propensity, was,
that when Theadore attained his twenty-

M 2

third year, Sigismund his twentieth, the elder brother was the glory of his father's heart, the beloved of his friends, the pride of his countrymen, as a distinguished protector of his country, and the admiration of the fair; while the poor younger was the ridicule of the indiscriminating multitude, and loved only by a very few.

Nothing could rob the naturally fine countenance of Sigismund of it's attractive sweetness, and eloquence of expression; but the pallid tints of sallow sickliness and languor overspread it's surface, whilst his figure, formed on a slight fragile scale, had sunk in the ungenial nursery of sedentary employments, from it's natural height; and drooping to the line of weakness, curved into almost deformity. His mind, while enriched by all the stores of science, had still, by indulging too deeply in all the fascinations of poetry and music, cherished and encouraged the natural susceptibilities of his heart; and now, with all the propensities to romantic enthusiastic love in his mind, he found himself, in form, an antidote to the inspiration of reciprocal attachment; and whilst thus,

too, in pursuit of sedentary love, his naturally weak constitution was enfeebled;
until infecting his mental powers by it's sympathy, it gave to them the unfortunate im-
pulsion of wooing sickness; and, in the imbecile malady of hypochondriacism, he learned to rest his chief happiness in the fancied
accumulation of every incurable disease.

Theadore, covered with Fame's immortal
laurels, had a second time returned to his
father's castle, from Venetian contests with
the Infidels, when the smiles of propitious
love hailed his approach; and, under the
auspicious approbation of their mutual
friends, he was happily united to the lovely
and accomplished niece of the Duca di Modena.

The susceptible Sigismund had long beheld the matchless fascinations of this daughter of the house of Modena, with admiration too powerful for his repose; but
promptly finding she was the beloved of his
brother's bosom, he sighed in secret hope-
lessness; and when she became the wife of
that brother's choice, he heroically exterminated the glowing flame, and gently fan-

ning it's embers into tender friendship and
esteem; he bestowed both with sincerity
upon her whilst she lived, and then gave
them, transformed into parental affection, as
an inheritance from her mother, to her only
offspring, the little Angelina, who experienced the dire misfortune of losing this
young, lovely, and incomparable parent,
ere she had completed her fourth year.

. Shortly after this period of sorrowing
mourning, in the family of Montalbano, the
partial mother of Sigismund also paid her debt
to nature; and her death was speedily followed by that of her husband; who, irritated
and disgusted by the nourished weakness of
his younger son, cruelly and unjustifiably
cut him off with a shilling; in the vain hope
that necessity might arouse him into vigor,
and teach him the blessings and comforts of
activity, in the pursuit of maintenance.

But Theadore, tenderly attached to his unfortunate brother, in despite of all his adven-
titious foibles, no sooner found what was his
revered father's last testament, than, in the
zeal of paternal affection, (but with every
precaution to save his late parent from cen-

sure, for injustice), cancelled this partial will; and not only cancelled it's disinheriting clause, but added considerably to the formerly-arranged patrimony of Sigismund; in the considerate belief, that bodily infirmities and defects, like his, absolutely required affluence, to secure attention and respect; and further made it as his most importunate request to his grateful brother, that he should henceforth consider the Castle di Montalbano as his home.

From the hour he sustained the deeply-rooted affliction, the early loss of his adored wife overwhelmed him with, Theadore seemed to acquire a still greater fondness for a soldier's life; as if, in the toils of war, and the din of battle, he could only lose the poignancy of that grief, which consumed his happiness; and the Venetian contests with the Turks gave him full and ample field for the indulgence of this specific, against the increasing malady of his woe; and the family of Montalbano, like the Alvianos', being Venetian, (although their property chiefly lay in Tuscany), he gladly laid his claim to Venice as his country, and fought

it's battles, as one of it's most successful
champions, leaving his adored child to the.
care of his brother at Montalbano Castle,.
during his campaigns; except in the last.
unfortunate one, when he lucklessly per- -
mitted her visits to the wily family of Tolmezo.

From the period of Theadore's marriage,
Sigismund, exerting some particles of the
native energy of his mind, carefully guarded his bosom against the inroads of the tender passion, until the unfortunate time of
Minora Tolmezo's accompanying Angelina
to the Castle di Montalbano.

It had been the original plan of the specious and insinuating family, of Tolmezo,
when they instructed the beautiful Minora
to ingratiate herself into the favor of Angelina
so completely, as to obtain from her an invitation to the castle of her father, that the
heart of that father should, on his imme-
diately-expected return from the Morea, be
assailed by his daughter's fair visitor, with
the ambitious view of her becoming Duchessa di Montalbano. Well instructed by
her wily preceptors, Minora judiciously

paid the flattering and seductive incense of respect and attention to the susceptible Sigismund; well initiated in the knowlege of his brother, highly reverencing his opinions, and being likely to make no second choice without his approbation. But the effect of these assiduities went further than was first intended; and, where she only aimed at inspiring esteem, to insure commendation and kind services, she made a tender impression on the heart of Sigismund.

This secret, the penetrating Ezzelino, then on a visit to the really-amiable and unsuspecting Viletta di Tolmezo, soon developed; instantly he wrote home an account of the discovery he had made. " The presumptive heir to the dukedom was captivated; the duca himself, from all that he had artfully learned in the family, most likely to prove invulnerable. The duca might not live to return from the supposed embassy he was gone upon; and, without further trouble, the ambition of the family might be gratified."

A new line of conduct was now marked

out for Minora; and, with seductive, half-retiring, half-encouraging tenderness, she promptly secured that conquest she had un-intentionally made.

The astonished vanity of Sigismund here proved a powerful auxiliary; he thought himself voluntarily beloved by a most fasci-natingly-beautiful, and, as he believed, in-nocent and amiable young woman, whom he had not even attempted to woo; and his gratitude now aiding his love, he offered himself to Minora, who had, by her blan-dishments, lured him into making this offer, without even waiting for the approbation of his brother; and with eagerness she ac-cepted him, for her heart, only devoted to Fredrico di Alviano, was now writhing in the jealous pangs of unrequited, nay, even rejected love; for she had here quitted the villa di Castrioto, revealed to him her pas-sion, and had been politely, but unequivo-cally repulsed; and wishing to marry im-mediately, to prove to this young man she did not break her heart in despair for him, cared not to whom her hand was given : and further, to promote this her plan for braving the slights of Fredrico, she readily obeyed the commands of her subtile relations, in luring on the ardent and infatuated lover Sigismund, not to delay their nuptials, even until the arrival of his now hourly-expected-brother; as they dreaded that arrival, lest Theadore, in alarmed solicitude for his child's threatened succession to the titles of her ancestors, might devise means to break off the union.

But scarcely had the nuptial revellings commenced, when Conte di Ordelaffo, a friend, and eau-de-camp of the Duca di Montalbano, arrived, with the afflicting intelligence of his having fallen, with Conte Nicastro, in their unfortunate rash pursuit of the retreating Ottomans. Their bodies not having been found among the slain, had given to the generalissimo, the gallant Francis Morosini, a soothing hope of their having become prisoners; and, whilst he had been exerting all the influence of his power to ascertain their fate, he had forborne to announce to the world, or to his family, the irreparable loss the Venetian arms had sustained by the death of the Duca di Montalbano, and thus had caused that apparent mystery, relative to the duca's return by varied routes, which for so many weeks had prevailed; and during which weeks of anxious, and, at length, fatally terminating inquiry, the generalissimo had deceived his family by a rumor of the not-more-gallant soldier than profound statesman, Theadore of Montalbano, being engaged in a secret negotiation for the Venetian senate.

The grief of Sigismund for his brother, in it's first anguished feelings, subdued the recollection of every other idea in his mind; but as time poured it's assuasive balm into that wound, he recovered the faculty of thinking, and his affliction changed to despair, inspired by the misery of self-upbraidings. Infatuated by passion, and the blandishments of a syren, he had married, without bestowing one thought upon possibilities, and their concomitant consequences. He was now, by his brother's premature death, become Duca di Montalbano; his heirs must, therefore, unquestionably inherit the titles; and, from his brother having cancelled every disinheriting clause in his

father's will, the estates also of his ancestors, and by his reprehensible marriage,
he had ungratefully, cruelly, and perhaps
irrevocably, injured his darling Angelina,
the orphan of his brother, and of his own generous benefactor.

The anguish of his mind soon spread it's
baneful influence to the ever-too-easily affected frame of Sigismund; and those ideal
maladies which love had given a temporary
suspension to, now returned with renovated
violence from their banishment. When
moping, in his own apartments, a prey to
every fancied ill, he left his beautiful wife to
her own devices; and his estates, and
worldly affairs, to the mercy of his duchessa's numerous family, who now, like
locusts, came pouring in, to devour and destroy.

Secluded in his chamber, Sigismund
brooded over the ruin he had brought upon
Angelina, without taking one active measure to prevent it's full extent. The late
Duca di Montalbano, knowing his own determination against a second marriage, was
too deeply rooted in the stamina of his heart

ever to be exterminated; and fully believing his brother's ever entering the pale of matrimony, out of the nature of possibility, considered his adored daughter's inheritance of the wealth and honors of her forefathers, as secure, as if she had been a male heir; and therefore, unwarily, made no kind of provision for her, in case of contingencies; and Duca Sigismund, not enduring the, to him, terrible idea, of her being excluded by him from the succession, felt invincible horror at the thought of making any settlement upon her; weakly fancying, that, by doing so, it would seem like a wish, or foreboding implication, that she was to be disinherited.

At length that event, so much dreaded by Sigismund, was exultingly announced by Father Ezzelino to him. The duchessa's pretended pregnancy was declared; and, though Sigismund tenderly adored her, (in despite of his repentant grief for his marriage, and her inattentive and unamiable conduct towards him, since she had become his wife), yet with horror he anticipated the birth of his supposed child, as a being who would come more forcibly to attest his ingratitude to his brother; and a severe nervous fever now aided his imaginary sufferings, in weakening his ever-feeble frame, and in taking strength from that mind, which nature had gifted with superior energies.

In these dormant moments of the duca's bodily and mental imbecillity, the expulsion of Lady Angelina was planned and executed. She was maliciously sent off to the then obscure convent of Santo Valentino, with every appearance of ambiguity, in invidious management, to make the world believe she had unkindly forsaken her sick uncle, when most he had wanted her attentions; and had absconded to gratify her not-to-be-vanquished propensity to a conventual life.

The poor heart-rived invalid was easily persuaded into a belief of it's being Angelina's own choice to quit the castle, but he also believed, from the unkindness he well knew she had been treated with, that she was driven to the rash measure; and, in all the anguish of his grief-torn bosom, he implored them to seek out the convent she had retired to, and entreat her to return.

This the perfidious league of Tolmezo promised; and this they assured him, their agents were dispersed about all the states of Italy to that effect; but, upon every report of such pretended search, " still, still, without success."

At length, in the full success of artful arrangements, the pretended accouchement of the duchessa took place, and the spurious child, the chance of whose sex the confederates had been forced to compound for, introduced at the castle as the heiress di Montalbano; and, to veil the circumstance of Minora's not herself nourishing her offspring, incapacity was pretended, from a cold caught; and to give plausibility to that excuse, she was compelled to lengthen, most annoyingly, the term of her confinement. Then great indeed was the chagrin of this iniquitous woman, on finding, in some months after she had submitted to the inconvenience and privations of a long seclusion from the gay haunts of revel; had endured all the agonizing alarms of detection in her fraud, that she was actually in that state she had affected to be in. She

had now, in her eager haste to cut off Angelina from the succession, perhaps as effectually, (should her coming offspring
prove a girl), destroyed her own child's
birth-right, by the imposture she had practised, and which she could not avow, without overwhelming herself with infamy. And
now the bitter recollection of the miseries of
confinement she had endured unnecessarily,
must, in time, be renewed inevitably. Her
mortification and ill humor surpassed
even the regrets she experienced for the injustice she had done her child.

The consternation of her confederate relatives, when this most unexpected circumstance was announced to them, was indeed
extreme. In the mind of Lorenzago it
strengthened some painful suspicions to the
disadvantage of his sister's purity, which
he had lately imbibed; while her lenient
confessor, Ezzelino, careless whether the
coming offspring was, or was not, the Duca
di Montalbano's, only felt concern that they
had shackled themselves with this spurious
child; which, he determined, should be got
rid of, and accordingly, with the barbarous

Ezzelino for it's fate, the helpless infant expired, in some weeks after, in terrible convulsions.

But, however, ere this deed of cruelty was perpetrated, Ezzelino, well knowing the horror with which Sigismund recoiled from the idea of further progeny, hastened with the intelligence to him of Minora's pregnancy, in the diabolical hope of it's fatal effect upon his shattered frame. As the ruthless Ezzelino expected, the information overwhelmed him with poignant distress; but, as Ezzelino hoped, did not terminate his existence; on the contrary, it seemed to awaken the slumbering energies of his mind, and instantly he sent for his notary, Brondelo; on whose arrival he immediately made a noble provision for the child of his beloved brother.

The integrity of Brondello the Tolmezos well knew was incorruptible, and they dared not to tamper with it. In his care, they contrived to learn, an important deed now was placed; but it's exact import, with all their art, they could not discover; and all they now had it in their power to effect for preventing this apprehended great decrease of wealth was, to aim at establishing a belief of the mental derangement of the duca, at the period this deed was formed. To aid in this atrocious purpose, yet under an appearance the most friendly to Sigismund, was Father O'Carrol introduced at Montalbano Castle.

Lorenzago, although keen and unerring in developing the characters and propensities of his countrymen, as the eagle eye of deep and searching penetration could make him, yet, in fathoming the disposition of a guileless Irishman, he was in many conclusions egregiously mistaken. From Father Patrick's still glaring defects in the polish of his manners, (for neither education, or improved society, had divested him of his natural want of the refinements of gentility), Lorenzago thought that, like the generality of low-born and unenlightened people, he would soon become a venal tool to those, whom it suited to bribe him to their interest; but, although he quickly found his integrity was invulnerable, and that no sum could lure him into becoming a mercenary abettor in villany; yet, from his propensity to blunder and repeat, he still hoped for the most essential services, in the advancement of their vile project, by Father Patrick's innocently retailing to all he met with, the eccentric whims of the poor fanciful invalid; who, in return, was likely to derive no consolation, as a friend; no comfort, as a companion; no benefit, as an adviser, from this unpolished, and imprudently unguarded man.

But at length the duca finding, that the medicines he was given seemed to increase, rather than diminish, (as they were calculated to do, being powerful soporifics), his alarming lethargic stupor, he determined to take no more of them; and a suspicion of the fact having, for the first time, dawned upon his mind, he firmly resolved no more to follow the prescriptions of his wife's family, which they were officiously fond of recommending to him; and from the time he discontinued the use of these opiates, he found himself materially better.

Father Patrick believing he was performing his duty, earnestly remonstrated with him against this total suspension of medicine, when the poor forlorn Sigismund judiciously told him, with the hope of it's being repeated to Lorenzago, " That he was determined no medicine should again pass his lips, until his beloved niece should return to administer them; and that if he soon was not gratified by beholding her, he should send his notary with a petition to his Holiness, to have her restored to him."

The duca's stratagem succeeded; the confederates shrunk from the idea of the pontiff's interference. Some late accounts of Father Patrick, related in a numerous company, had been calculated to give powerful support to their affirmation of the duca's insanity; and this, therefore, was the express moment in which they wished he should die. And ere Brondelo should convey the petition of sound faculty to his Holiness, Lady Angelina was, therefore, immediately sent for; as the almost enthusiastic tenderness of affection he bore his niece; the unrestrained joy he evinced at the idea of once more beholding her; and the slender thread, they believed, he held the continuance of existence by; had inspired them with the determination of adopting a diabolical manœuvre, which, they doubted not, would fatally operate upon his sensitive nerves. For the completion of their plan, they had recourse to agents; who, from former services, they believed might be depended on. Anfania, from arbitrary reasons, was in the full confidence of the duchessa; and she, therefore, was considered a safe auxiliary too; and as they had arranged every thing with plausibility, to turn from themselves, as they hoped, every shadow of suspicion; and had placed Father Ezzelino's strong box as the attractive incentive to such an outrage, they congratulated themselves in the happy prospect of having thus laid a successful train for the removal of every impediment to their revelling on the spoils they panted to obtain, by the death of Sigismund, through horror and dire affliction at the cruel fate of his niece, in becoming a hapless victim to sanguinary banditti; and by that of Angelina herself, by the fell hand of assassination, which they each, in their own bosoms, had resolved to give their pitiless mandate for. Nor did it ever once enter into their imagination, in this exulting triumph of expected success, that their agents in villany had the power, as well as the intention, of outwitting them ; or, that the merciful protector of the helpless could, even by the turpitude of the wretch they had employed to destroy, send a champion to defend and rescue the innocent from their diabolical snares.

CHAPTER XIV.

ON entering the chamber of her uncle, Angelina, to her infinite joy, unexpectedly beheld him up, and seated in his easy-chair, to receive her; but his pale, languid, and care-worn countenance assailed the heart of Pity at one glance, and awakened there it's tenderest emotion; and with these promptly-awakened pained sensations of compassion, now adding to her agitated feelings, she flew to the expanded arms of Sigismund—but the effect of her long fondly wished-for appearance, her affectionate look, and thrilling exclamations of tender kindness, proved too much for the almost-exhausted frame of the poor duca to bear; and he wept upon the sympathising bosom of his beloved Angelina, in joy at having her—the child of his adored brother—a being, who did regard him, who did really feel interested in his fate, restored to him; so affecting was the scene, that Father Jeronimo, respecting the feelings he beheld, retired, and left no one to witness the further ebullitions of the heart, in the first interview of those long estranged, attached relations.

" O, Angelina! loved, yet injured child of my sainted brother," exclaimed the agitated duca, as soon as he could articulate, " how powerfully your very looks affect me! How has time, in the nearly two long years of your absence, with it's unceasing pencil, touched and retouched your countenance, until he has completely finished you into a striking model of both your sainted parents, and sweetly combined, from persons so opposite in aspect, the most harmonious assemblage of Nature's beauties to blend together in you. O! may you in mind inherit too this striking resemblance! Your father knew no weakness, no guile; his heart contained not a fault. Your mother was — O! she was perfection! She loved your father, and deceived him not with the phantom only of tenderness. In sickness, or affliction, she would never, no, never have forsaken him. But I was unlike my brother in mind and form; I could not expect to be loved as he was: I ought to have been aware, that interest only could lead the venal beauty to kneel at the altar of Hymen with me. I know it was egregious folly, reprehensibly absurd vanity,—but yet my disappointed heart writhes in the anguished feelings of being unjustly treated."

In this moment, when Angelina could only look her sympathy, Father Jeronimo, anxious to attend his other patients, re-entered, to prescribe for the ducá, and to inform Lady Angelina of what he wished to have done to promote his recovery; and, when these necessary arrangements were made, the good monk departed; and Father Patrick soon after entered, to inquire his patron's commands?

"The duchessa knows of my niece's arrival, I presume, holy father?" said Sigismund.

' ".Why, then, indeed, it is she, who knows it, sure, enough, monsignòre," replied Father Patrick.'

" I should have thought," said the duca indignantly, "that the duchessa would have been eager tò evince her sorrow and sympathy for the direful distress my beloved niece has been exposed to (through the mismanagement of those intrusted to convey her home), by hastening hither, with cordial congratulations, upon her providential escape from destruction."

" O! sorrow come, will she come, at all, at all," exclaimed Father Patrick ; " for she has got a black dog on her back, because Lady Angelina, did not think of paying her, the respect to be waiting upon her, to thank her, for her condescending letter; ere her nature led her, to embrace her own kiff, and kin." .

" Since the duchessa considers me defective in attention to her, I ought certainly not to allow a longer continuance of that impression to operate in obtaining for me a less kind reception than I might otherwise

N 2

receive. May I not, dear *zio* *, attend the duchessa?" Angelina said, rising, and beseechingly taking the hand of Sigismund.

"I will have you treated with what I consider as respect," he replied with energy.

"But let us not enforce it, my dear, kind uncle; let us win it; for surely that will prove the pleasanter mode for all parties. Besides, I know not but I was much to blame when I last was here: I had not then learned to forget — that is, I mean, I — I had not learned my duty; I was often refractory, and then knew not how to conciliate. I now am older, I trust a little wiser too, and I hope we shall live better friends than we parted."

The duca now clasped Angelina with affectionate, approving exultation to his bosom. "Sweet child!" he exclaimed, "in every way your parents' counterpart: with such noble rectitude would your father act; with such fascinating, mild forbearance your mother win all to her own path — the path of gentleness and peace. Father Patrick,

* Uncle.

have the goodness to convey this lovely olive-branch to the duchessa's apartments."

"No, no," said Angelina considerately, "I will find on my way some other conductor; for this reverend father will, I am sure, have the goodness to comply with my first request to him."

"That I will, my gem, of the world, or myself is no true knight, of the shamrack. Is it comply, with your first request? why then to be sure, I will; and your last too, with the greatest pleasure in life; ay faith, if there were nine score of them; and if the performance of every one of them, was an impossibility."

"O! thank you," replied Angelina smiling; "but I shall not exact from your knight errantry the achievement of impossibilities for me: I only now ask you to remain with my uncle until I return, and amuse him with all the pleasant, interesting, and lively anecdotes you can think of; but, if you enter upon the retrospection of the alarms of last night, or of any past grievances, I will become unchristian, and never forgive you."

" Faith jewel, if you keep your anger off myself, until I offend you; we will continue, the best Darby and Joan friends, that ever sipped in the honey-pot, of harmony, together," returned the good priest.

" And now to begin this sweet career of amity, do pray tell me, ere I depart, what you meant, holy father, by your expression of a black dog upon any one's back."

" Why jewel, it is a sort of a barometer, in the form of an ugly mongrel, cabbin cur, that some people are apt to be mounting upon their backs; to growl, and be snapping at people's heels, to show the temper is under a dark, and lowering cloud."

" This definition however, Angelina, portrays no inviting prospect for you, in this condescension of yours in visiting the duchessa. If such is the gloomy aspect of the atmosphere, I shall not choose that you should be exposed to it's inclemency," said the duca gravely.

" Fear not for me, my dear uncle," Angelina replied, trembling in heart, but assuming the aspect of unfaltering courage; " weather can change, and time flies swiftly,

Although it was winter when Father ·Patrick quitted the clime I am going to visit, it may be spring when I arrive there; and, I trust, it may be summer ere I depart from it: but, if not, I still shall find, upon my return, those genial sun-beams here, that cannot fail to cheer me through every threatened storm."

The duca pressed her hand in gratitude, and summoned his own *camerière** to attend her on her amiably condescending visit; when Angelina was grieved to see, that the old and respectable servant of her uncle, was exchanged for an insolent looking coxcomb, whose countenance at once proclaimed him to be one of the most unfitted persons in the universe for an attendant upon a constantly-suffering invalid.

At length Angelina reached the apartments of the duchéssa, which had once been her own mother's; and where now the alterations of showy fancy had superseded, with her gaudy fopperies, the chaste and simply elegant arrangements of refined and genuine taste. Her supercilious conductor,

* Valet.

Signore Rospo, threw open the folding-doors, and announcing "Lady Angèlina," she entered the dressing-room of Minora, who now was making her toilet; and who, believing she was little less than the goddess of beauty herself, had the Graces, in the form of three waiting gentlewomen, to attire her; yet not in perfect similitude to the attractive attendants of the Cyprian queen, she had selected her handmaids from among the least charming of their sex, for the judicious purpose of all the advantages to herself arising from the force of contrast.

One of these homely damsels was now employed braiding the long and glossy tresses of the duchessa's hair. Another, with her strikingly coarse and ruddy hands, was twining strings of pearls around the finely polished alabaster arms of this vain woman, whilst the third was arranging those jewels about her beauteous throat and bosom; which the sanctified and pompous probationary Archbishop di Mazzarino, with right reverend zeal, was carefully selecting from a casket, to adorn this modern queen of love.

Four pages, rivaling Cupids, or the Zephyrs, in youthful charms, and fancifully attired, had here perpetual employment, scattering odors round the room, and replenishing innumerable costly vases with fragrant incense, or the most beautiful and sweetly-scented flowers; whilst, at a luxuriously-adorned veranda, Conte Lorenzago stood, warily observing, with no sensations of satisfaction, the further confirmation to those painful suspicions of his sister's purity; which the levity of her conduct had awakened, in her present reception of the impassioned glances of the archbishop; and at the toilet table, filling up another department of this vain woman's suite, sat a dependent cousin, as plain and as subservient as a dependent cousin need to be, with a beautiful small greyhound in her lap; one hand of hers engaged in tenderly stroking the popular favorite, asleep on her knee; the other supporting her own head, in the attitute of contemplating the beauties of her cousin, the duchessa, which she failed not to extol in the highest flights of rapturous panegyric, as she pointed them out to observation, as each new adornment, or judici-

ous movement, displayed them to her watch-
fully-adulating eye.

And now this luxurious apartment, so
fitted, so dedicated to attractive adornment,
the only and orphan child of the elder
branch of the illustrious house of Montalbano entered, attired in the plain grey stuff
habit, worn by the boarders in the rigid
convent of Santo Valentino; it's form like
the costume of a Persian slave; her only
ornaments, a plain ebony conventual cross,
suspended from her neck, and a correspond-
ing rosary, hung by the knotted cord of
black silk, which encircled her slender waist.
The long and flowing veil of the order had
fallen, unconsciously, in graceful drapery
around her, and left her exquisitely-formed
head, and lovely face uncovered; displaying
her luxuriant hair, unrivaled in beauty and
silky burnish, twisted and twined in graceful meanderings, by the simple and unstu-
dying hand of intuitive taste and fancy; it's
only confinement, a curiously-wrought gold
bodkin, the gift of the abadessa of Santo
Valentino to her.

The blush of agitation and alarmed expectation heightened the bloom of beauty upon the cheeks of Angelina, on her entrance, whose name and appearance seemed to electrify the faculties of the principal persons present. The dignified pride of heartfelt, superiority taught her to recoil from the debasement of humbling herself in courtesy to such worthless beings, as they had proved themselves to be; but it was for her uncle's sake she bent to them; and never did conciliating sweetness, tinctured with unsubdued dignity, appear more attractively lovely than Angelina, unhesitatingly advancing to the duchessa, and, with a smile that seemed gifted with the magic of effacing from the heart the remembrance and the feeling of all enmity, presented her hand, accompanied by a short sentence, expressive of that pleasure which politeness instructed her to assume the semblance of, upon meeting, after such a lengthened absence.

But the now exquisitely-finished figure of Angelina, with the beauty of her countenance matured into surpassing loveliness, was more than the duchessa was prepared for; more than she possessed firmness to behold, unmoved by an invidious envy that would betray itself. Scarcely articulate was her unconnected reply, given in the unharmonious tones of vexation and' asperity, while coldly she took the offered hand of amity; but the moment she beheld the transparent whiteness of that hand, yet, stamped by health, with it's delicate carnation hue, it's streams of life meandering through their slender tubes of blue and violet, the full rose-tinted palm, and the taper fingers, with their unrivaled terminations, touched it's smooth surface, and felt it's downy softness, than, electrified by her envious propensities, she dropped the hand with a recoiling motion, expressive of her real feeling, although she maliciously meant that it should evince disgust.

The moment Lady Angelina di Balermo was announced, the probationary prelate felt ashamed of his employment; and, awkward in a situation, so little according with that pious austerity he had labored to impress her with a belief was his dignified characteristic; while the sagacious

cousin; Signora Zola di Tolmezo, promptly
taking her one from the duchessa, turned
up her thin and bloomless lip in strong contemptuous disapprobation of the whole appearance of Lady Angelina, whom Conte
Lorenzago, to the infinite amazement of
every one present, with a countenance of
smilingly-flattering welcome, rapidly advanced to her with extended hands to greet,
and to receive.

Conte Lorenzago was then in his thirty-
eighth year, and told most forcibly by all
he still retained undiminished of uncommon
beauty, how superior it had been, to that
generally possessed even by the most favor-
ed sons of nature, when the potent spells
of youth aided, resistlessly, the enchant-
ments of surpassing personal endowments.
But, although great and alluring were his
beauties of form and face, they had ever
been considered, by all who knew him, as
even less seductive than the fascinations of
his manners, thrilling with the soft magic of
bewitching all who were unacquainted with
the secrets of his heart and disposition; secrets, which no glance of his amenable

eyes, no tone of his well-regulated voice, no expression of his obedient countenance, ever betrayed; leaving to those only, whom the habits of unrestrainted intimacy, or who, from experiencing it's effects, had discovered his dissimulative powers, to know, that his mind resembled a deep translucent well, whose surface yields the purest liquid of the fountain; but which, on fathoming, is found to shelter some of the most noxious deformities of nature in the reptile form, of mining art, and treacherous design.

Proud and ambitious, beyond all control of reason and of justice; and even stung with the unceasing recollection of the mean origin from which he sprung, he, early in life, strained every power to please, to adulate, and to charm; to give their seductive aid in extricating him from the humble state of his family; and to lead him on to soar in that exalted sphere. He resolved no boundary of honor or of conscience, whilst in secret he could overstep them, should impede his way. Under this aspiring influence he climbed incessantly, but not to that eminence he panted to arrive at, until

the combined arts of his wily family threw
the Duca di Montalbano into his power.—
On the mind of the refined and highly-ac-
complished Sigismund, this specious man, of
winning graces, was most likely to make
every favorable and partial impression;
and, ere poor Sigismund could form an
ideal fear of the spells which were encom-
passing him, Lorenzago had fascinated him
out of the government of his own household; nay, almost out of the absolute disposal
of his own revenue. This power secured, as
he now believed for ever, Lorenzago no
longer sedulously sought to shade, with the
deluding mask of perfection, his unamiable
qualities, from the victims of his ambitious
views; and, ere the expulsion of Angelina,
both she and her uncle had discovered, that
Conte Lorenzago could be unfeeling, insolent, and presuming, like too many individuals of his insidious family.

Although his inordinate pride and ambition had filled his breast with many a noxious weed, ungenial to humanity and to honor, he still, from that polish of the mind
he possessed, could see, could estimate,

each treasure of the stores of virtue; and even love and approve in others what he could not himself practise. Of female beauty he was ever an avowed admirer. Of female mental charms, and purity of heart, a greater lover still; and this homage to the sex's most lovely attraction, led him to those observations upon his sister's conduct, which taught her to fear him, and him to censure her.

At that period of Lorenzago's life, when the boy was fast approaching to the maturity of man, the dawning ambition of his soul led him to unite his fate to a wealthy relict of a Venetian senator, who, enamoured of his beauty, offered him her hand; and who, in his eyes, possessed no charm but the wealth she had to bestow. Disgust on his part, neglected love on hers, soon made this union a fate of misery to both; and at length, once more in corcordance, they agreed to separate. And the hourly augmenting pride of Lorenzago teaching him to recoil from what he now deemed the low connexion he had unadvisedly made, as one leading condition of their separation, decreed the Contessa Lorenzago should fix her residence with her own relatives at Pavia, in Milan, far from his rising greatness, which her obscurity would tarnish.

One child only had sprung from this unhappy marriage, Conte Hilario, who was, at this period, receiving the last polish of the most refined and expensive education at Rome. For this son's aggrandisement the wary Lorenzago was ever anxiously musing; and, upon a most unexpected discovery he had that very morning made; and which, he doubted not, to turn to that son's interest. He had been ruminating, when called from his meditations upon his new-raised airy fabrics of ambition, to form mental strictures upon the conduct of his sister; and which, too, in their turn, found their speedy interruption, by the unthought-of entrance of Lady Angelina, whom he hastened, as we have before mentioned, to greet with every trace of former supercilious insolence, vanished from a countenance, on which now sparkled joy, almost amounting to the transports of superlative happiness, at beholding once again some long-lost, most loved, and valued object of esteem.

" Heavens !" he exclaimed, after taking an earnest survey of the blushing Angelina, with eyes expressive of the most animated admiration, " how much you are grown in the tedious interval of your absence from us ; and how exquisitely have you fulfilled your more juvenile promise of future surpassing loveliness !"

" Conte Lorenzago forgets," said Angelina gracefully, with the happy combination of youthful timidity, and inherent dignity of mind, " that, through the cloister wall, the sound of earthly flattery could not reach my ears ; and, in pity to the poor recluse, should spare her the probable consequence of subduing her senses by this intoxicating homage of unmerited incense."

" In mind, as in form, perfection !" exclaimed the conte, in a subdued voice, instructed to express how heart-felt was his admiration.

Angelina was surprised and embarrassed at this new and unexpected line of conduct adopted by Lorenzago; but, not choosing to betray her being so, made a successful effort to rally her rather faltering spirits, and smilingly replied:—

"You have, I fear, indeed, fathomed my understanding; and, from that experiment, have formed the belief of it's being too easily overset in the overwhelming tide of unqualified praise."

"I have, indeed, fathomed it, and must devise some other method more congenial to it's sensitive delicacy, to regain your now highly-prized lost good opinion," replied Lorenzago gravely, bowing with the marked reverence of profound respect.

"And so!" exclaimed Signora Zola, "Lady Angelina never heard flattery in her cloister. Of course she never heard nothing but truths; and we cannot, therefore, wonder at her humility."

"Oh! Conte Lorenzago," said Angelina smiling; "I may now, indeed, defy your eulogiums; since, if you present the poison of flattery to my understanding, this kind signora will, I perceive, humanely supply an antidote."

Signora Zola, highly disconcerted at this open discovery of her malicious propensity, and more so, at it's failing in it's intended effect of mortifying and provoking, now coloring in passion, vehemently caressed her sleeping lap-protegèe, who growled at having his slumbers so roughly broken.

" Heavens! Zola, how barbarously ungentle you are," cried the duchessa, pet-ishly, " you will absolutely spoil the temper of my darling *Fèbo*, by your savage treatment. Come, my love, my precious treasure, to your adoring mistress." And, with affected tenderness, she drew her favorite into her beauteous arms, and seemed almost about to smother him with caresses.

" I am, I am, surprised at this attachment," said Lady Angelina, in a tone of more reproach than she wished to betray, " for I thought you had an unconquerable antipathy to dogs, duchessa?"

" So I have to *old*, hideous, and annoying ones," replied Minora, scornfully.

" Mine certainly had grown *rather* old in a faithful service; yet even his approach to-age, had not made him in the least an-

noying. ' May I take the liberty of asking
you,' duchessa, what was the fate of my
poor Fedelio ?"

" His fate!! The fate of your dog,
girl!!!—Can you really conceive, Angelina, that I condescend to shackle my mind
with the remembrance of such growling
things? Ask my people. Was the animal
shot, drowned, or strangled, domestics?" '

" Neither, illustrissima signora," replied
one of the pages. " By your excellènza's
orders I gave him to a blind beggar you
saw kick his leader to death in the forest."

The thrill of horror and grief that now
struck upon Lady Angelina's heart, stole
at once the roses from her cheeks; and, in
despite of every effort of that rule for her
conduct, which reason and reflection had
pointed out for her to pursue, tears started
to her eyes, and forced a passage thence.

" Heavens! girl," said the duchessa,
contemptuously, " weep for your favorite's
being restored to his original station!—
Surely a renewal of those habits he pursued
in early life, must be a restoration of comfort to him."

" What the origin of my poor degraded sacred trust's family may have been, I was not old enough, when they first became the leaders of the venerable Richardo, to recollect. But a restoration from an exalted, to a degraded situation, although it might possess the charm of early habit to recommend it, might not always be deemed a comfortable change. And to many, whose origin I do remember, I am sure it would prove no source of pleasure," replied Angelina, aroused irresistibly to sarcasm, by that ferine cruelty wreaked on her protegèe, solely for the purpose of giving pain to her.

The low-born Tolmazo keenly felt the retort; and Angelina, ashamed in finding herself surprised out of that forbearance she had hoped rigidly to persevere in, made a successful effort to regain her lost composure; and, with that genuinely impressive dignity of a superior mind, that never fails of it's effect, calmly admired the beauties of the surrounding plants, and judiciously contriving to turn the conversation from personalities to general topics, was enabled, to extend her visit to the duchessa for some time longer; and, until the arrival of more company, afforded her a fair pretence for withdrawing, when she hastened to the apartments of her uncle; where, in her detail of her reception from, and interview with the duchessa, she, in the goodness of her heart, suppressed all that she believed would be heard with pain by him.

CHAPTER XV

BUT scarcely had Angelina completed
her lenient account of her unpleasant visit
to the duchessa's apartments, when the
housekeeper, sent by the wily Lorenzago,
appeared, come to inquire,' " What apartments in the castle Lady Angelina wished to
occupy ? Her ladyship's own had unfortunately been fitted up, during her absence,
for Conte Hilario; but Conte Lorenzago
had instructed her to say, " ' That if Lady
Angelina retained the smallest predilection
for them, a number of hands should instantly be employed to remove the book-
shelves, &c. &c. of the young conte's
study; and, as promptly as possibility
would admit of it, all should be restored to
it's original order.' "

Angelina sighed at this deprivation of

apartments, rendered dear and interesting to her, both from local attachment, and from their having been selected for her by her still tenderly-beloved father; but with due civility to the apparent courtesy of Conte Lorenzago, politely declined giving such trouble to his goodness, or disturbing Conte Hilario so unnecessarily. But, upon being importuned to know upon what other apartments her choice should fall, in her haste to get rid of a matter so immaterial to her, knowing that all the rooms in the castle were spacious and comfortable, she mentioned the apartment which had been the nursery of her infancy.

The moment Angelina named this set of rooms, the housekeeper changed color, looked embarrassed, and, at length, hesitatingly said, " That these, too, were unfortunately pre-occupied."

" By whom?" the duca demanded.

" A—a person, a—a lady; an invalid; to whom the duchessa had lent them, for the benefit of—of the salubrious air of Tuscany;" replied the housekeeper, stammering in evident confusion.

" Why should you feel embarrassed, woman, at disclosing the virtues of your patroness?" said the duca, rather sternly.—" For my part, I rejoice to hear any apartments in my castle are now so benevolently filled. But, Angelina, my child, forgive me, if I feel pleasure in your disappointment; those apartments are a fearful distance from mine."

. Angelina blushed, and looked grieved at what she now felt; seemed like an unpardonable unkindness, and omission of dutiful attention.

" Forgive me, my dear uncle," she ingenuously said, " I never once thought of that, which should have influenced my choice. Pray, signora, are there no unclaimed apartments, adjoining the duca's, that I may be permitted to inhabit?"

" None. Father Patrick had the only one belonging to that range; not immediately appertaining to his excéllenza's own suite."

" What mean you?" asked the duca. " Who, what invalid can have taken possession of those apartments belonging to this suite; which, since my late severe indispositions, I have never used?"

The housekeeper again colored, and hesitated, in the confusion of embarrassment; but at length, finding she must reply, said, " Being so very approximate, I did not think monsignore would permit any one to inhabit them."

" Oh! by Lethe's, cordial water, but it's game your making, *madàma confettúra!* Success to yourself and memory!—Sure, one Signore Vasco Tolmezo, has them, for his gorgeous tenement, when the castle has him, for a guest," exclaimed Father Patrick, in his manner for ingenuous communications.

The indignation of the Duca di Montalbano now ebulliated into a degree of anger Angelina had never before seen him evince; and which, she believed, the sweet serenity of his temper incapable of feeling ; but now passion conquering almost reason, led him, with the strength of frenzy, from the supine lap of indolence; and vehemently and virulently he reprobated the insolence of his wife's younger brother, in daring to take possession of any of his own suite of rooms, without his permission; and rooms, too, the most sacred to him, as there were deposited in them many important family papers, many gems, and other costly things belonging to his museum.

"But no longer," he at length added, "shall that free and easy signore possess them. They are my niece's from this very hour; and do you now go, woman, attend Lady Angelina to those her own apartments; and see that whatever she commands to have done for her accommodation is instantly complied with. Go, my love, go; order every thing, as if in your own castle; for while it is mine, I consider it as yours; and, while life is spared to me, I will have you respected, I will have you obeyed."

Scarcely had Lady Angelina returned to her uncle, and given him every assurance that the apartments he had so kindly selected for her promised all possible comfort, and every accommodation she could desire, when Florio, the eldest and most beautiful of the duchessa's pages, appeared, bearing a most courteous message to Angelina, from Minora, requesting the pleasure of her company that day at dinner.

Angelina was amazed at such an unexpected innovation of politeness; but, preferring the idea of dining with her uncle, was proceeding to send her excuses for declining the honor intended her, by such a condescending invitation, when Sigismund, signifying that it was his wish she should comply, she sent her cheerful acquiescence to the duchessa, when the graceful page departed, who shortly after was followed by Father Patrick, who considerately reflected, that uncle and niece might have family secrets to discuss, after so long a separation.

Father Patrick was not mistaken; for, when left alone with his beloved Angelina, the poor suffering duca first deplored to her his bodily maladies, many of which, she feared, were real, many more, she believed, imaginary; but whichever they were, she doubted not of their being incurable, and that at no very distant period of time, even if fairly acted by, that she should have the misery of seeing herself bereft of this beloved tender relative too.

Sigismund next, even more pathetically than he had recounted his other ills, entered upon the long and melancholy catalogue of all his mental anguish; enumerating for her, all the slights, the unkindness, the cruelties he had experienced since she had left him; comprising all the sorrows which had preyed upon his mind, since last they met, save one; but that one, direful and agonising, menacing destruction to his existence, even to Angelina he shrunk from the idea of disclosing.

The helpless and interesting appearance of her uncle; the touching pathos of his grief-tuned voice; the melancholy resignation of his countenance, combined with this recital of all the heart-wounding array of injuries he had sustained, most sensibly wounded the affectionate and susceptible feelings of Angelina; and the pain of sympathy found an agonising increase in the terrible conviction, that she possessed no power to shield him from such cruelty.

" Grieve not, my love," said the duca,
endeavouring to soothe his beloved niece,
" grieve not for what is now inevitable. I
brought all my woes upon myself, every
misery upon you; and I cannot, cannot
bear to see you sorrow for the infatuated
monster of ingratitude who has undone you.
I—I ought to dissolve away in Affliction's
saddest tears of penitence; and yet I weep
not for your undoing and my own. No,
no, no, in my heart are my griefs, like the
desolating Sirocco, blighting, withering, all,
and expelling the salutary dew of tears.

" From my birth, to the evil hour of my
infatuated marriage, I was gently treated by
all around me; and, though ruthless maladies
afflicted me, yet, from all who approached
me, I learned the belief, that the native
dwelling of kindness was in the human
heart. Terrible, then, my Angelina, was
the shock which undeceived me; and led
me to feel, in contrast, how I had miscon-
ceived the whole of my species. In all my
latter months of misery, I have had no
sympathising bosom to repose my griefs in;
no friend to unburthen a heart breaking

with sorrows; no one to beguile into pity for me; but now my beloved Angelina is restored to me, that grief is removed, and again I shall know, that kindness and affection are inhabitants of this world."

Angelina, with reverence and filial tenderness, took the sorrow-withered hand of her uncle, and pressed it to her lips, to her heart, now throbbing with sympathy for his miseries; miseries for which she had no consolation; and feared to give utterance to those sensations her pity, grief, and indignation had awakened, lest they might too much affect him by the novelty of their kindness; but, at length, after a successful combat to subdue the violence of her emotion, she gently inquired, " What was become of Father Erasmo ? who had been her uncle's preceptor, his confessor, his friend."

" Alas! my child, gone; torn from me, because he was inflexible in virtue, firm in his purposes, exalted in understanding, and zealously my friend. He disapproved my marriage; exerted all his influence to prevent it; was never forgiven by Minora

or her family; and was expelled my castle
in that fatal illness of mine, in which you,
too, Angelina, forsook your helpless uncle."

"Oh! say not, say not, dear zio, that
I forsook you. Believe not I could have
been so barbarous, so ungrateful; for, in
very truth, force only tore me from the
chamber of him I then believed to be my
dying uncle."

"Wretches!" Sigismund exclaimed,
with powerful indignation. "Yes, yes,
they can tear all tender ties asunder; rend
hearts; burst bonds of friendship. My
friend, my second father, Erasmo, was, I now
doubt not, forced, like my Angelina, from
me. No common means were those made
use of, to urge him to quit me in sickness
and sorrow. In vain, upon my restoration
to perception, did I entreat, implore, to
have him recalled. In vain did I write letters of supplication to my friend to return;
but, alas! he came not, wrote not; and the
direful pang was added to my miseries, in
the torturing belief of his being no more.—
But that rankling grief was taken from my

bosom about six months since, when I saw,
in a list of new publications, that he had
-recently presented to the world a work of
great celebrity, at Rome."

"At Rome!—Know you, or can you
learn, the name of his bookseller?"

"Know it!—Oh! yes. I treasured up
the page wherein his name was so honorably
mentioned; treasured it up, with all your
father's letters to me, with one little beauteous lock of hair, belonging to her who is
now a saint in heaven; your mother's, Angelina. I stole it from my brother. It was
the only act of fraud I e'er committed.—
But when I married, I took it from the
locket in my bosom, which I profaned with
a syren's hair; a serpent's sting. Here,
Angelina," and he unlocked a drawer in a
writing-table before him, "behold my treasures, and remember, upon you I depend
for compliance with my solemn request, for
having them inclosed in my last resting
place with me."

"But, my dear, dear, uncle," said Angelina, endeavouring to shake off all mournful sympathy of voice, and to look enliven-

ing cheerfulness, " we will, at present, if you please, make a better use of one of these treasures; I will write to Father Erasmo, under cover to his bookseller, if you will permit me, and give it to the care of Father Jeronimo to convey securely for me. By this plan we shall elude all inspection and interception; for I cannot but think your letters never reached the reverend father, no more than my numerous ones did you."

This project of Angelina so overpowered the sensitive Sigismund with hope and joy, that the emotion it created so alarmed her, that she hastily poured out some of a cordial which Father Jeronimo had left with her, to administer at her discretion.

The duca, smiling touchingly and gratefully at her, as she presented it, said, " I would swallow it when presented by you, even unknowing who prescribed it for me, because you would offer it only in the hope of it's proving efficacious to me." He now eagerly drank it, and then added, " It warms me with thy affection, my child;" and then, after a pause, in which he found considerable renovation from the medicine;

but much more from the innovating sunbeam, penetrating with cheering influence to his heart, in the flattering hope of once again hearing from the friend of his earliest youth, his looks began to assume the aspect of much-diminished sadness; for he no longer doubted the success of Angelina's project; and that his ardent wish would be promptly realised, by the return of Erasmo to Montalbano castle.

"Not, Angelina," said the duca, at length traveling full speed in the fascinating regions of hope. "Not, though my beloved and venerated friend should return to me, will I send poor Father O'Carrol from me, or displace him as chaplain to my household; for although he still retains, unimpaired, many of the vulgarisms of the sphere in which he originally moved, he yet possesses too many virtues of the heart not to have obtained my cordial esteem."

At length, after much more earnest and confidential conversation between the Duca di Montalbano and his lovely niece, Angelina found, by the intimation of the duca's dinner bell, that it was time for her to go and arrange her hair, and re-put on her gown, as the only preparation she had it in her power to make, for appearing at the duchessa's table; but infinite was her astonishment, on her arrival in her dressing-room, to find Anfania waiting her coming; and who immediately hastened, with the innovating appearance of civility, to announce—

" That as her ladyship had unfortunately lost her great stock of clothes the preceding evening, the duchessa kindly and considerately wishing to remedy, as much as possible, the inconvenience she must suffer from the circumstance, had sent her thither with a temporary supply; and, with an order, to offer her services in the honor of assisting to put them on."

Angelina made her grateful thanks in sincerity, for this apparent kindness, ere she turned to the table where the clothes were laid; but soon she found how unmeritted were those premature thanks. Yet still she possessed sufficient command over her feelings not to betray the smallest symptom of chagrin, as she calmly looked upon this supply of pretended kindness, although she beheld the dresses were a collection from the castle theatre; where, at a stated period every year, some comedians from Florence performed before the Montalbano family, from time almost immemorial; and so grotesque and hideous were the forms and texture of the habits selected, she could only believe they were sent her to make her ridiculous, for the pastime of Minora and her satellites; and when all was carelessly inspected by her, she quietly said—

" I shall retain the linen, and be thankful for it, Signora Anfania, until I can procure some of my own. The dresses and ornamental parts of this very kind supply, I must beg leave to return, having no present occasion for them. So long accustomed to the close stuff habit I wear, I should run great hazard of taking cold, was I at once to throw it off."

" Bless me !" exclaimed Anfania, visibly disconcerted at the failure of this plan of ridicule in every expected effect. " Surely you will never have the rudeness, the unpardonable disrespect, to appear before your superiors, at the duchessa's table, in a paltry stuff gown?"

"It is a religious habit," replied Angelina, gravely, "and the duchessa is too innately pious to object to it."

Anfania could make no possible answer to that plea, without implicating the piety of her lady, therefore most unwillingly she found herself compelled to acquiesce; and finding there was no employment for her in disfiguring Angelina, and having no intention of offering her assistance, as a real service, soon after withdrew.

CHAPTER XVI.

SHORTLY after the departure of her tormentor, Angelina returned to her uncle, who instantly expressed his surprise on seeing her still in her conventual dress.

" My uncle forgets," said Angelina, " that I have no other. You know I lost my whole wardrobe last night."

" But the duchessa did not lose hers; and surely it was in her power, as it ought to have been in her inclination, to supply your present necessity."

" She was very kind, and did supply me with linen," replied Angelina, blushing at an evasion, which her amiable wish of sparing this unfortunate relative every unnecessary pang inspired; " but the duchessa is formed so much on a larger scale than I am, her clothes could not very well fit me;

and, and, beside, I feared to throw off my long-accustomed warm dress all at once."

Father Patrick now made his appearance, as the duca's last dinner-bell had summoned him, to be in readiness, to perform his duty of saying grace for his patron, with whom he partook of all his meals.

At the request of the poor invalid, Angelina performed the honors of his table for him; and performed them with such peculiar grace, and winning kindness, and so resistless he found her affectionate and dutiful attentions, that he was beguiled by them, into taking more food than his flown appetite had long permitted him to partake of. But, although he looked, and was grateful for her kindness, he appeared often abstracted in thought, and the moment the attendants departed after the termination of his repast, he mournfully said :

"Ah! Angelina, the ingenuousness of your nature betrayed to me, that there was evasion in your excuse, for still retaining your conventual dress; and I fear, alas! that I have penetrated the true cause.— You, you continue it, Angelina, from predilection; and I have not been deceived, when assured, you meant to take the veil."

"My dear uncle," said Angelina, with a playful smile, yet accompanied by a conscious blush, "whenever, or rather I should say, if ever the mate, whom I could be content to coo in a cage with, for life, should appear to demand me from you, I will soon convince you, that I have no passion for the life of a *menoca."

"Ah! then, who would have suspected," exclaimed Father Patrick; "that your dress to day, jewel, should have given such a big fright to his excellenza, and myself. The duca in thinking, you were so bewitched, as to turn nun; and myself in fearing, you would be creazy enough, to be putting on, some of those, hogmagog coats, and petticoats, the Duchessa, Signora Zola, and the maids, caballed about sending you, to try, and make a bugabow, of you, to amuse them."

The duca instantly demanded an explanation, to which Father Patrick, not feel-

* Nun.

ing Angelina's delicate scruples upon the subject, unhesitatingly gave in as glowing colors, as the grotesque clothes had been composed of.

Sigismund was painfully disconcerted.— "Ah! my child," he said, " and the amiable kindness of your heart led you to conceal all this low malice from me. · But yet, they have not deprived me of all pecuniary power. I will have you dressed as the child of your father ought to be. I will have your dress beyond the shafts of ridicule to aim at. I will have you wear nothing belonging to that narrow-minded, ungrateful woman; whom, in the climax of folly, I made my wife. Write, therefore, as speedily as possible, to the most approved tradespeople for such purposes; and order them, forthwith, to supply the wardrobe, in appropriate magnificence, of the late Duca di Montalbano's daughter."

Angelina was deeply penetrated by her uncle's kind consideration for her feelings of female vanity, but she knew not the names of any trades-people; for ere her expulsion from the castle, her respected governess had ordered all things for her wardrobe; and since that eventful period, all she wore had been made in the convent of Santo Valentino, or presented to her by the abadessa, procured from she knew not whom ; and these insuperable impediments to acompliance' with his desire, she hastened to impart to Sigismund.

While making this statement to the duca, Father Patrick stood behind his patron's back, making the most ludicrous grimaces, and unintelligible gesticulations, to her, to desist; but at length finding them ineffectual, he came round to her and, whisperingly, said :

" Take him, in the humor, take, the elegant coats, and petticoats, a *vurneen*, for I'll be bail, we will find out, some clever hands, to sew for us."

" Alas! Angelina," said the duca, " and I cannot assist you in this most singular dilemna; I have been cut off, by the antipathy of my wife, from all society; and from the seclusion I have lately lived in, I know nothing of modern fashions, or their most celebrated artizans; and were we to apply to the duchessa for information, we now cannot shelter a doubt, of her meanly, and invidiously misleading you."

"That's what, she would," exclaimed Father Patrick, eagerly. "So I would not be, telling her about it, at all, at all. Let us have tit for tat, my darlings; and find our vengeance, in surprising her. Sure myself, has not been cut off, from society all, my born days. Was I not, after living nineteen months, at Naples, until I was starved: looking for bread, and more grief to me, for sorrow morsel, would pop into poor pat's mouth, though I gorged day, and night, on my troubles; ay and success to my memory, of those days of yore; for it helps me to an elegant, modern friend, for you jewel; my particular acquaintance, the Queen of Naple's barber."

"But," replied Sigismund, beguiled of one of his melancholy smiles, "but though her majesty of Naples may require the aid of a barber, my niece does not, you plainly see, reverend father."

"Ah! then be easy; and don't be joking

us, Monsignòre," returned the zealous, Patrick. "Sure barber's can have wives, though priests must not; and more grief to us and my friend Signore Modo, is married to the queen of Naple's, right-hand. Och! such an elegant fashion-monger; makes and fancies, all the queen's dress's and undress's, her coats, and her aprons; her stays, and her topknots. — Oh! flounces, and furbelows! but 'tis she's, the real, dandy."

"But," said Angelina smiling, both pleased and grateful for the good priest's zeal to serve her, "I have no gown to send to Signora Modo for a pattern, being reduced to one; and since she never saw me, we can devise no method for her fitting me."

"Oh! jewel! where there is a will, there is always, a mighty accommodating, way. I'll bid her step to Florence, and measure the Venus di Medici, there; only to make the coats, and petticoats, somewhat longer; since in the race, of sprouting upwards, you outtopped her, or if that, would be taking up too much time: I'll bid her to cut out all, for the form of perfection; and they will find the model here, ready to slide into them."

" Upon my word, Father Patrick," said the duca, again smiling, " your kind in‑ terest for Lady Angelina, can only be equaled by your gallantry."

" Och! then, who thanks any man, that is not blind, for being gallant, to youth and beauty? but never do you mind my gal‑ lantry, my good duca, but proceed to busi‑ ness. If myself had a morsel of tape, I think with your assistance, we would con‑ trive to send some sort of a bungling mea‑ sure, jewel, to Signora Modo; who, would work for the bare life, to serve poor pat, or so for that matter, would her husband; only you want no wigs. But to prove, its no palaver in myself; and that I have interest, with them; and that they are no botches, whom I want a job for; I'll be after telling you, just, how I got into the cockles of their hearts, and good luck to them.

" Why, one day, when the starving fit, was mighty bad upon me; I went into the first church, I met; to pray for bread; and some how, when one prays earnestly, the exertion I suppose, is mighty apt, to make one's eyes, a little humid; so mine began to keep company with my teeth; and water for bread; so myself thought, would some one give me, even a hard crust, the tears were ready, to moisten it for me; and just at that moment, a beautiful, elegant young lady,—Och! such a creature! arose from her knees, nigh hand me: and passing near, in her way out, dropped a pistole, into my hat, which laid beside me. Well jewels, you may well suppose, how my heart blessed her; but though ravenous I was, myself had the grace, to stop, and say, all that was so highly due, to the great inspirer, of charity: but when my thanksgiving, was ended; may be I did not run! faith I did; for the bare life, to the first baker's shop, that came in my way, and bought a young loaf; for says prudence, says she:—

"Pat my boy, sure you would not be, improvident in the days of prosperity; for remember the knawings of hunger, may come again, like the bitings of remorse.

"Well my darlings, in the days of pros-

stly, the
to make
ie began
nd water
ild some-
the tears
and just
nt young
from her
near, in
)my hat,
wels, you
t blessed
s, myself
l that was
r, of cha-
as ended;
for the
hat came
loaf; for

not be,
rity; for
er, may
norse.
s of pros-

perity, the pride, of us Irish gentlemen, is mighty apt to rise, with our fortunes; so myself, that was glad, a minute before, to receive alms, was now forsooth, ashamed to eat my loaf, in the street; for fear, some internal impulse, should make me cram it up, greedily, as if I wanted it. So off I trots, to the first obscure lane; and down I seated myself, upon a bench, under a gateway; and was beginning to devour; when myself, suddenly saw, two eyes, swimming in the rheum of sorrow, rivited upon my loaf. So I looks, in my turn; and finds they belong, to a creature, as old as the hills; and as crippled, as a dunce's capacity; for he had lost his supporters in the wars; and was now carried about, by two wooden spindles; like a good œconomist, he was clad in remnants; and he shook, och! concussions, and ague fits! how the creature shook, with age, poverty, and sorrow, as he falteringly, articulated—

"'I have tasted no food, these two, days!'

"'Faith, nor myself either, since yesterday; for that matter,' says I—'but first come, first served; you got the start of me, it seems, at the goal of poverty; so there's my loaf, for you, and I'll go bring myself, its brother.'

" ' Oh! my countryman!—my dear, countryman!' exclaimed the old cripple, in genuine Connaught Trist.

" ' Och! by dad!' says I, ' but there is no blarney, no sham, in that same; but true as the gospel : so be after waiting for me here, until I bring the staff of life, for myself—'

" So with that, off I set, bought my loaf, and taking my old post, opposite the cripple.—' Tell me your name; says I?'.

" ' One Patrick O'Carrol,' says he.

" By dad! I stared!—and so question, and answer, went, ding dong to its catechism; and drew out, at last, that this remains of a warrior—a reduced gentleman, like myself; was a bit of a relation, of mine, indeed a sort of great uncle; being the twin brother, of my grandfather—but any how, poverty was no disparagement to either of us; as long as we came honestly by it; and now in our cabal, finding we were both rank beggars, we agreed, to unite our fortunes, henceforth together.

" Well jewels, my landlord, in the miserable tenement, I had, was a mighty civil, decent man, and as myself, was going out of hand, to pay the modicum of rent due, to him; which he always made me pay, before hand, I thought I could, with a better face, take poor uncle Pat, home with me, and as the creatures, was so spent, with the whacks of Mar's journeymen; and the hardships of poverty, in a strange land; where the angry waters, had spouted him out, of a wreck; that myself did all I could, to comfort him; and so I got a morsel of dinner for us both; which from its novelty, by dad, we relished mightily.

" Well, my honeys, at night, there was but one bed; and that was a stone-quarry; —for when I lay upon its highland, and lowland diversities, myself would always be thinking, it was made of the hard hearts, I had met with, in my troubles; but bad as it was, it was better than none, at all, at all; so I made the, creature, uncle Pat, get into it,. as a luxury of his improving fortune; and myself was wrapped in; a monk's old habit, which I had come by, in my days of prosperity, and which now served me, for a big coat; and choosing the softest board, of the worm-eaten, floor, I made it groan with my weight, for I was heavily laden, with sorrows; having got the old cripple's, to groan under, as well as my own; and there I lay, ruminating, until myself was bothered; thinking how, I should get bread for uncle Pat: and so I thought, it was best, to go, to sleep, and put it out of my head; until morning; when fresh and fasting, my poor pericranium, might be often finding out, the relationship, between necessity, and invention.

"Well, I had been some time, clothed in my sorrow-hushing, vestments of sleep; when uncle Pat, began to belabor me, with one of his limbs, that lay on the chair, beside him. Faith myself was frightened, thinking it was crasy, he was.

"'Arrah Paddy,' says he, 'get up

with yo
death.'
"Sure
fire, blaz
was not
bonfire;
the back
perceivin
Pat, I r
to see w
the time
lady, w
wringgin
bawling,
per roo
"W
last got,
ment; a
got out,
sound,
"'T
boy?'
the mo
nurse,
"'I
the ha

with yourself; or we will be burned, to death.'

"Sure enough, there was a terrible big fire, blazing like Mount Vesuvius; but it was not our tenement, that was making the bonfire; but a fine house, in another street, the back of which, exactly faced us; and perceiving no danger, would befal uncle Pat, I run for the bare life, into the street; to see what use, myself could be of. By the time, I got round, there stood a young lady, whom they had got out of the house, wringging her hands, and screeching, and bawling, for her infant; who lay in an upper room, which she pointed out.

"With great difficulty, a ladder was at last got, long enough, to reach this apartment; and some nimble lads, went up; and got out, the spalpeen of a nurse; safe and sound, but sorrow one of the child.

"'Where, where, is my child; my boy?' exclaimed the distracted mother, the moment she perceived, the jade of a nurse, was come without him.

"'I could not find him, signora,' says the hard-hearted, gurren, and bad luck to her! 'for the smoke was so thick, I could not find his bed.'

"So with that, the poor mother, made at the ladder; and, after mounting a few steps, back she fell, as dead as a door nail, in a swoon; and now the Neapolitans, began to howle in recitative sorrow; for the ladder, some one who had ventured up, found was broken, and it was no longer considered safe, to be mounting it.

"By this time, I had made my way, to the side, of the poor *kilt* mother; when och!! Saint Patrick! and Shamracks! who should she be? But the very child of charity, who gave me the pistole, in the church! so with that, sorrow step, I stopped, to think even what will I do? but up the ladder I shot, until I came to the broken part; when off I tore the rope, which girted the monk's old habit, round me, and spliced the ladder, while y'd say 'peas!' and got safe, and sound, into the poor darling's nursery; which I found thickly inhabited, sure enough. Och! bubbaboo! but all was as black, as a bad conscience, and roll, and roll, came the smoke to give me the quinsy.

and if I
enemy,
wonder
guide me
a bed-po
welcome
one mi
and foun
lambs-w
raging i
brings h
which I
my ske
should
that the
be save
"Oc
how the
joy, wh
gave he
"'tl
you?'
"'
your c

ing.'

and if I did not embrace, armfuls of the enemy, as I groped about for the bed, I wonder at it. Sorrow cry was there to guide me; but at last, whack I came against a bed-post; and by dad, it was the most welcome whack, I ever received;—for in one minute now, I fished out the child, and found the innocent babe, as warm as lambs-wool; and fast rocked asleep, by the raging furies around. Well doon myself brings him, wrapped up in the big coat; which I fastened as tight, as a drum, about my skeleton's sides; in case the ladder should give way, any how, and I fall, that the little, duck of diamonds, might be saved.

"Och! guinea-pigs, and screech-owls! how the dear mother of it, sung out with joy, when she came to life; and myself gave her the boy, safe and sound.

" 'Who—what, angel of mercy are you?' she shouted out.

" 'But a mercenary one,' says I, 'for your charity purchased, the services of his life, with a pistole, in church, this morning.'

" ' Ah! poor *pàdre!* I remember you,' says she— ' Come, come to me, to-morrow. Alas! I have now no house, to ask you to, but come to me, at my mother's.'

" Well jewels, to make short of my story, I waited on Signora Modo, for it was her own sweet self, next morning, and I was obliged to stop in the entry, of her mother's house, for ever so long, such stacks of grand ladies, were come, to bother her, about the loss of the elegant coats, she had making of theirs, and all accusing her, of carelessness, in suffering such an accident, to occur, when such costly things, were in her charge. One lady telling her, ' she ought to be ashamed of herself, for not taking better care, of her daughter's new coat; that had come, in not less, than three ships, from India to her.' Another; scolding, and whimpering, by turns, because her wedding clothes, were burned; and her nuptials in consequence must be postponed, until more were purchased, and made.

" Well, in the thick of this hullabaloo,

arrives a noble lady; from the queen ; with
messages of condolence from her majesty,—
' who was in great grief, at Signora Modo
sustaining such a big fright, when her husband was not in Naples, to take care of,
and console her, but as to the pecuniary
loss, not to let that, disturb her serenity,
at all at all; for as soon as an estimate,
could be obtained of it, all, should be
remunerated, from her majesty's privy
purse.'

" Och the ficle elements, how the wind
changed!—Signora Modo, was no longer,
' a careless creature, scarcely fit to be work-
ing for the *canáglia*, let alone, for ladies of
fashion.' Och! no, my honeys, they
now placed themselves quite cute, upon the
queen's civil list; and at once adopting
courtly manners, to prove their loyalty no
blarney; they gave her a royal salute, in
the fine congees of condescension; and it
was now 'Pray, pray, take care of yourself, dear signora ; and do not be attending
to business, too soon, after this sad, sad
accident ; but when you are sufficiently
recovered, to attend to such trifles, you

will have the goodness, to assist our taste, in replacing these things, this fatal cata- strophe, has destroyed.' Agh, then sor- row fashion, was ever led more neatly by her majesty, than that same, of civility to the poor signora.

" Well jewels, by the queen desire and success to her! Signora Modo, took a grand house; and went on, more, elegantly than ever; now who but she, and who but, Fa- ther Pat, for myself was made so much of, by the grateful husband, and wife, as the queen made of the latter, and so by their kindness, uncle Pat, and myself, got out of the sinking bog, of poverty; and through their kindness, I have been enabled, to settle the old warrior, in comfort at Naples; for it was through their recommendation, that Conte Lorenzago took myself up, and gave me the big honor, of being chaplain, to the Duca di Montalbano.

" So, now jewels, you see, by my rig- marol story, it is not a hedge mantua maker, I am after recommending to you; and that I have a big morsel of interest, with Sig- nora Modo; which will all be exerted, to

make her work expeditiously, and beautifully, and elegantly, for you."

Angelina gracefully expressed her gratitude for the intended kindness of Father
Patrick, whose anecdote of himself, and
Signora Modo, was not calculated to lessen
either in the estimation of his auditors; and
as the duca seemed determined that she
should avail herself of the assistance of Father Patrick, in the present instance, it was at
length arranged, that at night Angelina was
to take proper measures from her gown, for
the reverend father to send off, the subsequent day, to Naples, accompanied by a
letter from him, to Signora Modo; with
an order from the duca himself to the signora, to spare no expence in procuring
every thing necessary and proper for the
wardrobe of Lady Angelina di Balermo.

After every thing relative to this business,
had been adjusted, and that Angelina, with
affecting sweetness, made her acknowlegements to her generous uncle, Sigismund
said :

"I wish this arrangement of ours might
be kept secret; for I own I have littleness

of mind, sufficient to enjoy the idea of retaliation, in the mortification of those who were so malicious, as to plan the mean project you have recounted to me, reverend father; by our suddenly and unexpectedly showing to them, it was no longer in their power to disfigure Lady Angelina."

"Sure, that will be the beauty of it," exclaimed the good priest.

"And yet, I fear, your ingenuously acknowleged propensity, to disburden your heart of every secret, may betray us. How can we contrive to lure you into silence, upon the subject?" said Sigismund.

"Faith I know not, monsignòre; for if my wish to comply with your excellènza's desire; and to retaliate for that sweet creature there, cannot keep the long tongue of me silent; nothing in the wide world, can."

"We will try some expedient, however," said the duca. "What think you of the efficacy of a wager upon the subject? Come, I'll bet against your new missal, an annuity of twenty pistoles, for your uncle Patrick, during his existence."

Tears started to Father Patrick's eyes: hastily he arose from his chair, pressed the duca's hand to a heart throbbing with gratitude; and profoundly bowing, precipitately withdrew, to conceal the overflowing of his feelings.

" Good and benevolent creature !" exclaimed Sigismund.

" Good and benevolent creature !" repeated Angelina, taking her uncle's hand, and looking at him with an approving and affectionate expression, that identified her application.

In a very short interval after the collected firmness of Father O'Carrol permitted his return to remain with the duca, during the absence of his niece, Lady Angelina was summoned to attend the dinner-party of the duchessa; and with a heavy heart, recoiling from that society she doubted not, either from inclination or precept, would be found by her most ungenial to her feelings, she followed the gentle page, Florio, who appeared with the mandate for her attendance.

CHAPTER XVII.

IN the drawing-room Angelina found assembled, beside the family party of the duchessa, (composed of herself, father Ezzelino, Conte di Lorenzago, and Signora Zola) the Princess di Belcastro, and her daughter, by a second, imprudent, and rather degrading marriage.

The princess had been a celebrated beauty; and her love of admiration still continued, what her charms did not, unimpaired; although with the utmost exertion of art she strove to retain the appearance of youth, long after it's reality had flown; but in despite of her personal vanities, and consequent follies, she possessed strong intellectual powers, most highly cultivated; but intermingled with her mental endowments, were the base alloys of worldly interestedness and mining art; and although her aggrandizing faculties had been superseded in her second choice by love, she had long resolved that her two children, a son by her first marriage, and a daughter by her second, should fully compensate to the declining fortunes of the House of Belcastro, by wealthy and advantageous alliances, her own lapse from peeuniary considerations. For her son she had, early in her speculating visions of ambition, marked out the heiress of Montalbano; but Duca Sigismund's most unexpected marriage destroyed all the allurements of that embryo project; and at this period of her introduction to Angelina, she was sedulously wooing the reversion of the duca's beautiful wife for the prince, who, never having felt the power of love, quietly acceded to that of interest, and made no objection to his mother's plans for him. The beauty of the duchessa pleased his fancy; and although her mind and manners were not exactly suited to his taste, yet as her family intimated, that, upon the duca's decease, her wealth would be immense, the charms of riches

preponderated the scale against his chances
of happiness with her.

Bertha Osimo, the princess's daughter,
whom her highness had arrogated to herself
the privilege of dignifying by the title of
Lady Bertha, was destined by her ambitious mother for the bride of some illustrious
man, of immense wealth; but this girl, now
in her nineteenth year, had unpropitiously,
for her highness's projects, imbibed an invincible horror, at the idea of every alliance,
not founded upon enthusiastic love; and
with a mingled tincture of strong susceptibility, and romantic propensities in her disposition, she was ever, in fancy, subdued by the
tender passion, sighing for some lovely
youth, but hitherto without any reciproca-
tion of sentiment from any of the varied objects of her numerous ardent attachments;
nor was she very likely to prove a successful
votary of enthusiastic love, since Nature, after lavishing every personal charm upon her
mother and brother, took a sudden capricious
turn in the family, and gave to poor Lady
Bertha no attraction but in a pair of soft lan-
guishing blue eyes. The present object of

this romantic girl's passion, was, in defiance of her mother's ambitious precepts, Florio, the already-mentioned beautiful page, who the enamoured Bertha, with all the painful alarm of jealous apprehension, beheld stop to steal a glance, of unequivocal admiration, at Lady Angelina, after he had conducted her to the duchesa's presence.

Not even the seclusion of a cloister could despoil Lady Angelina of the native graceful elegance of deportment with which Nature had so eminently gifted her, and the striking beauty of unstudied ease in her movements, on her entrance, befitted the dignity of high birth, and the refined polish of an elevated situation.

The moment Lady Angelina appeared, Conte Lorenzago flew to meet her, and, conducting her to the princess, introduced her, with a most flattering eulogium, to her highness, and Lady Bertha; then attended her to the seat she seemed to choose, (after paying her civilities to the rest of the circle) took a vacant place beside her, and strove to engage her in conversation, exclusively to himself, until dinner was announced;

when he handed her out, seated himself next to her at table, and appeared determined, by the most profound adulation, to efface, if possible, from her mind, the recollection of all former bad impressions of him.

The other individuals of his family, present, not comprehending the motives of this new line of conduct in Lorenzago, and angry at his seeming thus to have adopted plans of his own, without making them participators in his secrets, their rudeness and ill-nature to the lovely object of his intentions rapidly increased, as his politeness augmented; and making, by strong contrast, his courtesy appear more conspicuous. Incessantly he talked of the virtues and mental excellence of his son, with the most parental enthusiasm; mentioned his intending shortly to visit the Castle di Montalbano; and bespoke her favor "for a youth whom sympathy ought to attract her esteem, since in every perfection of the heart and mind he was her counterpart."

But scarcely had this small dinner-party adjourned to the saloon, after their repast, when the cicisbeo of the duchessa, the Mar-

-chese di Cantazaro, arrived. He had been
detained for the last two days from his duties
at Montalbano, by the hourly-expected
death of his wife, a lovely and amiable young
woman, of immense fortune, whom he had
married just at the period the Duchessa di
Montalbano had elected him her cicisbeo.
Father Jeronimo had about one hour since
pronounced the Marchesa di Cantazaro out
of danger, when the marchese set out on the
wings of diligence, to perform again the suspended attentions and devoirs of his department, at the Castle di Montalbano.

This man was young and handsome; but
had a boldness of expression in his countenance, a strong character of dissipation in it,
that could not fail of disgusting a mind of
delicacy; and promptly he became an object
of recoiling aversion to Angelina, on whom
he fixed his undeviating gaze the moment
he first beheld her, and strove by every
means, most sedulously, to evince his power-
fully-awakened admiration of her.

The brow of the observant Minora contracted to a scowl, her lip fell in pouting
sullenness, and Angelina felt infinitely dis-

tressed and alarmed. Less in the power of
the duchessa, and her treacherous family,
than fate had seemed to place her, she might
perhaps have felt amused at this visible degree of envious mortification she had invo-
luntarily awakened in this vain woman's
breast; but as it was, she dreaded every
cause of increase to her enmity; and soon
impelled by her apprehension, she pleaded
extreme fatigue, from the unfortunate occurrences of the preceding night, and requested permission to retire; a permission
which Minora readily granted; and gladly
and gracefully Angelina withdrew, and hastened to the apartments of her uncle.

Angelina found the melancholy Sigismund
full of imaginary symptoms of new maladies, all brought on by fretting at her being
so long detained from him, although it was
unreasonable to have expected her one moment sooner; and the irritation of his nerves
at this, considered by him, long retarded absence, leading him to conceive she would
never more be permitted to return; and
when his lovely niece beheld the state he
was in, full of amiable solicitude for his re-

storation to health and happiness, she exerted all her varied powers to interest and
amuse him; nor did she quit his apartments
to retire to her own for the night, until she
soothed his gentle spirit to an aspect of
tranquillity.; and when returned to her own
apartments, she sought not " tired Nature's
kind restorer," until she had obeyed the last
charges of her uncle, and his good-natured
chaplain, to prepare her measures and directions, to be forwarded to Signora Modo
on the morrow.

So completely subdued by fatigue was
Angelina, that the moment her aching head
rested on her pillow, she sunk into a profound repose, which continued undisturbed
till morning, when an almost southern sun
stealing it's penetrating rays through the
laths of her window-blinds, (for having no
domestic appropriated to attend upon her,
no one thought it incumbent on them to
awake her) roused her from her pillow.

Angelina, distressed at her trespass, in in-
temperate sleep, hastily arose; and as soon
as her sacred duties, which nothing short of
absolute necessity ever induced her to abre-

viate, and neatness, the idol of her toilet, would admit of, she was ready to emerge from her chamber; and after an earnest gaze at the venerable towers of Rossarno Castle, of which from every window of her apart- ments she had a full view; and hearing some deep-drawn sighs, for the sorrows of the too interesting Fredrico, she hastened to pay her duty to her uncle, and to apologize to him for so late an appearance.

But though infinitely chagrined at having lost those hours in sleep she meant to have dedicated to the important purpose of writ- ing to Father Erasmo, to entreat him to re- turn to Montalbano; and to have her letter in readiness to intrust to the care of the good monk Jeronimo; on his promised early visit to the duca, she soon experienced an unexpected pleasure to cheer away her men- tal murmurs, in the visible amendment in her uncle's aspect; a tranquillized calmness that told a great decrease of Sorrow's touch- ing traits.

But soon were the internal murmurings of her self-upbraidings resumed with renovated force, by the almost immediate appearance

of Father Jeronimo, who quickly announced, in exulting professional pride, "that he
was sent for to the Grand Duchessa of Tuscany; and that, as he should be detained at
least two days on this visit, it would be impossible for him to see the Duca di Montalbano during that period, and therefore he
must make up sufficient medicines to last
through that interval; but as he found the
pulse and looks of his patient almost miraculously amended, he trusted his absence
would prove of no material consequence."

With that activity of impatience, which
seemed to proclaim every delay was an infliction of misery, Father Jeronimo set about
the preparation of his medicines; so that
Angelina instantly perceived he would not
delay for the composition of even a short
epistle, which hers to Father Erasmo could
not, from the nature of it's subject, prove;
so that at least two days of delay would arise
from her unfortunately protracted sleep.

Immediately after the departure of the
pride-flattered Jeronimo, the duca feeling
highly indignant at no domestic having
been appointed to attend his niece, which,

amongst other proofs of it's being essentially necessary, would have prevented the unlucky circumstance which had now postponed her. writing to Father Erasmo; and feeling also, that now having passed her childhood, his brother's daughter ought to have an establishment of her own, he directed Father Patrick to write to Signore Brondelo, to seek out proper domestics for her, since no dependence could be placed on any selected by the Tolmezos, who could, as they had given terrible proof, admit domestics into the castle, of characters so little investigated, they had turned out to be even associates of a banditti. "But as to her equipage," he said, "as that must be regulated solely by her own fancy, Brondelo must be directed to order the proper tradespeople for that purpose, to wait upon Lady Angelina for her orders."

"But, sure, *Monsignore*," said Father Patrick, after receiving those instructions, "this Signore Brondelo is only a bit of an old bachelor, and more grief to him! as formal as the musty deeds, he draws out, to gain his solitary living by. To find out characters, and hire steady servant-boys; and sober, careful coachmen, 'tis he that will answer, mighty well; but, how he should come to be knowing any thing at all, at all, of waiting maids, myself would be glad to know. One servant-girl, would, answer the purpose, in his mind, as well as another; and, so she is prim, and ho- nest; sorrow look will he look farther; and she may prove, a perfect botch, at dressing elegantly,; so that myself, thinks, I had better, be sending a morsel of a post- script, to the letter I dispatched only two hours ago, by express, to, Signora Modo, and desire her, to send us, with the beautiful coats, and fans, and caps, an elegant wait- ing maid, that will know, how, to put them, on; with her head full, of the Queen of Na- ples; fashions; and her hands full, of Sig- nora Modo's grand dresses. As to charac- ter, the Signora's own, is staunch; so she will have no flaws, in her dealings; and I'll en- gage, 'tis she, that will be sending us an elegant girl; long before old Brondelo, would have got half through, the Saints Calender, in search of a tirewoman, for Lady Angelina."

"Upon my word, Father Patrick," said the duca, smiling; "you are the most complete lady's man I have lately met with; and in my niece's new establishment, I think I must resign you to her, as her fac totum. If you are really convinced, Reverend Father, that we may depend upon this same Signora Modo of yours, for the moral part of the business, I acknowlege your plan wears a better promise of success than mine."

"Depend!" exclaimed Father Patrick, coloring with zeal; "is it depend, on Signora Modo?—Ah! the creature!—Myself only wishes, you were just to see her, and sorrow doubt, would spring up any more, to be choking the free passage, of firm reliance, by dad, her heart (although she is only a handicrafts woman) was made, of a little remnant, of the same beautiful stuff, that composed Lady Angelina's own; and she would sooner die, I'll be bail now, than recommend any one, she ought to be ashamed of herself, for disparaging her own discretion, by."

"Well, my beloved Angelina," said Sigismund, "which shall your Abigail be of, Signora Modo's choice, or Signore Brondelo's?"

"Of Signora Modo's, certainly, since Father Patrick will have the goodness to take this further trouble for me. But, Reverend Father, will you have the kindness to remember, that I should wish to find something more in her head, than merely the fashions of her Neapolitan Majesty; and should wonderfully like to have *her* heart formed of some beautiful stuff too."

"Yes jewel.—Of the wholesome dowlass, made in my country for common wear; —sound, strong, and unblemished, in it's manufacture; and made sightly to the eye of refinement, in the beautiful bleach ground, of honesty, fidelity, and obedience."

"Such a piece of manufacture, procured for me, by such accurate discernment, I shall value as a treasure, above all price," replied Angelina; and the good priest,

happy in the idea of obliging, hastily withdrew, to put his plan in execution.

Since the delusive period in which Conte
Lorenzago had, by his specious conduct,
and flattering attentions, infatuated the Duca di Montalbano, into appointing him
agent to his estates, he had never visited
the apartments of the invalid dupe to his
wiles, except upon absolute business, so
that infinite was the astonishment of the
long-neglected Sigismund, upon receiving a
visit this morning from his brother-in-law,
of mere courteous compliment, or rather was
of opinion to form conclusions from appearances of strong cordiality.

For nearly two hours, the visit of Lorenzago was extended; and during that period,
so well did he manage the fascinations which
Nature gifted him with, that no one could
form a wish for his departure; for, beside
all the topics of refined conversation likely
to please Sigismund and his lovely niece, he
entered into every thing interesting to them
both, with an air of friendship which seemed
to take a warm part in all that concerned

them; and had they not already known he was not to be depended on, he must have succeeded in deceiving them into a firm belief of his sincerity. ...

At length, Lorenzago, alluding to his being about to quit Tuscany, the duca inquired, " Was his absence from the castle meant to be a long one?"

" Not very," he replied, " he was going to Rome, where he should be happy to execute any commission of his Eccellenza's, or Lady Angelina's. My son," he added, " has just completed his studies there: I am going to make his departing arrangements; and mean, with your permission, *Monsignóre*, to bring him back with me to the castle, to pay his compliments to your *Eccellénza* and the duchessa, ere he sets out upon his travels."

" To me," said Sigismund, impressively, " your son must ever prove a welcome guest, since to me his conduct has uniformly been that of undeviating respect, and attentive kindness."

Shortly after, Conte Lorenzago departed, first obtaining the duca's permission for

Lady Angelina to dine with the duchessa's party;—an invitation which Minora (to appear amiable, and conceal her envy and hatred from the eyes of her guests and admirers,) found herself compelled to give.

CHAPTER XVIII.

WHEN the moment arrived for Angelina's retiring to arrange her hair, for appearing at dinner, and re-dress herself in her only gown, nothing could exceed her astonishment, on finding all her baggage, which had accompanied her from Santo Valentino, in her dressing-room, laid out in complete readiness for her to unlock, and all the vases around her apartments filled with the most fragrant flowers.

Angelina's amazement at this most unexpected restoration of her wardrobe, took from her every power of bestowing even a thought from gratitude upon the attentive kindness of some friend, in this beautiful present of flowers.

" Oh! who," she mentally ejaculated, " can have procured for me this restoration

of my baggage? Assuredly not the Tolmezos; since that measure, by betraying
intercourse with the banditti, would at once
implicate them in the villany that threw
me into the power of Salimbini. Who,
then, possessed sufficient interest in the
brigand's fortress, to draw my treasures
thence?"

" It was—Oh! it was Fredrico di Alviano!" she exclaimed, and eagerly her heart
welcomed the suggestion; for while it told
her she lived in his remembrance, proclaimed at once that the employers of Salimbini
were indeed in Fredrico's power; that he
had successfully compromised with the ferocious chief; and his safety was no longer
endangered by his gallant rescue of her.

And now, with a heart bounding in joyful measure, and a countenance illumined
with it's glad feelings, Angelina flew back to
the duca, and announced to him and Father
Patrick, the unexpected restoration of her
clothes; but knowing the peculiar delicacy
of Conte di Alviano's situation, already too
much implicated by supposed friendship
with the banditti, she forbore to point out

him as the being she conceived herself obliged to.

Sigismund was thrown by her intelligence into the most powerful astonishment. The same ideas, relative to the Tolmezos not being the restorers of her baggage, that struck with conviction upon Angelina's reason, could not operate upon the mind of her uncle; since he, like her, had neither proof or suspicion of their bearing any part in the villany of Salimbini until now; when, after a train of deeply-mental investigation, the horror of a suggestion, that it was possible they might be guilty, struck upon his recoiling-heart; and now, as some clew to confirm or banish his agonising surmises, he rang for Rospo, and ordered him to inquire, minutely, who had brought Lady Angelina's baggage to the castle, and who had deposited it in her dressing-room?

Rospo remained absent some time, and then returned with the extraordinary information, "That nothing belonging to Lady Angelina had been delivered at the portal; and that nobody had seen her ladyship's baggage, or had deposited it in her dressing-room."

The duca could not give credence to such intelligence; and requested Father Patrick to immediately investigate the business for him. Shortly after Angelina again retired, now invested really with the power of dressing for dinner; for, although she really possessed nothing of the costume of the world, she yet had been presented, a very short period before she quitted Santo Valentino, by her beloved abadessa, with a very beautiful convenient habit to wear on gala days in the cloister; for as out of it she never now appeared, any other style of dress than that arbitrarily arranged for the boarders would have proved useless; and Lady Constantia, wishing to see her, on every festivity, attired according with her rank, had every part of the boarder's habit made up with the most expensive elegance. The robe long, and gracefully flowing, was made of soft grey silk; the veil and drapery for the neck, of the finest Mecklin lace; the cross and rosary were composed of jet; and

when all combined and worn by Lady Angelina, nothing could appear more simply
pleasing and becoming.

But while Angelina made her toilet for
this day's dinner, the flowers, which per-
fumed the surrounding air, attracted her
attention, and, for a time, drew her thoughts
from the interesting Fredrico, and her supposed new obligation to him, to wonder
whom in the Castle of Montalbano she
could be indebted to for this fragrant incense, when she soon determined it to be
some piece of insidious flattery of Conte
Lorenzago's; some spell to lure her into his
sinister projects against her uncle; and, in
this belief she firmly resolved, while she admired the beauty of each rose, to beware of
the thorns they bore to wound.

The moment Angelina's dress was completed, she returned to the apartments of
the duca, where Father O'Carrol shortly
after made his appearance, bringing with
him intelligence not more satisfactory than
Rospo's had been, relative to Lady Angelina's baggage.

" Sorrow morsel of Father Ezzelino's big

treasures are restored," said Father Patrick, with an arch smile, " and what was a mighty queer thing, he forgot all about them, until myself, roused up his memory, and reminded him of the rage, he ought to be getting into, by just wishing him joy; supposing for all the world, that he had come in, for his share of the restitution.—Faith my joy to his suspended grief, came like electricity to a benumbed faculty;—it made him sensible, in a moment; and alive to misfortunes, that were sent to repose, in the repository of his philosophy;—but now the hulabaloo he is kicking up for the loss of his essays, that are gone to improve the rogues, instead of making him a cardinal! Och! Thunder and hurricanes! if he is not the man, for an extempore passion, the vocabulary mint, of little Ireland, never clapt it's sterling mark, upon it's own coinage " 'Humbug!' " and now he says, " ' by that very scandalous partiality shown, in the business; the diabolical Conte di Alviano, is at the bottom of the restored baggage.' "

" Alas! no," said Angelina smiling, and

with playfulness, to hide a conscious blush; " for had hé been there, I should have unpacked every thing to find him out, and bring him hither, for my dear uncle to thank the preserver of his Angelina."

" Whoever was at the bottom of the business," said Sigismund gravely, " I cannot feel very comfortable in the idea, that some invisible emissaries of a banditti have the power of visiting my castle at pleasure."

" Faith," replied Father Patrick, " was the castle mine, the first time, ever these invisible agents, appear again; I'd make them give an account of themselves,—'tho as the bringing back Lady Angelina's clothes, was a good, and honest thing, sorrow harm I'd harm them, for that, same my honey."

The mystery of this matter gave to the duca an infinity of uneasiness. It seemed to argue his being in the power, and, perhaps, devoted to the villany of the banditti of the forest, with whom, and some individual, or individuals, beneath his own roof, there could exist no doubt of there being a perfect understanding of mutual interest;

and, without delay, he issued orders for Signore Prondelo's being instantly summoned, that he might consult with him upon the most effectual method of discovering this secret correspondence.

- At length the duca's dinner-hour arrived, and in some time after that repast was ended, his lovely niece joined the duchessa and her guests, at the summons of the last dinner-bell. This dinner-party had no increase from the preceding day, except by the Marchese di Cantazaro, who, subtile and wary, had learned by this time, to shape his manners to Angelina, by those of the duchessa and her satellites.

Angelina, coldly received by all but Conte Lorenzago; his flattering attentions became more glaringly conspicuous, by the force of contrast; and soon, by their exuberance, led the penetrating object of his homage, to more complete conviction of his having some new project in view against the peace or interest of her unfortunate uncle, and, to lure her out of her acquiescence, he thus assailed her by this overwhelming tide of adulation: and thus impressed with apprehensions' of further evil awaiting her helpless uncle. She stole many a moment, while she apparently listened to the fascinating conversation of this man of art, to meditate upon what possible mischief he had in view; in hopes that, could she anticipate it's purport, she might find out the means of averting it; but at length, from one of these painful ruminations, inspired by alarm, every faculty was aroused, and centred into the one, of sound-devouring attention; for the general conversation of the table had, by the malicious manœuvring of Father Ezzelino, turned upon Fredrico di Alviano.

"The more you hear of that execrable dæmon of iniquity," replied the invidious Ezzelino, to a remark of the Marchése di Cantazaro's, "the more you know to condemn and to recoil from. Beside this direful murder of his relative, and his shameless intimacy with the banditti of the forest, another very nefarious fact has lately transpired, of his having seduced a most lovely and fascinating young female, Hermione by name :—tore her from her mother's sheltering care, and drove that wretched parent to the most dreadful of human maladies; and who has since continued a raving maniac, without a hope of cure."

A dreadful thrill of agonising horror vibrated through the sensitive heart of Angelina; and the chilling creep of terrible conviction pervaded her whole frame, until the bigoted belief of Fredrico's calumniated innocence, consecrated into hallowed faith at the altar, where he smiled in pious resignation, arose in severity, of mental censure, for her own momentary injustice; and, full of indignation at Father Ezzelino, for circulating this invidious tale, (which, although she had herself heard, in the very semblance of undoubted truth, she yet disbelieved, as the wild phantom of a maniac's ravings), she turned to him, with cheeks of glowing resentment, and eyes of deep research, and impressively she said—

" How came the Reverend Father Ezzelino so well acquainted with the history of the Brigand Salimbini's family?—Did his son Orsino inform you, in his tête-à-tête walk to the convent of San Stefano?"

check soon

The expression of Angelina's countenance, and her questions, surprised the
cheeks of Ezzelino by a conscious blush; but
soon the crimson effusion changed to the
deepened tints of anger, and haughtily he
answered—

" The interrogations of good-sense and
politeness I am ever happy to reply to; but
the questions of impertinence I uniformly
disdain an answer to."

" Nay," returned Angelina impressively, " my questions were not those of impertinence, nor, I trust, the reverse of
good sense; since their source was a Christian spring, arising from the laudable wish
of reminding your reverénza, that Conte di
Alviano's knowlege of the terrible banditti,
from whom he gallantly rescued me, and
even his removal of Signora Hermione from
her mother's care, may have sprung from
means and motives as pure and innocent, as
those from which your information came."

Lorenzago, not choosing that Lady Angelina should encounter more of the betraying intemperance of his uncle's violence,
eagerly and judiciously proposed an imme-

diate excursion to visit a lately-erected edifice in the neighbourhood; and the party separating to prepare for their ramble, Angelina gladly availed herself of this opportunity of retiring to the apartments of the duca, which she quitted not again, until the hour arrived of separating for the night.

Although Angelina generally arose with the sun, Anfania was in her chamber before she left her bed the succeeding morning, with a peremptory command, more than a request, to her, " to lend the silk robe she had worn the preceding day, to be sent to Florence to have one made by, for the duchessa to appear in at a masquerade she was invited to in the neighbourhood. And I suppose," added Anfania, " that you may possibly have it back again by to-morrow."

The natural disposition of Angelina delighted in obliging, and promptly benefiting others by any advantages she possessed, but in this instance she felt an innovating unwillingness to acquiescence, for well she divined the request was propelled by the mean ill nature of depriving her of the only dress she possessed, befitting her rank to appear in. However, wishing to avoid every thing that might lead to warfare with the wife of her uncle, she quietly yielded to the unreasonable demand, and Anfania, with a malicious sneer of triumph, soon bore this spoil of invidious policy away.

The departure of Conte Lorenzago for Rome took place this day, according to his arrangements; and Angelina, during this morning, made the painful observation of the energy of mind her uncle had evinced since her arrival, being but the momentary flashes of animation, awakened by the joy and action given to his mental faculties, since her restoration to him; and that now the tumult of anxiety and pleasure, with the novelty of her presence, were in part subsided, his intellectual powers were sinking back into their unfortunate imbecile weakness, encouraging his propensity of welcoming each real bodily ill, and wooing every ideal one; and, with all the gentle incentive of humanity, Angelina determined sedulously to combat this dreadful mental weakness, not by argument, but by address; and promptly she resolved to remove all books upon medicine, from time to time, from his view, and to replace them by others, selected from the different branches of reading her uncle used to take delight in, yet only upon such subjects, as, while they possessed fascinations to allure his thoughts from their favorite and destructive contemplations; were calculated to awaken the energies of his mind and talents to their original firmness; and to accelerate and assist her laudable design, she took an opportunity of deploring her own imperfect knowlege in many branches of literature, in which she felt most anxious for proficiency, and entreated the duca's aid to perfect her in; which, with all the amiable kindness of his nature, he cheerfully promised her.

The duchessa had, the preceding evening, intimated to Lady Angelina, that she should expect to see her every day at her dinner-table; an appearance of courtesy assumed for the purpose of gratifying her own malevolence, in seeing her placed there as an object of contempt and derision, where once, she had presided, and had been loved by each inmate, and esteemed by every guest.

Angelina, to preserve that appearance of concord most likely to conduce to her beloved uncle's tranquillity, determined to accept the specious invitation, in defiance of whatsoever humiliations it might subject her to, whenever the state of Sigismund's mind permitted her to leave him, without deviating from that kind attention his distressing situation called for; but this day, beholding in him many symptoms inimical to that mental health she earnestly wished to behold in him, she made an effort to accomplish her desire of dining with him; but the duca persisting in his anxiety for her joining the duchessa's party, she was compelled to acquiesce; and, at the accustomed time for making her dinner toilet, she retired to effect the only alterations in her dress which the invidious Minora had now left in her power to benefit by.

When arrived in her dressing-room, Angelina beheld a new selection of the choicest flowers; but firmly believing their arrange-

ment there was by order of the wily Lorenzago, took no further notice of them, than
what their fragrance and their beauty
claimed; for she had many a momentous
theme for contemplation, and found the
time occupied by her toilet, too short for
indulging in her manifold perplexing and
afflicting cogitations; for now her uncle's
spirit drooped, she no longer dared to look
for happier prospects through his exertions.

CHAPTER XIX.

AT length the dinner-bell summoned
Lady Angelina from the apartments of her
uncle, to go and enter a formidable circle
of the gay and fashionable, in mean attire;
but she had been early taught by her excellent governess, justly to appreciate dress;
neither worshiping it as the deity of her
idolatry, nor despising it as beneath her attention; and fully convinced, that mind
and manners were the unerring drapery
which best proclaimed pretensions to respect, she rallied promptly all the firmness
she could muster, to sustain her, without
betraying humiliated discomposure, as she
took her seat amongst a large assemblage of
fashionable personages, of that thickly-in-
habited neighbourhood, herself the object of
universal gaze, scrutiny, or interest.

Many of this numerous train of guests had known and estimated the parents of Angelina, and many had known her when fortune smiled upon her, as heiress of that castle. Her early disappointments and misfortunes could only affect the hearts of the worthy with pity and solicitude for her fate; nor were the fascinating graces of her manners, nor the mild dignity with which she bore such a transition of fate, likely to diminish the esteem or admiration of those who were not actuated by attachment to Minora, to view her through the perspective of prejudice and envy; and soon the invidious duchessa found the intended mortification she had prepared for the lovely niece of her husband, recoil upon herself, by quickly beholding Lady Angelina paid, by the majority of this large assemblage of guests, the most unequivocal homage of respect and admiration; for while in self-delusion, she believed she had devised means of lessening the charms of Lady Angelina, she had prepared odium and abhorrence for herself; for memory now faithful to the rumor of Minora's never-effectually-concealed detestation of her husband's lovely niece; awakened the well-founded conjecture, that it was through her machinations the wardrobe of the bereaved heiress of Montalbano was so shabbily supplied. It had been circulated too, that the duchessa had influenced her infatuated husband to destine Lady Angelina for a conventual life; and her habit not giving conviction to that belief, all cried "Shame!" in mental indignation at the diabolical projector of such a sacrifice.

But although Angelina received the most gratifying respect and attention from many individuals, of whom this dinner-party was composed, yet sincerely she rejoiced when the moment arrived, in which, with propriety, she could withdraw from it, since she had felt completely miserable in a society, where all, influenced by universal prejudices, were unanimous in condemnation of Fredrico di Alviano, and each eager to repeat some direful tale in proof of his depravity; and though Angelina considered all as calumny, although she was firm in her conviction, that he merited the world's esteem, and not it's censure; and that she

felt the most painful indignation at all the
injustice she was thus compelled to hear,
yet a consciousness that she could not attempt the defence of Fredrico, without the
almost certainty of betraying the carefully-
guarded secret of her unconquerable attachment to this aspersed young man, silenced
all that her enthusiastic gratitude would
otherwise have urged her to plead in his vindication, by a fair and candid statement of
his amiable conduct towards herself, in his
heroic rescue of her from the villany of Salimbini, in doing which, she believed, she
could give an unanswerable refutation to
one, at least, of the calumnies she had been
doomed to hear. " Of his friendship with
the banditti being incontestably proved, by
it's chief having been seen that very day
mounted upon the conte's celebrated war-
horse Ràpido," an anecdote that, by still
more powerfully awakening her gratitude,
led her, in the glowing tumult of her feelings, to consider her own conduct as inex-
cusably reprehensible, in not generously
braving all apprehension of betraying herself,
to scorn, by attempting to pay some part of

her incalculable debt to her preserver, by
undauntedly proclaiming how Rápido had
become the property of Salimbini; but, in
every effort to give utterance to what she
wished to tell, her bounding heart, her conscious agitation, destroyed at once her faculties of articulation; and, with a bosom
saddened by self-upbraiding, she fled from
society, the moment she found herself at liberty to retire, and was rapidly hastening
to give free scope to her self reproaches, in
the seclusion of her own chamber, when her
design was frustrated by the pursuit of Lady
Bertha, who, half breathless with speed,
had followed her to implore an hour's conference in a walk together.

Politeness, combined with the natural
sweetness of Lady Angelina's disposition,
forbade her offering any negative to a request so earnestly made; and, although
panting for solitude, she accompanied Lady
Bertha to the most sombre part of the castle-
grounds; for the pensive Bertha, in concord with the romantic turn of her mind,
and to suit her love-sick fancies, ever where
inclination could guide her footsteps, bent

her way to the scenery most congenial to.
the nurture of the tender propensities of her
susceptible feelings.

And as Lady Bertha now led her lovely,
companion to the chosen spot of her present gloomy fancy, she, in a preface formed of the sweetly-flowing words of sentiment, and uttered with all the melting softness of heart-subduing pathos, gave Lady
Angelina the unwelcome information, that
it was to confide in her a tale of love, and
maternal persecution, she had solicited a
private conference.

Angelina, by no means anxious for such
a distinction, would fain have turned her
from the project of this intended confidence, but the fair inamorata was resolved
upon disclosing her tender weakness; and,
eager to fulfil her wise determination, hurried her lovely and unwilling companion to
a secluded spot, where, on a rustic bench,
beneath the shelter of a luxuriant willow,
she purposed the deliciously-interesting
communication should be made; but how
was her project demolished; how her susceptible heart palpitated, when, on ap-

proaching the grand scene for Friendship's
sweet and sacred disclosures, she beheld
the object of her fancied passion, the beautiful Florio, reclined upon the very bench
she was proceeding to, weeping bitterly as
he seemed arranging some papers into a
small packet.

Angelina, pitying and respecting affliction wheresoever she found it, would instantly have retreated, to leave the sacred
haunts of sorrow unmolested, but Lady
Bertha was resolute in her determination to
stay, and intrude upon the griefs of the interesting mourner.

" My destiny calls," she emphatically
exclaimed. " See you not sympathy led
me hither, to meet the ecstasy of an eclaircissement; to give transports to his bursting
heart, and ease my own? Ah! see you not
they are my pathetic billets, my melting
sonnets, that have thus unmanned me?" *him*

Nothing could exceed the astonishment
of Angelina, at exclamations which at
once revealed to her the object of Lady Bertha's passion, except her indignation at being so ungenerously drawn in to become a

confidant of a clandestine, ill-suited attachment.

"Lady Bertha," she cried, with cheeks
mantled by the brilliant glow of the delicate resentment of wounded propriety, "if
you have forgotten your rank, your duty, I
cannot cease to remember mine. If you
are thus resolute in degrading yourself, in
opposition to both, you must excuse my becoming a witness to a scene that, under
every existing circumstance, I feel, could
not exalt me in my own opinion."

"Ah! cruel, cruel girl! leave me not,
I conjure you, at this awful moment, the
very crisis of thy poor persecuted Bertha's
fate," exclaimed the enamoured fair one, in
so elevated a tone of energy, that the accents vibrated on the ears of the astonished
Florio, who, overpowered by confusion on
being so surprised, started from his seat,
hastily hid the papers in his bosom, and, in
the most painful embarrassment, would have
retreated from the gaze of his observer, had
not Lady Bertha called to him, in the gentle
voice of tender entreaty, to approach her.

Florio, in the trembling perturbation of

shame and chagrin, respectfully obeyed the
tender summons; but, while his varying
cheeks betrayed his emotions, he turned his
timid eyes, with a supplicating expression,
upon Lady Angelina, as if to implore her
aid, in extricating him from this perplexing
situation.

" Oh! Florio!" exclaimed the lovelorn
Bertha, and then she ceased, conceiving
a pause would then have an interesting effect, and, by its sympathetic operations,
work in her cause; but Angelina promptly
destroyed it's effect; for feeling powerfully
the impropriety of Lady Bertha's conduct,
the degradation of her own situation, as her
confidant, and, in pity to the well compre-
hended tacit supplication of poor Florio,
she, with intuitive delicacy, resolved to free
all from the errors and embarrassments of
their situations, and mildly, yet hastily, addressed the trembling page—

" Signore Florio," she said, " Lady Bertha has been most unfortunately taken ill
on her walk, and has not been herself for
some moments past. I must therefore entreat you to fly to the castle, seek out Lady

Bertha's own woman, and send her instantly to me, to assist in conveying her ladyship
to her own apartments."

The decisive dignity of Lady Angelina's
manner, as she announced by her request,
her wish for Florio's absence, would have
insured immediate obedience from even the
most presuming; but the poor agitated
page's wishes so exactly co-operated with
her own, that he was prompt in compliance,
and with eyes beaming gratitude to her, for
thus relieving his painful embarrassment,
and with a profound and graceful bow, he
precipitately retreated.

And now we find our feeble powers of
delineation totally inadequate to the task of
portraying, in the full force of the fierce
colors it appeared in, the everescence of the
hitherto-apparently gentle Bertha's resentment against her lovely companion, on beholding the prompt obedience of Florio, and
that his parting look was directed to Lady
Angelina: her cheeks glowed, her eyes
glared, her lips quivered, and franticly she
flung the arm of Angelina from her, that
was linked in hers, and, in the tremulous,

almost inarticulate voice of ungovernable passion, she exclaimed—

" Base ! cruel ! ungenerous ! diabolical perfidy ! Yes, yes, I see, clearly see, the developement of your insidious scheme, of preventing the eclaircissement I panted for, you smiling hypocrite."

" These are harsh sounding epithets, Lady Bertha," said the astonished Angelina, with mild, yet impressive dignity, " and will, in your cooler moments, give your heart as severe a shock for having inspired their utterance, as my amazed ears received on hearing them addressed to me."

" Oh ! yes, calm and collected like all consummate dissemblers : yes, yes, thus you would veil your treacherous design of insnaring the heart of my adored Florio from me."

" Be assured, Lady Bertha, the heart of my aunt's domestic is not the prize the daughter of a Duca di Montalbano will ever aim at insnaring from you," calmly returned Angelina.

" Dare not to call the lovely youth a domestic !" exclaimed the almost-phrensied Bertha : " Does not his majestic look and mien, his rare acquirements, his every word and action, proclaim his being the disguised heir of some illustrious house?—But, well, well, I see through your blandishments.— You affect this disdain to conceal your ambitious views upon this exalted youth. Oh! why, ere I threw away my confidence upon you, did I not credit the assertions of the dear, angelic, unerring duchessa! She told us truly what a smiling hypocrite you were; ay, and instructed my mother to devise pretences to keep my brother from the castle, until you are securely disposed of."

The glowing resentment of Angelina was now chilled at once, by the freezing thrill of horrid alarm, and falteringly she repeated, half breathless with dismay, " Securely disposed of!"

" Yes, securely disposed of," replied the enraged inamorata, deprived, by resentment against this fancied rival, of every recollection of the solemn promises of secresy she had pledged herself to, upon hearing the invidious communications of the duchessa: " Yes, securely disposed of; for she will not rest until you are insnared into some convent for life, where your powers of doing mischief will be destroyed; for, until that is effected, she cannot be secure of the affections of my brother, who is to be her spouse, the moment decorum will permit the union, after the duca's decease; for well is she aware that you will exert your insidious machinations to win his highness from her, the moment you behold him."

The dismay of Angelina, at hearing there existed another diabolical project of depriving her of liberty and happiness, chained her trembling frame to the spot, from whence indignation, at hearing such unfeeling and indecorous arrangements for a second marriage, during the existence of her beloved uncle, such unfounded aspersions thrown upon her spotless rectitude, would have instantaneously led her; and, with a desperate hope of learning all that menaced her safety, she condescended to inquire, from the infuriated Bertha, " What cause the duchessa could possibly have for supposing she should endeavour to withdraw the Prince di Belcastro's affections from her?"

"What cause? Does she not already know your propensity to such honorable achievements? Was not Conte di Alviano her devoted wooer, until your envious malice led him to believe all evil of her; and, in the moment your misrepresentations swayed his mind, she, in the just indignation of aspersed innocence, became herself the victim of your arts, by bestowing her hand upon your hateful uncle. And now, to my own affliction, have I not further proof of the baseness, the perfidy of your heart, in your thus treacherously aiming to insnare my Florio from me?"

The wounded feelings of Lady Angelina now peremptorily inforced her instant retreat, nor one moment longer to subject herself to the insults of this infuriated young woman, on whom she fixed the unfaltering eye of offended rectitude, as impressively she said—

"When your present unfounded irritation of temper permits your reason to resume it's influence, Lady Bertha, you will do what yet I have never had cause to do for mine—blush for your conduct." And now, winged with desire to escape from so ungenial a companion, Angelina made her rapid way to the castle.

CHAPTER XX.

EARLY the succeeding morning, Angelina appeared in the duca's apartments, full of anxious impatience to commence that plan, which dutiful affection had suggested to her; and with all the energy of a fair built hope in his ultimate success, she entered upon her course of instruction, from the highly-informed Sigismund; but much as her ardent heart panted for the prosperity of her project, so auspicious in promise, of peace to her uncle's mind, and knowlege to her own, her truant thoughts would often stray to the events of the preceding day; to the recollection of the direful censures pronounced against Fredrico di Alviano; and of the conventual imprisonment which menaced herself. Of each imputed crime, Fredrico's smile—that smile which piety beamed, and seraphim in kindred sympathy had borne to heaven—assured her he was innocent: but still those alleged crimes filled her breast with terror; for it was possible that enmity might prevail against even innocence; and then, indeed, the convent, so direful in it's present aspect, would lose it's horrors for her: or should the assertions of Anfania and Lady Bertha prove true, and that the beautiful Minora had indeed superseded the image of the lovely Violante in Fredrico's heart, then should she care not what cloister entombed her sorrows.

Fredrico's union with Violante St. Seviero Angelina had long contemplated as one of the first wishes of her heart, because she then believed them reciprocally attached, and that such an union would insure the happiness of Fredrico; but when undeceived by Claudia, as to the existence of that supposed attachment, it was then that hope first kindled into glowing sparks those embers of dormant love, which lay concealed amidst the almost idolatrous veneration, her heart had disinterestedly cherished for Fredrico, ever gifting him in her fancy's visions

with happiness bestowed upon him by another; but when the possibility arose, that
she herself might constitute the happiness
she wished to be his lot, she shrunk from
the appalling idea of a rival, and most of
of all, a rival in the Duchessa di Montalbano.

The Duca di Montalbano seemed to derive both pleasure and benefit from the
new and salutary employment Angelina had
devised for him; but still his thoughts often
reverted to the singularity, of neither the
Monk Jeronimo or Signore Brondelo making
their appearances. This was the very day
the former had assured his patient he should
return from Florence; and Brondelo had
never before omitted the most punctual attendance; yet the whole morning passed
away without the expectations of Sigismund, of the arrival of either being realized; and with murmuring impatience he
mourned his disappointment, as he felt almost assured of having received benefit from
the prescriptions of Father Jeronimo, and
earnestly wished to consult him further;
while, beside the investigation of the ban-

ditti's connexion with his household, he
wanted to arrange, with his notary, an inde-
pendent establishment for his amiable niece,
and found each moment would be felt by
him as an age of pain, until that important
business should be completed; while Angelina herself, caring little about establishment, felt grief only for the protracted absence of Father Jéronimo, since that might
retard the recovery of her uncle; and would
in certainty still longer delay the conveyance of her letter to Erasmo.

This day Lady Angelina again most unwillingly appeared at the duchessa's dinner-
table, where the party assembled, was only
comprised of the Marchese di Cantazaro,
and the castle inmates; the latter of whom
had that morning been increased by the
arrival of Vasco di Tolmezo, the duchessa's
younger brother, an addition to the guests,
of no pleasurable kind to Angelina; for of
all the Tolmezo race whom she disesteemed,
this young man was the most obnoxious to
her. Ere her expulsion from the castle of
her forefathers, and indeed during her visit
to his family in the republic of Venice, he

had avowed the most ardent love for her,
but uniformly made his impassioned ad-
dresses to her clandestinely, which even
child as she was, she repulsed with the most
dignified determination of rejection; and
disgusted with the glaring impropriety of
his conduct, which had every thing in it
repugnant to a mind of delicacy, strongly
devoted to every duty, she took no pains to
disguise her sentiments of condemnation
and dislike from him; so that baffled, mortified, and enraged that partiality which
had added fuel to his ambitious projects,
changed to the feelings of vindictive hatred;
and no heart could find the deadly passions
of the human soul more congenial to it,
than this very man's.

Vasco Tolmezo was, at this period of his
return to Montalbano Castle, in his twenty-
sixth year, and was, in person, tall, athletic,
and boldly moulded in the rough cast of
colossal symmetry. Nature, to display the
incalculable varieties of her powers, had
seemed, when she modeled this man, to
form him in the capricious fancy of showing
how she could give charms, even to a ruf-

fian's aspect; for while she portrayed the assassin's ferine character, in every line, still all was stamped with uncommon beauty. With such an exterior, his intellectual faculties most aptly corresponded; and the strong lines in his face and form found their congenial energies in the composition of his mind, where all was clear from the inert masses of imbecillity. His passions, too, were mighty, formidable, impetuous, and ungovernable; so love, or hatred, ebulliated to excess in his determined breast, where the faltering pause of hesitation rarely entered; since their inactive station, borne on Celerity's expanded wings, was ever to be found the spontaneous power of prompt, yet firm, inflexible decision. Of evil propensities, his heart was the iron repository: of good, it contained one solitary virtue—candor; for his exertion told his disposition was savagely ferocious, and scorning dissimulating, he threw no veil over the deformities of his nature, where the arbitrary vengeance of the law enforced not the concealment of his misdeeds, or diabolical designs.

With implacably envenomed malice, Vasco now beheld the sweetly-expanded blossoms of Lady Angelina's beauty, which, in their bud, he sighed for and adored. Now he cursed the partiality of fate, which had not blighted them as they opened to perfection; now he sickened with hatred as he viewed her charms; and as the possessor of such transcendent fascinations scorned him, he vowed, "since he could not blast her to deformity, that he would sweep happiness from the tablet of her dawning life, and remorselessly yield her to destruction."

Morose and gloomy in meditated vengeance, Vasco scowled his hatred on the lovely Angelina. Lady Bertha, in jealous enmity, aided every slight and insult which the duchessa, Signora Zola, or Father Ezzelino seemed disposed to level at her; and they were not inactive in the pursuit of that kind of pastime, for they seemed to possess no other business or pleasure in existence, but that of sneering at and bestowing their invidious sarcasms at poor Angelina; who, firm in her resolution of doing all things to promote her uncle's peace, sat in placid dignity, bearing all with a calm philosophy, that infuriated her tormentors; and drew at leng.h the tears of vexatious disappointment, in the form of a violent fit of hysteric sobbing, from Minora, who, the moment the convulsive agitation of her passion permitted, articulation, answered to the adulating inquiries made, as to the occasion of this sudden indisposition, " That Angelina was the cause."

" For this horrible composure of hers," she, sobbing, said, " I cannot, cannot bear; it paralyses me with direful alarm; since in it I clearly see rapid approaches to that state of lunacy her poor maniac uncle is reduced to; and, horror of horrors ! in finding it thus, indisputably, a family malady, I have the maternal anguish to know, my poor devoted unborn babes are doomed to the most direful calamity that can befal the human specie."

This was a chord which vibrated instantly upon every discordant tone in the mind of Angelina; not for the invidious and puerile stigma, attempted to be thrown upon the sanity of her own mind, but for the more diabolical one leveled at her beloved uncle; fearing it as the confirming progress in the execution of that pitiless plot, which Anfania had informed her was in agitation, to bereave her now sole parent of liberty, and every hope of earthly happiness; and alarmed, and irritated from, for her plan of stoicical serenitude, she darted the lightning of reproach, from her eloquent eyes, upon the malevolent Minora; as, with all the energy of offended affection, she expressively said:

"If the minds of your unborn babes, duchessa, expand into half the sound intellectual endowments of the Duca di Montalbano, you will, indeed, have just cause to triumph, in the amiable pride of maternal exultation, at the superior talents and unclouded judgement of your offspring; but, with his mental superiorities, I sincerely hope they may not inherit the sensitive susceptibility of his nature, 'lest, in their path of life, they should be doomed to meet unkindness, which, feeling to excess, as he does, might leave it in the power of those who wished to find it so, to mistake the sad ailments of a wounded heart, for the still more direful distempers of an unsettled brain."

"Insolent girl!" exclaimed Vasco, almost infuriated to madness, at beholding now the enthusiastic animation of her countenance, the graceful dignity of her manner, heightened that beauty he sickened at beholding. "Insolent girl! how dare you hold such impertinent language as this to your superiors? You seem totally to forget whom you address, whom you utter such sarcastic insolence before."

"No, Signore Tolmezo," Angelina replied, with provoking calmness; "my memory is very faithful to all you fear it has failed in. I forgot not that it was a wife, who proclaimed her husband a maniac, I addressed; and as to the recollection of whom I spoke before,—had my remembrance been inclined to so good-natured an oblivion, your style of language would have most forcibly aroused it to full reminiscence."

"Leave the room; instantly quit the du-

chessa's presence, presuming babler!" exclaimed Vasco, envenomed now, almost to
the blasting power of the basilisk; for in
aid of other deadly passions of his breast,
which she had innocently awakened, was
the baleful mortification of finding no dark-
furies deformed her aspect; but still, even in
resentment, that she looked amiable and
lovely. " Instantly quit the duchessa's presence," he exclaimed—" How dare you,
an atom in creation as you are, insinuate
a censure against the Duchessa di Montalbano, as an affectionate wife! Defaming
presumer! you forget the existence of truth;
you forget...."

. " Not the respect that is due to a daughter of the illustrious house of Montalbano,"
Angelina proudly replied, " and therefore will
certainly not await a second mandate from a
Tolmezo, to quit an apartment in the castle
of my ancestors:"—And with such a striking
grandeur of mien, she arose from her seat,
and left room, that it created a new source
of vexation for the Tolmezos present; since
it drew the Princess di Belcastro, and the
Marchese di Cantazaro, from their chairs,

to make to her the homage of profound respect at her departure.

Swiftly and unmolested Angelina winged
her way to her own chamber, where, for
some time, she gave free indulgence to an
agonized flood of sorrowing tears, for her
own insulated situation; exposed to all the
persecutions of insolence and malice, without a friend, who possessed the power of
snatching her from such injustice. Feelingly, she there deplored every source of
grief which filled her heart with anguish,
until, in the wide scope her thoughts now
ranged in, they soared to the great Throne
of Mercy; and there, catching the bright
spark that re-kindled the pure fire of unmurmuring piety in her bosom, the truant
resignation returned with it's placid aspect
to her breast; and by the sweet serenity it inspired through every faculty,
proved it was, indeed, a gift from heaven.

At length, the hour for the duca's awakening from his siesto arrived; and Angelina, with a countenance irradiated by the
sweetest smiles of cheerful duty, entered
the apartments of her uncle, to give him

all the comfort' her solitary efforts could
yield to his maladies and misfortunes ; but
in the tenderness of her affectionate, undeviating anxiety to please and amuse him,
he found a host of consolations.

This evening passed more pleasingly, and,
on the part of the duca, more cheerfully
than any preceding one, since Angelina returned to the castle ; and when the hour
for rest arrived, she retired with the heart-
felt satisfaction of having, by her dutiful
attention, soothed the sorrows and lightened
the cares of her unfortunate relatives ; and
when she breathed her last orison to heaven
for that night, in it was mingled a devout
aspiration, for the re-appearance of Father
Jeronimo on the morrow, to bear away her
packet for the good Erasmo, which she
doubted not would soon bring that reverend
father to Montalbano, to comfort and befriend her amiable uncle; and in full hope
of the speedy completion of this, her anxious project, she sunk to rest; and slept the
tranquil slumber of innocence.

But severe were the disappointments
which awaited Angelina; the morning came;

but not Father Jeronimo. The store of medicine was exhausted, and apprehending the inauspicious consequence of a cessation of what had seemed to prove of such essential benefit to her uncle, and more and more anxious for the conveyance of her letter, she proposed to Sigismund, to dispatch a messenger to San Stefano, to learn if the Monk Jeronimo was yet returned from Florence? when instantly the duca ordered Rospo to proceed on that embassy to the convent, and to bring back an immediate answer; but Rospo, a worshiper only of the rising sun, took his own time in returning with intelligence, " of the holy father not being yet returned; nor did it appear, that he was expected even that day at San Stefano."

Angelina was, if possible, more disconcerted at this unwelcome information, than even the disappointed duca himself; for in addition to her other serious causes for regret, she had to deplore the loss of expected necessary assistance, from the medicines of this cruel monk, to support her uncle through the unpleasant account she had to give him, of her having been commanded to quit the duchessa's presence, by the turbulent Vasco Tolmezo; intelligence which, she had just reason to apprehend, would have the most distressing effect upon his sensitive and shattered nerves: but for the amiable purpose of deferring her unpleasant communications, until the aid of Father Jeronimo could be obtained, she determined, as the only means her feeling heart was left the power of adopting, for once, to to deviate from sacred truth; trusting the motive might expunge the stain from the record of her offences, yet not without a blush of ingenuous shame, for what, however, by circumstances extenuated, she yet felt as a transgression,—she entreated the duca's permission for dining with him that day, as her silk dress had not yet been restored to her; and, as she understood the duchessa was to have a large company to dinner, she owned she had discovered, upon a former occasion, that she possessed not sufficient philosophy to subdue her female vanity, **and** therefore wished not again to exhibit herself, in her almost shabby stuff habit."

The duca, considering the reason, assigned by her for this entreaty, a most natural one, readily granted her request; and this day's dinner proved to him the most pleasing repast he had made for many a day; the smiling face of his lovely niece, partaking of it with him, gave it a cheering comfort, that brought with it a zest, his long-declining appetite had ceased to feel; and his gentle spirits were exhilarated to an unusual pitch for him. Angelina, in delight at this auspicious change, caught from his cheerfulness an augmentation of her own. Father Patrick unoffendedly gay, and whimsically ludicrous, increased their disposition to forget a while their cares, until something relative to the ungracious manners of the Confessor Ezzelino, being said, the good priest replied:—

" It was myself, that fell, among some of the flourishing briars, of his rhetoric this morning, when I went to take the air with him, in his little close carriage: that is as nárrow as his conscience; and as uneasy too, for that matter.—He is mighty fond you must know, to be showing his learning, to these, who are blind to it; and he is for ever coming over myself, with his botheration about his logic, and his mathematics; and all his brain works, (which I am mighty apt to believe, are but botch works, if the truth was known) on purpose to make me look small; but sorrow mind, I mind him, for success to myself! but I tell him, whenever he wades out of my comprehension, in any of his little puddles of knowlege, 'I was after learning that matter,' differently; for every nation, has it's own rules: for what is called learning, in one country, may be thought, the bigest ignorance, in another; without disparagement to the parts, of either; as for instance, what would the most learned Laplander, in the wide world, have to say for himself, in Trinity College Dublin? or the most enlightened wild Indian, in your Italian Universities?' and then I glibly run a change, upon all their hard names, until I bother him out of all recollection, of what branch of knowlege, I fell off of, into

the bogs of my own dear country, that hid
my deficiencies from his detection.▲

, "But when he gets into his palaver, about
religion; it is I, that am up sides with him;
for what myself wants in it's theory, he lacks
in it's practice; so my darlings you know,
when he comes shaving with his sharp ra-
zor, the poor bald pate of my ignorance; I
came whack with a brandish of my shilala,
across the knuckles, of his omissions."

"And in such a contest," said the duca
smiling, "I should consider your shilala the
most cutting weapon of the two."

"Faith honey and you may say that;
but then he is provided with a stiptic, in his
indulgences, and absolutions; and sorrow
thing, for a wounded conscience, like Friar's
Balsam, from the Pope's laboratory.—But
in our cabal to-day, he began a palaver,
about what country, the Catholic faith, was
first established in.

"'Ah! then, what does that signify, my
jewel?' says I, 'we all know, where it is
to end; and if it begins in the heart, there
is it's true primitive seat; and mighty satis-

factory, to the curious researchers, of self-inquiry.'

" 'Then he went about, with his flourishes, of gall, and wormwood, laid with his holly-bush, upon the thin canvass, of ones feelings; about how a wise man, was to obtain know-lege, if he only looked inwards, upon him-self; and then off he trots, through all the narrow lanes of his information, to prove that Rome, was the mother of the true faith.

" '"Och! hold your palaver,' says I.—' Little Ireland, was it's father, and must take precedence. From it's soil, the neat illustration of the Trinity sprung; so the best saint in the calendar, Saint Patrick himself, took up our shamrock, beautifully to exem-plify, the Holy Trinity in the trefoil leaves, proceeding from one stem; and there, where, the simile was it's native growth, may be he did not erect the first standard, of faith.'

" ' What !' exclaimed he, ' in that country, of proverbial error; that nation, re-nouned for blunders!'

" ' Ah ! then be easy,' says I, ' for

there his the proof. What are the Pope's edicts, called? Why bulls.—And what are blunders, called? Why bulls.—Now may be, says I, ' the first Pope, did not issue his first, edict from Ireland; and not being deep in learning—for I'll engage knowlege was but a poor puling infant, in the cradle then—it might have been a blundering performance, sure enough; and so ever after, from this notorious mistake; an Irishman's errors, from becoming known in this edict, got interwoven with it's name; and so from thence forward, every lapsno linguæ of ours, obtained the stigmatizing appellation, of a bull.'

"So my honey, with this bit of waggery of my random maybe's, I staggered this vauntingly learned man's belief, of the precedence, in the true faith, of his own country, over mine; and while I laughed in my sleeve, at my glaring humbug of him, he stuttered out, two or three botching efforts, to prove my statement erroneous; but being in this point, every morsel as deep in the bog of ignorance, as myself, he thought it

the best plan, to get on firm ground once
more; and so with that, out he leaps of the
mire at once, upon the back of the Trojan
horse; and brings me behind him, without
leave or license, before the walls of Troy;
where he carried on the siege for some time,
with the odds in his favor, for sorrow an op-
ponent was there, since myself was the only
Greek to be found; and I was as peaceable,
as the wooden beast, he bestrode; which at
length in some sudden piceering, reminded
him of poor Laocoon; and with that, off he
pranced to Florence, to review, and praise,
the merits of a cast, he showed me there the
other day, of Laocoon's sons, one of whom
he thinks, strongly resembles, his beautiful
nephew Vasco; and so it would to the life,
that's true for him, if the serpents instead of
going-in, to feed on himself; were made to
be coming out of his heart, ready to sting
others; for all the world, like his envenomed
breath, when he yesterday had the audacity
to bid you get out a *vurneen*."

" Bid my niece, get out!—Lady Angelina di Balermo, get out!" exclaimed the

duca, his languid eyes kindling to the fiery
flashes of vehement indignation.—" Vasco
Tolmezo, bid my niece get out !'!!"

Angelina, in the most distressing consternation, threw an upbraiding glance at Father Patrick, followed by a beseeching look
of supplication, to extricate her from the dilemma he had plunged her into; and the
good priest, promptly perceiving his error,
and all contrite anxiety to rectify it, hastily
said to the duca:—

" Yes my honey, to *get out* of the way;
when one of those spalpeens of servant boys,
whacked down a dish of of—a ice cream,
just at Lady Angelina's feet; and Signore
Vasco, in a mighty gallant fit, was afraid
she would be scalded, if she stayed in her
place; and he looked so fierce, at the *gossoon*, who caused the accident, that myself
thought of serpents; and all manner of wild
beasts; that is I mean.........

" Pshaw! pshaw !" exclaimed the duca,
petulantly interrupting him, " I clearly
perceive that Lady Angelina has been insulted;—her ingenuous countenance, and
your want of practice in the plausible fabri-

cations of artful evasion, announce at once to me that Vasco Tolmezo has dared to bid her quit the room she was in, and which is the true reason of her dining with me to day; and not the cause which she, in kindness to me, assigned for it. Ah! Angelina, why attempt to conceal this outrage from me? Why not tell me every degradation you met with? Why benevolently strive to spare my feelings, when I it was who gave the mortal wound to yours? Oh! Angelina, my child, my child! this amiable forbearance, more keenly—deeply pierces my contrite, my bursting heart, than the most eloquent up-braidings of resentment could have power to do. Oh! Angelina! am I not your direst foe? Is not every insult you receive, of my infliction? and yet, oh heavens! how kindly, how tenderly, you soothe my ills, and be-guile me of many a bitter potion of my sor-rows!"

Poor Sigismund, now overpowered by re-morse and excess of gratitude, wept abun-dantly; and Angelina, infinitely distressed, strove, with all the sweet affecting kindness of her disposition, to hush the self accusa-

tions, and painful regrets, of her uncle; but
the more the benign and forgiving gentleness of her amiable nature evinced itself, the
more poignant became the contrition of Sigismund; and Angelina in alarm, on thus
beholding him subdued by his penetential
sorrow, to that imbecile tenderness of soul,
which she dreaded every inauspicious consequence from, resolved at length to obey the
duca's mandate, for her repeating the insolence, in full description, of Signore Vasco;
believing that the best antidote against the
slow poison of melancholy retrospections,
would be found in arousing the energies of
his mind into indignation against present
offenders.

With the view solely of such an effect,
Angelina now hastened to detail all the occurrences of her last appearance at the duchessa's dinner-table, only softening down
the insolence she had encountered, where
she thought a faithful tinting might strike
too painfully upon the sensitive chord of her
susceptible uncle's self upbraidings; yet
even with the veil of caution and gentle forbearance thrown over it, the representation

presented such a glaring tissue of insult, that
it almost phrenzied the poor duca with passion; who now, in the resistless impulse of
his powerful resentment, dispatched by Father Patrick a peremptory command to the
younger brother of Minora, to take his immediate departure from the castle, couched
to the following effect :—

"TO SIGNORE VASCO DI TOLMEZO."

"THIS moment only have I learned
how you have dared to insult a daughter
of the illustrious house of Montalbano, and
that outrage cannot be committed with im-
punity. The castle in which you have presumed to command Lady Angelina di Balermo to quit an apartment in, shall no
longer afford you shelter. Learn my peremptory mandate, and yield it immediate
and becoming obedience. Quit my castle
instantly,—and for ever !

"MONTALBANO."

Angelina, though with dutiful respect,
gently ventured to entreat so violent a mea-

sure might not be adopted; one so little calculated to conciliate peace and harmony between him and his duchessa; but the duca was arbitrary; the billet was sent, and Father Patrick soon returned with the following laconic reply; bearing all the proper *illustrissimo's*, *eccellentissimo's*, and *colendissimo's*, in the superscription, that could denote profound respect.

" MONSIGNORE,

" I only obey *such mandates* as suit my inclination; therefore learn *my* determination. I will *not* quit your castle, *now—* or *ever*, until my own wishes lead me from it!

" VASCO DI TOLMEZO."

The displeasure of Sigismund, at such unprecedented insolence, now flowed into it's proper channel, and arose to the mingled resentment of dignity and contempt; that whilst it glowed at the presumption, felt too much scorn for the offender, to allow his insolence to arouse the more turbulent sensations of his mind; and firmly he now resolved to take effectual measures, under the guidance of Signore Brondelo, to rid his castle, without delay, of such a dauntless offender;, and Father Patrick accordingly received instructions to proceed to Florence, in a chaise and four, the subsequent morning, to bring Brondelo to the duca, to make arrangements for this object of his inflexible determination.

"I'll engage," replied the zealous priest, "I'll be off, like the mist of the morning, when the sun rises to light me;—but as for the matter of the carriage; sorrow better one, than my mare at full gallop, for expedition; for she can trot ten miles an hour, without flagging; so I had much better go on horseback, for then, I can take a short cut, round about the new mill; and then I can hire a carriage at Florence, with four nags, fresh and fasting, to rattle the old Notary here, in a trice; and I can take the Convent of San Stefano, in my way back,

for 'tis only just two miles out of my road,
—that is, if myself can't find brother Jerry
at the Archduke's, for I'll be bail, I'll
scent the old druggist out, dead or alive,
to learn at once from him, if it is humbug-
ging of us he is?"

CHAPTER XXI.

SCARCELY had Lady Angelina entered her uncle's apartment the succeeding morning, when Father Patrick, with a flushed countenance, and an air of much discomposure, appeared to perform the matin service for Sigismund and his lovely niece, according to their established custom.

" Father O'Carrol here!" exclaimed the duca, in powerful and chagrined astonishment : " Why, I thought you promised to be on your road to Florence long, long ere this time ?"

" I'll tell you what duca," replied the good priest, in the hurried tones, of emotion " I promised, that's a sure thing; but the will of others, has performed for me. By dad, this same castle of yours, is Liberty Hall, and in the spirit of freedom,

that reigns, your people have made a prisoner, of my four bones."

" A prisoner! a prisoner!" reiterated
the duca, shuddering with anticipating apprehension; " What is it you can mean, reverend father?"

" Och! jewel-we are bastiled, and more
grief to us! that's my meaning; and bad
luck to Master Vasco!" replied the agitated Patrick. " Myself was up by the
dawn, for I never went to bed, at all at all,
for fear of oversleeping myself; so the very
first moment I found the grooms were stir-
ring, off I goes to the stables, to get my
mare; but sorrow morsel of her would they
give me; but up and told me, ' they had
orders not to let me have her.'

" 'Why then by dad,' says I, ' but
I must have a carriage, with four nags'
—' No by mam' says they ' but you
must not, for we are forbidden to let you
have any conveyance, to take you from the
castle' 'What!' says I ' is it dis-
obeying the duca's orders you are, you re-
bels of the world?' ' Yes' says they
' the duca's but a cypher now, and we

obey, the duchessa,' ' A cypher! Och!
you raps!' says I ' A cypher! why then
tis a cypher, that will be summing up a
pretty long account against you, out of
the multiplication, of your impertinence.'

"So with that, they snapped their saucy
fingers at me; and bid me go to the porter,
for further information; when myself, like
the biggest fool in Christendom, trots off to
the hall of judgement, to hear my sentence
of imprisonment, from stern Cerberus there,
for out of the gates, he had orders not to let
me pass. ' Why,' says I, ' sure you
would not, be making a prisoner; a jail-
bird, of me? I that escaped such disgrace,
even when I was famished to death, at Naples? But I'll tell you what's, what, Mr.
Turnkey,' says I ' if you are after com-
mitting the sacrilege, of imprisoning a consecrated priest, I'll make you sup sorrow
for it, out of the bitter cup of fasting, and
infliction. I'll soon surprise your fat sides,
with an unexpected view of their own ribs,
I'll treat you with a striped jacket, from the
wardrobe of Penitence ; and may be, I won't

write to the bishop, to complain of your conduct to me.'

"' And who will convey your letter?'
says he, grinning ' for I can tell you, no
letter, message, or messenger of the duca's,
Lady Angelina's, or yours, are to be suffered
to pass these gates.'"

Angelina looked on her uncle in dismayed consternation, but soon her emotions
were centred in a more powerful alarm; for
the agitated Sigismund, now believing himself and beloved niece completely insnared
in the toils of those who had resolved upon
their destruction, with a convulsive shiver,
sunk back in his chair in a death-resembling
swoon.

Every thing which the affectionate Angelina and the goodnatured priest could devise for the restoration of the duca, they
promptly tried, and at length with success.
Sigismund recovered, and, with the renovation of his faculties, returned a powerful
sense of the destruction which seemed inevitably to encompass him and the child of
his beloved brother, when his censures upon
his own infatuated folly, as the source of all

these evils, were so severe, his lamentations
so affecting, they called forth every soothing effort of Angelina, to calm the tumult
of his troubled soul; and when, in pious
conviction of where the only efficient consolation for sorrows could be found, she
gently led his thoughts to build firm hope of
succour upon the mercy of heaven. She
feelingly reminded him, "that in the moment of her almost-phrensied despair, when
believing in the fortress of the banditti there
was no deliverance for her from wretchedness and horror, the ministrant angels of pitying Providence sent forth a champion to
her rescue."

"Just" said, the sensibly-affected, Father
Patrick, "as when myself was starved to death,
and thought my skeleton was ready made, for
the anatomists, the beautiful gift of heaven's
own daughter Pity, came glittering in the
sterling form, of a pistole, pop into my
badge of poverty, my tatterdemalion hat;
that lay beside me; and allowed me to fos-
ter my poor uncle Pat; and what but Providence, sent the bedpost to come whack
against me, to the rescue of Signora Modo's

child, from the devouring flames, that would have made tinder of him? and what myself would be mighty glad to know, but divine mercy, sent me, to Montalbano Castle, to be with you, and comfort, and befriend you, in this time of trouble? So now my honey, to effect the great purpose of Providence, which sent me to stay with you, discharge me out of hand."

"Discharge you!" repeated the astonished and agitated Sigismund: "What mean you, sir? I do not comprehend you."

"Och! but 'tis I, that comprehend myself, and that's the same thing; so be quick; discharge me; pack me off; pick a quarrel with me, instantly jewel; 'tho on my safe conscience, that's the last thing, you will ever be picking out of poor Patrick, in earnest;—but now dismiss me your service.—Sure you can do it, on account of my failing to go to Florence, as you ordered me."

"But, holy father," said the amazed and indignant Angelina, "will your desertion of my dear uncle, in such a moment, perform that mission of a comforter, a friend, which, you believe, divine mercy confided to you."

"'To be sure it will, jewel; for when I am packed off, they must let me out; for who keeps a discarded chaplain?—so then, I can be after following the bent, of my own inclination; which will bring me to the world's end, to serve you; and farther too, for that matter; so as I suppose there will be no search warrant, issued against me, I can bring all your letters, and messages to the old notary, Father Jeronimo, or any other friend, who can redress you; and sorrow a more faithful Mercury, ever flew on the pinions of diligence, than sturdy fat Pat;—and if any of the leaguers, come to knock me on the pate, with their wily tongues, of inquiry; success to them! but they'll find, they have got the wrong, sow by the ear."

Both uncle and niece were considerably affected by the good priest's genuine kindness; but the duca firmly, yet gratefully rejected the plan, unless subsequent despair should compel them to adopt it.

" No, most good and reverend father," he said, " I will not deprive my Angelina, and myself of the only friend we yet have spared to us, unless we should indeed have the painful conviction, some future day, of such a sacrifice being our only mean for attempting to rescue ourselves from the snares of our daring enemies. But that we may lay some claim to the protection of heaven, let me not forget my duties to it; let us, in humble reverence, unite in prayer, and then we can, with surer hope of success, enter upon our consultations for projects to emancipate ourselves from this vile Vasco's toils."

In meek and heart-inspired devotion, Sigismund, Angelina, and Father Patrick joined in prayer; thanking heaven, in ardent gratitude, for mercies past, and imploring it's protection from impending evils; and at length, from this duty, so renovating to Christian fortitude, they arose, with all the consolations of hope, the calm of resignation it awakened, and after a few serious moments passed in a solemn pause, while recalling their thoughts from heavenly to sublunary themes, the unfortunate duca proceeded to the projected consultation.

" But first," he said, "that we may know if the porter's information to Father Patrick is authentic, I will order Rospo to set out to Santo Stefano to inquire, ' if Father Jeronimo is yet returned?' "

A peal was therefore rung for Rospo, but which was obliged to be several times repeated, ere that consequential gentleman deigned to answer it by attendance. With an aspect of conspicuous insolence he at length made his appearance, and Sigismund inquired " the cause of such a tardy performance of his duty?"

" I was otherwise engaged," he replied saucily.

" Engaged!" repeated the duca sternly, " Do you not know, man, that the engagements of a domestic must ever bend before his duty to his master?—And now, in spite of your mal-apropos engagements, Signore, it is my command that you instantly go to San Stefano, with my request, to see Father Jeronimo, if he is yet returned."

" We are about preparations for a magnificent masquerade," returned the cameriero, insolently, "and the duchessa has full employment for us all, therefore your commands I cannot at present obey."

" Not obey my commands!" exclaimed the duca, starting from his chair with a firm elastic bound, that filled the minds of Lady Angelina and Father Patrick with pleased surprise: "Dare to disobey my orders, and instantly you quit my service;" and stamping his foot with vehemence, as the signal for Rospo's departure, the astonished valet, in alarm at a renovation of mental and bodily faculties so little expected, recoiled to a more respectful distance, and, despoiled of a considerable portion of his insolence, with something of an air more according with his station, he, bowing low, replied—

" I dare not obey, Monsignore; as we are all prohibited, in the most absolute manner, from passing through the castle gates, without a special permission from the duchessa, Father Ezzelina, or Signore Vasco; and, upon the peril of the most severe infliction of punishment, " 'commanded not to perform any service for your excellenza or Lady Angelina *out* of the castle.' "

" Leave my presence; and learn to tremble at my infliction of punishment, when I decree them for you," said the ducá emphatically, and with an impressive dignity, that enforced the instant and respectful departure of the crest-fallen Rospo.

" So, my friends," Sigismund despondingly added, " we have gained nothing by this experiment, but a mortifying confirmation of Father Patrick's intelligence."

" Yes, my dear uncle," replied Angelina, her brilliant eyes beaming with the animation of Hope's cheering influence, " we have received the heartfelt pleasure of being assured your bodily faculties are not so enfeebled by your ailments, as we all had cause to apprehend. It is many a month, as you have told me, since you were able to arise from your chair without assistance; yet now you did so, unaided; and the effect of this successful effort I hailed as an auspicious omen of future benefits. Your astonished servant no longer beheld in you the enfeebled master, sinking fast into the imbecillities of closing life, which he had considered you: no, he saw in you the renovated fire of energy, which awed him into instant respect, and I imbibed conviction from the circumstance, that if you could but summon up sufficient resolution to encourage the renovation of many of your long-apparently dormant faculties, by calling them daily into action, they would gather strength by exercise, and in a short period, I doubt not, you would be enabled to appear, to your usurping persecutors, in full possession of the power to guide your own affairs; and, taking the reins into your own hands, govern your family and your vassals, as the lord of Montalbano, with justice, benevolence, mildness, and steady firmness, happily combined.''

The duca listened with grateful pleasure to his beloved niece, while with animation she portrayed the probability of his restoration to health and strength, which her affection so flatteringly presented to her imagination; but, in the true spirit of hypochondriac despondence, the poor valetudinarian shook his head despondingly, and

pronounced her hopes and project a visionary flight of impossibility, never to be realised ; but Angelina's observations had
struck her with conviction, that, would he
but give her hopes, the basis of his exertions,
to rest upon, her prophecy would soon as
happily be verified.

And now believing the execrable Tolmezos had indeed adopted every unjustifiable
measure for severing himself and niece from
the aid of every friend or redress; the unfortunate Sigismund earnestly communed with
his companions upon the most judicious method to pursue, for obtaining the means of
effectually conveying intelligence to Signore Brondelo, of the imprisonment his
wife's family had inthraled him in; that he
might adopt those means most likely to insure immediate redress. And so successfully had the Tolmezos spread their toils
around him, that he found himself compelled to the degrading necessity of seriously
considering who among the domestics was
likely to be won from the Tolmezo interest,
to befriend and assist him; and after deli-
berating for some time with Father Patrick

upon the subject, they united in opinion that not one among them could be confided in, when Angelina, erecting faith upon the tenderness of feeling, which Florio had demonstrated for some powerful afflic- tion when intruded upon by the roman- tic Bertha and herself ; upon the de- licacy and propriety with which he shrunk from the imprudent advances of the infatuated Lady Bertha, and upon the re- spectful courtesy he upon every opportu- nity evinced for herself, ventured to say, " That she thought the page Florio would faithfully deposit any letter in the post for her."

" Florio !" exclaimed the duca, " What possible interest can you, my child, have with any of the duchessa's pages ?"

" Faith," replied Father Patrick, " the interest, which youth, and beauty, is mighty apt to find, with such sort of gentry; and it is possible, jewel, he will promise in the honey, of his courtly pala- ver, the secret conveyance of any letter ; for those tricks, come like mother's milk,

to such spalpeens; but if myself knows
what, is what, trust the gossoon, no further
than you could throw him; for sure 'tis he,
the rap! that is the Pan, or, Pandora (sorrow one of me knows which, the name is,
since it is not of Irish extraction), to the duchessa, that is, one of her go-betweens, her
love-letter carriers, her........"

" The duchessa's pander! the duchessa's
love-letter bearer!" the duca exclaimed,
again starting from his seat, with almost
phrensied elasticity.

" Yes jewel," Father Patrick, promptly
replied, with a transient flush of cheek, as
he recovered his recollection, of the impropriety he had uttered. " Yes jewel, to a—
letters, to her own kiff, and kin, to her uncles, and brothers, you know."

" Love-letters to her uncles and brothers!" repeated the duca, with a ghastly
smile of contemptuous incredulity.

" Och! yes, such as one affectionate relation will indite to another; which in my
blundering impetuosity, I miscalled,—but
that same, was natural too; for sure 'tis not

the province of a priest, and worse luck to
to. him!—to know much of the true genea-
logy, of love, epistles."

Sigismund, with a groan of heart-riving
anguish, sunk back into his chair, the pallid semblance of despair.

Angelina, in all the pained sympathy of
her affectionate bosom, felt this new source
of anguished sorrow, given so inadvertently
to the bursting heart of her grief-stricken
uncle; but eager to attempt, at least, to
withdraw his thoughts from the new tortures
presented to them, she hastily spoke at
random upon the first subject which presented itself to her imagination, by asking
Father Patrick, " had they no hope of assistance from the lady who occupied the
nursery of her own infancy? Has she no
domestics, holy father?" added Angelina,
mechanically speaking, her every thought
devoted to commiseration for her uncle's
woes.

"She has only one, belonging to her, a
vurneen; and that's herself; for never was
seen. such a bigoted domestic animal, as

she is; for sorrow morsel of her, ever leaves her own fire-side, at all at all."

"What! here for the benefit of the air?" said Sigismund, endeavouring to abstract his thoughts from a new page of misfortune, the perusal of which inflicted anguish too mighty for his heart to bear. "Here for for the benefit of the air, and yet lead a solitary confinement?—How is this accounted for, reverend father?"

"Why my honey, if, when my brother reverence Ezzelino, steps into his confessional, to hear the transgressions of others, he dropped on his own knees, and uttered a shrift, for himself, we might know, and his precious soul, might be all the lighter, for unloading a heavy burden:—but he's the man, that can be keeping his own secrets, until doomsday; let them be ever so uneasy, in their place of rest; but as no one ever yet, could accuse myself, of being a churl of my knowlege, you shall hear every morsel of the matter, 'tho' myself knows hardly a sylable:—but conjecture is a mighty notable helper out, of an imperfect

manuscript,—so the way of it was darlings,
the very day eight days, after myself first
heard of this good gentlewoman, who came
here for the benefit of the air—fixed air, I
suppose it was, as she has been shut up with
it, ever since her arrival—one of the scul-
lions was mighty bad, and wanted absolu-
tion for his sins, 'tho sorrow one he had for
that matter; and I was sent for to him :—
for you must know, when I came to the
castle, Father Ezzelino divided the household with me, giving all the men's conscience, to my jurisdiction, with the old women's to boot; taking on his own shoulders,
the sins of all the young damsels.—At first
myself thought, it was a bit of a humbug,
to give me so much the bigest half of the
duty; but by dad, I soon saw, what a dear
lover of infliction he was; and when he
found no good, cause for a penance, sooner
than be disappointed of the pleasure of pu-
nishing, he would contrive by the hocus-
pocus of his art, to put sins into the heads,
and hearts of those, whom Nature made,
pure, and spotless."

" And all these sins, and these inflic-

tions, will be registered as my misdeeds!''
exclaimed the duca, in bitterness of soul,
'' for, by my infatuated union with his syren
niece, I fixed him in my family, to corrupt
the morals of the innocent.''

'' But, Father Patrick,'' said the distressed Angelina, wishing to turn her susceptible uncle's thoughts from their agonising
self-upbraidings, '' you have wandered from
this lady, whom you told us is a prisoner in
this castle.''

'' Faith and you may say, that jewel;
for it was I that wandered, sure enough,
when I lost my way, in going to the poor
scullion's chamber; and at last, I strayed
from the menials rooms, quite and clean;
until I found myself in a long corridor,
across which, as I entered, Father Ezzelino
flitted, like the grim ghost of an executed
assassin, pale in the visage of death, and
with a countenance, which kept no secret,
of the catalogue of crimes, for which he
suffered; and while you would say trap-
stick, by dad he unlocks a door, glides in,
and locks the door after him. Och! turn-
keys! and jugglers! how neatly, he per-

formed it!—Appeared—high presto! Disappeared, for all the world, as if he had been bred and born, an invisible spy; so with that, myself stood staring at the door, as if that would tell me, the legerdemain of the business; when presently I heard a fine hullabaloo of hysteric sobbings, and at intervals, the words—' perfidious Ezzelino!' delivered in a female voice, sweet and plaintive; so with that, says I, to myself

"' Sure Pat, of the cloth, you are not turned a rapscallion listener? Agh! then wheel off with yourself, my reverend fellow, and don't be making a blackguard of a priest, and an Irish gentleman; for here you can do no good, with a door locked in your face, as a knight-errant'—so off I was trotting, when my heart boiling with indignation, cries out

"' Och! Murder! Murder! Pat! sorrow speed the traveller! sure you wouldn't be turning your back, upon a woman in distress, without one effort, to redress her? Och man alive, is the fire of Irish courage, of Irish humanity, dead within you?'

"' Och! sorrow bit,' says I, glowing

up into a champion, at once, and was making at the door, to burst it open, when suddenly at the very door master Ezzelino, had entered the corridor by, I beheld a black curly head, and a large pair of eyes, starting from their sockets, stuck at the jam, in a posture of observation.

" 'Och! botheration!' thinks I, 'this is some accomplice in a deed of darkness, and I will be getting a stiletto through my vitals, for standing in their light.—Well never mind that same, Pat of gallant Ireland; if you can help the creature, sobbing within, ne$_v$e$_r$ bother your head about a quietus from a stiletto, for should you survive it, it will be a matter of pleasure, and comfort to your conscience, ever after.' So being possessed with a belief, that the head must have a throat, I made an unexpected grasp at that, and as I throttled this observer, demanded ' What brought him there?'

" 'Ah! ha! Father Patrick,' he exclaimed, half laughing, half alarmed. 'So you have discovered me, by sympathy, both in the act of watching the secret haunts, of the sly confessor.'

"'Myself is no watch-dog, whatever you may be.' I replied, taking my hand from his collar, for by this time, I saw it was Jaques, one of the decentest behind among the servant boys, belonging to the household. 'It was accident; brought me out of the way hither, to find, there is some distressed female, confined in this room.'

"'And don't you know, who the prisoner is, holy father?' says he

"'No by dad.' says I—

"'Nor I either' says Jaques, 'although I have been on the watch, several nights, to see would he bring her out, to walk in the corridor; but not he;—he is too cunning for that; so not a soul ever sees her, but himself, and his own *camerière*, who is a close one, like his master; but this much I do know, without being told it; that she is young, and handsome, or old Ezzelino, would not keeep her in his strong box.'"

"Miscreant! sanctified, diabolical hypocrite!" exclaimed the ducà, in vehement indignation.

"That's what he is, my darlings, I'll

tell no lie; for upon further cabal with
Jaques, I found, he, had put his curious
ear, to the key-hole one night and heard,
the woman call Ezzelino, ' a base deceiver,
who no longer lovedher.'; so my honeys, that
was so completely, letting the butter out, of
the stirabout; that myself gave up my project of knight-errantry, at once; for what
could I do, to make peace, between jealousy, and perfidy; but it was as much as
ever I could do, to hinder myself, from rap-
ping at the door, civilly to ask. ' Would I
bring a glass of water, for the lady in hys-
terics?' just to give him a hint, that I knew,
he was a scoundrel, and a disgrace to the
function, he presumed to dirty, by professing."

" Diabolical! daring miscreant!" again
Sigismund exclaimed, in augmented ire,
" to bring thus his iniquities into my castle,
even beneath the very roof of his own
niece."

" Oh!" said, the blundering, priest
" they stand upon no scruples of delicacy,
one with another, for scruples, bear no
weight, in their consideration; but indeed,

they abound, in such, family secrets; and so, are mightily. given to toleration; for should one of the set, show an Oliver for a lance, another could produce, a Rowland for a shield; and so they could thrust, and parry."

" Oh! unfortunate, wretched, infatuated-fool! what a connexion have I formed! What a nest of vipers have I attracted round me, to sting my peace, to prey upon my vitals, and to destroy the happiness of this sacred trust my deluded brother bequeathed to me! Oh! Angelina! why do you not hate me, execrate me as I deserve?" exclaimed the almost-convulsed Sigismund, wringing his hands in the bitterness of heart-felt anguish.

Such appeals, while they vibrated on the finest tones of Angelina's tenderest sensibility, ever led her, in pity to him, to stifle the softening emotions they excited, and to exert all her firmness to aid her, while still, with melting kindness, she soothed, she comforted him, and lulled the poignancy of his self-accusations, the bitter anguish of his grief; and in this dutiful employment, performed with an affecting sweetness, that could not fail of being rewarded with some degree of success, she passed the remainder of this morning, until the duca's dinner was served up, and brought in by the lowest drudges of the household; the repast itself, composed of the coarsest viands, and all appointed in the meanest and most slovenly style, indicative of the striking insolence of premeditated disrespect.

CHAPTER XXII.

ANGELINA, the moment she beheld this new establishment and arrangement of her uncle's table, shocked at the insolence and cruelty of such a measure towards him; and anticipating at one glance every possible evil in future, from such a commencement of unprecedented daring, burst into a flood of tears, the first she had permitted herself to shed in the presence of the unfortunate Sigismund; who now, in heart-rived anguish, at beholding her so moved, endeavoured to repress feelings of varied poignance, some of the most violent he had ever before experienced; and after a severe conflict of mental warfare, but of momentary duration, he, with eyes flashing resentment, and cheeks glowing with Indignation's deepest tints, yet with calm and striking dignity, requested Father Patrick to proceed to his duty, of performing grace.

The reverend father, not finding that he could, in conscience, utter a thanksgiving, for such a repast, presented to his unfortunate patron, hesitated for a moment, meditating a negative; but indignation swelling his warm heart, soon from the impulse of his exasperated feelings, led him to ejaculate, in his own native language, which he knew was unintelligible to his temporal hearers; and with as much soul-directed emphatic devotion, as he, had ever prayed, an extempore aspiration.

" That when, Parson Ezzelino, should show his nose, in the judgment-hall, of the world to come; it might, with the gizzard of his nephew Vasco, be sentenced to Satan's gridiron, to be made a d—l of; for the infernals to feed on, more to their taste; than the dinner before him, could, be to the invalid duca."

Such a repast, and so arranged, brought with it too many palling surcharges of the heart, inimical to appetite, to permit it's being lessened by the insulted duca, or his af-

flicted niece; but as they both soon perceived they were narrowly observed by the
attending domestics, they possessed too
much native dignity of mind, to give to
their daring persecutors, through the me-
dium of these servile inquisitors, the triumph of knowing how much they were
wounded by such indignities; they therefore, as if intuitively inspired with a knowlege of each others sentiments and resolu-
tions upon the subject, assumed the appearance of as much composure as it was
possible for mental exertion to command,
upon such a trying occasion.

Not so calm and dignified was the often
blundering, but always feeling-hearted, Father O'Carrol; who now helped himself to
some of every thing this repast afforded,
in the forlorn hope of meeting with some vi-
and amongst them, which it would be possible for the invalid duca, or his interesting
niece to partake of, but in vain; and when
this form of dining was past, and the aukward
and slovenly domestics had removed the cloth,
the reverend father, with a contracted brow,
evincing how infinite was the cause for in-

dignation, or that would not betray a frown, again hastily resorted to his native, language, and vehemently repeated, with guttural volubility, an anathema against the purveyor of so black a fast.

The evening of this day passed on, in the apartments of the duca; under the mournful influence of the most heart-resident melancholy, for they had no hope to cheer them through any scheme of probable succour; they were enveloped by creatures of the Tolmezo's; they were cut off from all intercourse with every friend; and even should they affect to discard Father O'Carrol, it was very unlikely their wily persecutors would permit his departure; since well aware, from the integrity of his principles, that he would give information of the unjust proceedings against the duca, to those who could redress them. The good priest was, however, still very urgent for the experiment to be made, as he thought every possible means now left in their power should be speedily resorted to for succour; lest the insulted prisoners, should, as he said, "be starved by fasting; and the elegant coats arrive from Signore Modo, to fall into the hands of the enemy."

The thoughts of Angelina, frequently reverted to the Cardinal Gulielmo's offer of friendship to her, and, for her uncle's sake, she would now have been tempted to disregard the cautions of the good Olinda; and, attending only to the advice of her beloved Lady Constantia, inform his eminence, how much she required "a friend, a protector, and adviser;" had any means been hers of conveying such intelligence to Rome; but that resource, seemed now, with every other, wrested most cruelly from her.

In mournful meditation or fruitless consultations upon how to outwit their persecutors, this sudden trio passed the tedious hours of this evening; for, unused to plotting, they found their powers inadequate to the task; until at length, Angelina, whose rapid ideas swiftly traveled through every region of possibility, and had even soared beyond probability, as a kind of forlorn hope, the only one she could, alas! find in her route, ventured to hint to Sigismund—

" That if he could allow the peculiar friend-
lessness of his insulted situation to act upon the energies of his bodily strength as indignation had spontaneously done, she
thought she could point out a certain mode
of rescue."

The duca shaking his head despondingly
at the invincible barrier, which he believed
impeded the way of her project, desired to
know " What it was?"

" My dear uncle," replied the ardent
Angelina, " you have had conviction, that
a very useful faculty has not forsaken you.
By diligent practice, as children learn in
infancy, you may recover the power of
walking; and by the salutary exercise that
exertion would yield, much of your long
dormant strength would find it's renovation.
You will think me, I know, a visionary
schemer, but, indeed, I feel convinced of
the possibility of it's proving a vision, which
may be happily realised. What say you,
my dear uncle, to your making your unexpected appearance at the Mascherata,
about to be given?"

" Me! Angelina! What a phantom!

Me acquire sufficient strength ever to appear at a masquerade! Oh! Angelina!"

"And oh! *zio**! why should you not? The probable success of the project is surely worth the effort; for, supposing you could accomplish the arduous task; know you not the powers you possess in your unsubdued intellectual strength, to annihilate at once the invidious report, so industriously disseminated, of your mental deprivations; and there, while in the habit of disguise, think you not, amid the gay assemblage, you should identify some former friend in whom you might confide, and teach the way to emancipate you from your little less than bondage?"

"Och! then, if that be n't the highway to Freedom, little Great Britain, and Ireland, never heard the name of Liberty!—Who would refuse, I'll be mighty glad to know," said Father Patrick, "to walk out of a prison, when a pitying angel, opens the door? and good luck to you for it a vurneen! So come Monsignore, and be

* Uncle.

getting ready for the masquerade, in the new character, of a pedestrian ; and sorrow one will know you, 'at all at all—Come my honey, and begin, and creep, and creep, and creep ; and if yourself totters, never mind that same, for you shall have a firm crutch in Pat, made of the true shilala, that will never fail you ; and in your niece there, you will be having a sugar-cane, to support you,—a beautiful little precious wand, of an enchantress, that will lure you on, to incase you in the iron armor, of strength; to enable you to break the spells, of the cruel hearted wizards, who bewitched you into their ruthless clapper-claws.''

" It cannot, cannot be !'' exclaimed the, desponding Sigismund; '' your enthusiastic zeal, my Angelina, and the holy father's good wishes, lead you both beyond the regions of possibility. If, when matured by all the delicacies of a luxurious table, my strength failed me, how can I even hope to regain it, when the necessaries of life are almost denied me ?''

For a moment Angelina caught despondence from the cadence of her uncle's voice in his concluding sentence; but soon the buoyant thrill of not-to-be-extinguished hope cheered her to a brighter prospect; and, encouragingly she replied—" Surely, my uncle, luxuries are not the infallable nurses of health and strength."

" Faith, and that's, a sure thing!" ex-claimed Father Patrick, exultingly. " The poor bog-trotters, of little Ireland for that, who never tasted a morsel of meat, in their born days, except a bit of a salt-herring, now and then, by way of a relish; and sure 'tis they, are the sturdies; composed of the glue of potatoes, and butter-milk, that could crush a pampered shadow, from the poi-soned table of luxury, to atoms, with a whack of their little fingers. Agh! then my honey, 'tis theirs, is the strength, of the starvation of indigence, that to re-pay them for their forced temperánce, has clapt the hammer of death, and the sledge of destruc-tion, into the muscles, of their case-hard-ened limbs, so, as you see, what the whole-somes of necessity, can do; don't be after desponding, or throwing out weak excuses, to knock down the hopes of the creature hire, who would be giving you freedom, and peace, and an evening's amusement, with an excellent supper (when you are starving) into the bargain, and I'll be bail now, I'll keep a watch on my tongue, not to blab, that it is learning to walk you are again; and if you can get no better a disguise, for the occasion; you shall be as welcome as the flowers in May, to my best canonicals (which we can make shift to tuck, and take in for you) so if you provide your own footing there, I'll engage, I'll furnish you with a dress; and your friends no doubt, with redress; so if that won't be setting you a going, I wonder what's what."

The valetudinarian Sigismund still shook his head in despondence; yet, still believing it a propitious prospect, could it be adopted, after contemplating it's probable advantages for some time, at length actually summoned sufficient energy to make a deliberate exertion; and, with the aid of Angelina and Father Patrick, he accomplished what he had not attempted for many months,—he walked about his chamber for several minutes; and, to his own infinite astonishment, he found this effort did not subdue him with fatigue; when he made his anxious companions most happy, by assuring them, " he would renew his exercise on the morrow, and daily, if not overpowered by want of nourishment."

Shortly after the very unexpected event, of the duca's using one of his long dormant faculties, Father Patrick performed the vesper service, and then retired; but, to the agreeable surprise of Angelina, and certainly not to the displeasure of the duca, he almost immediately returned with the animation of joy, irradiating his guileless countenance, and bearing in his hands a small tray of refreshments.

" Here's for you, darlings!" he exclaimed " See with your own eyes, the Pity's gift, like the pistole of Signore Modo, which came pop, unexpectedly into my hat; and long life to the giver!—May be, I didn't find these beautiful cakes, and elegant little loaf; and three glasses of jelly, as clear as the conscience of true charity; with this flask of wine; and three neat glasses, to

drink out of, cocked on my table, instead
of my red night cap.—Och feasts, and ju-
bilees! how my heart capered, at the sight!
' Welcome as potatoes, and buttermilk, to
a famished spalpeen, are you to my longing
sight, my windfals!' say I, 'and more welcome still, in the proof ye bring, that we
have a friend in the market of Plenty.'—
All clear as the noon-day, ready prepared
for the poor jail-birds; so cheer up my honeys; eat and drink for the bare life; since
you are as welcome at the board, as the
board is to you; and then may be, we wont
be chanting a tedeum, that all the men and
woman about us, are not tigers."

Our readers can readily imagine, that
Sigismund and his lovely niece hesitated
not to partake of a repast, the merciful boon of some benevolent friend : the duca,
as he eat of it, mentally ejaculated a wish
(which his forgiving heart seemed fond of
cherishing as a realised one), that the com-
punction of the duchessa had actuated her
to this deed of humanity. Angelina, in
thankfulness, received it as the inspiration
of heaven itself, to some feeling-heart

among the household; while Father Patrick, certain it was not a repast sent by a cruel Tolmezo to them, partook of it with augmented relish from that belief; and when the grateful prisoners were satisfied, the careful priest, with many ludicrous expressions of forecast, collected the fragments, and put them neatly by, in a cabinet of the ducats; and after a sincere thanksgiving had been aspirated devoutly by all, and a parting benediction again pronounced by the reverend father, Rospo was summoned to attend his lord, and this small party of amity separated for the night.

The distressing occurrences of that eventful day proved a heavy addition to the already-oppressive weight of Angelina's sorrows; and she entered her apartments with a mind so subdued by the afflictions which seemed to surround her, that it appeared almost a miracle of chance, her attention being at all arrested by the appearance of a small ticket on her dressing-table, upon which was printed in black letters, Vase, No. 3.; but scarcely bestowing a thought upon it, as a

useless memorandum, she carelessly threw it
from her to the ground; and after about an
hour passed in many mournful and many
pious reflections, she retired to bed.

On the subsequent morning Angelina
found the unfortunate Sigismund not more
dejected than she had left him the preceded night. Father Patrick, at his accustomed time, joined his companions in the
indignity of undeserved imprisonment, and,
as usual, they devoutly united in their
morning duties; when, shortly after a breakfast was served, with the same insolence of
homely and comfortless arrangement, as the
dinner had been on the foregoing day.

"Agh! then, what do you charge a
head, for this snare of temptation, to a delicate appetite, my faithful cup-bearer, to
Belzeebub?" exclaimed Father Patrick; to
the menial, who appeared most prominent,
in the alacrity of furnishing appropriately,
this table of indignity, and what wages, has
Satan's factotum, Signore Vasco, promised
you, for insulting your lord, and master?"

"I am not paid by any one for bringing up this breakfast, I only do my duty, in obeying orders;" returned the fellow, sullenly.

" Why then, an airy death-bed, to you! is it game your making of your betters? you gibbet candidate!—Och! fire-brands, and faggots!—Doing your duty, to insult your master!—Och! bubbaboo! if that be do- ing your duty, only just *wait,—wait*, till I reward you, with the voluntary passtime, of the pleasures of penitential inflictions, the very first moment yourself, has the mo- dest assurance, to kneel before me, in my confessional, Master Hugo, the dutiful?"

" Oh! holy father!" exclaimed Hugo, in alarm; " do not punish me for what can be no sin.—You have always told me, 'to do as I would be done by;" and is not the meaning of that, also—' To do, as I am done by?' "

" Surely, friend," said the duca, mildly, " this is not exactly a case in point.—I ne- ver provided such food as this is, even for the meanest of my household."

" No," returned Hugo, insolently; " not provide, you were too great for that; but you ordered it for us.—That your other tables might be more profusely supplied, you ordained ours to be thus served, and every comfort your noble brother allowed us, taken from us. You cannot wonder then, that, when ordered to supply your table from ours, with alacrity we bring you specimens of what you sentenced us to feed upon."

"Oh, heaven!" exclaimed the duca, in powerful agitation, " how have my ruthless persecutors toiled, to render me obnoxious to my people. This, this is too much; their cruelty, in personal inffliction, I could better bear, than their traducing my humanity thus;—treating thus, as the lowest outcasts of mendicant wanderers, those whom the hardships of toil in servitude was a sufficient for, without the barbarous privations of such detestable parsimony, practised for the purpose of more amply supplying their own rapacious prodigality, united with the malicious project of throwing the odium upon me, who knew not of the measure; for if I had, I would have strenuously opposed it; not that my contravention might,

perhaps, have availed; but my poor ill-
treated people would then have known my
kindest wishes for their comfort were with
them; but when bodily infirmity took
from me the power of governing my own
household, I fell, my poor fellow-sufferers,
into cruel hands, and have become a
slave, even more harshly treated than yourselves."

The attending domestics now looked at
each other with countenances of amazement,
uneasiness, and something like contrite
shame; when Father Patrick, hastily brush-
ing away a starting tear, vehemently exclaimed:—

" Arrah what, now, can you be after
saying for yourselves? ye rapscallion bearers,
of revengeful specimens! to be coming up,
from your dens of malice, to insult a creature, who never to his knowledge, harmed
man, or mortal, in all his born days, bar-
ring himself, when bewitched by a Jezabel,
he gave himself up to vultures, and all manner of wild beasts, to feed upon."

" I can say nothing, holy father," replied Hugo, bowing, in penetential humi-

lity, "but that we are heartily sorry for having credited such evil of our lord; and for his suffering, like ourselves, from those who rule us with a rod of iron. It certainly, monsignore, is not in our power to supply much better food than this, but I think we might improve it a little."

"Och! then on my safe! conscience, you might a great deal; and yet make nothing good of it." returned the zealous priest "but my gay lads, have yourselves no sucking chickens, nor whiter bread, than this is?"

"No, they said; there were no chickens that sucked in Italy, and no better bread was allowed them."

"Och! black beans! and chaff grinders! what a burning shame, is that?—Why then I'll tell you, what you will do, my gay starved lads.—Go every mother's babe of you, to the purveyor; and tell him ' That as no one is after obeying the duca now, not so much, as the wife, who swore at the altar, to do it, you are not the boys, that will be eating the miser's cheer, he ordered for you, any longer.'—So then, I'll be bail,

if you are stout, and are sticking by one
another, you will either get provisions, fit
for Christians; or if the worst comes to the
worst, you'll only be discharged, from a bad
service; and then my advice is to you, to
take away, as hard as you can drive, to one
Signore Brondelo, a mighty humane notary
at Florence; and tell him, how it is yourselves have been used, worse than dogs, let
alone Christians, as well as the poor duca
himself, and his beautiful honey-bird, of a
niece, and his holy priest of a chaplain.
Tell him every morsel, that has come to
your knowledge; and I'll engage, it's he
that will be lining your stomachs, with the
very prime food of the most elegant markets; so now mind what myself says, and
don't be staying, to be made fools of, any
longer; and to be starved too into the bargain; as if ye were in training, to fill every
empty gibbet, in Tuscany.''

The domestics listened with profound attention to Father Patrick, who was an universal favorite with all the lower classes of
the household.; his advice seemed to make
some impression on their minds, and Hugo,

answering for all, said—"They would consult together upon what was most expedient
to be done; but as to murmuring to the
purveyor, they never did any thing else,
yet it obtained no redress; but now, since
they found their ill-treatment was not inflicted by the duca, they would go see if
they could succeed in procuring something
of a better breakfast for his excellenza."

They now all departed, taking with them
the untempting vians; and, in about half
an hour, they returned; but so changed by
the ever-improving hand of neatness, that
scarcely could they be recognised again;
and bearing with them a repast much
amended, in the temptation of it's aspect,
but yet of so homely a composition, that
necessity alone could have influenced the
duca and Angelina to partake of it; and,
when the domestics were again about to depart, the distressed Sigismund, imbibing a
little of Father Patrick's harmless wiliness,
presented each with a piece of gold, to reward them for evincing so much kindness and
compassion for the unfortunate.

" Why then, may be, it's yourself, that

understands the right path of bribery," said the sanguine priest, after the attendants had, respectfully retired. " I'll engage now, some of that same gold, will be changing in the markets, for our benefit."

Father Patrick augured truly; for, when dinner was served that day, a small white loaf, a chicken, and a flask of tolerably good wine, were smuggled in, under the veil of a clean cloth, covered over with what the cautious providers knew would be approved, in passing the review of the Tolmezo inspection.

The grateful Sigismund, and the no-less grateful Angelina, thanked their new-made friends in the most affecting manner for their kindness; and Father Patrick inquired, " If they had followed, any part of his advice?"

" Yes, holy father," Hugo replied; " we told the purveyor we would not feed like paupers any longer; and that he must either provide us with better food, or the castle with other menials; when he flatly informed us, " That he would not improve our provisions; and, that we might leave the castle—if we could;" and that we soon found was impossible, since there are double sentinels planted at every pass, and no one permitted to depart, on any pretence whatever, without a passport."

Angelina and her uncle interchanged looks of foreboding dismay, and the zealous Patrick's countenance lost at once it's expression of animated exulting expectation.

" But," said the good priest, after a pause of sad, and anxious thoughtfulness, " is it, not allowed to go out, you are, when you contrived, to get this chicken, and loaf, and wine, and elegant vegitables for us?"

" Surely, holy father," Hugo replied, " you are not now to learn, that the tables of the favorite domestics and confidants are so amply provided; they make a fine perquisite of the overplus; and so we purchased these things from one of them, pretending that being Georgio's birth-day, we wanted to make a feast."

The duca was infinitely shocked at hearing of such unfair, partial, and unjustifiable proceedings; such prodigal indulgence to some, and even the least deserving ; such tyrannical cruelty and oppression to others.

"How do the soldiery, of the castle fare?" asked Father Patrick.

"At our table, reverend father."

" Alas! my father's estimated veterans, who fought by and bled with him!" exclaimed Angelina, melted almost to tears.

" And who now, if they have luck," returned the eager *Irlandése*, intent upon his design, " will starve with your uncle, unless these fine fellows, are after putting a little morsel of their discontent, into the pouch boxes of the soldiers; and will be telling them, of that same rich, and humane old Signore Brondelo of Florence, and good luck to him; every day he sees the grass grow! and if one of these sentinels, when at an out-post, was to march off, and tell that staunch friend to justice (for sorrow better to be found, dead or alive, than Signore Brondelo) all about the ill usage he is meeting here, himself and friends; and the

duca,: and all of us; I'll engage, old Brondelo would be the making of him; and of
every one of you,, for that matter."

Hugo said, " he would immediately talk
to the soldiers upon the subject; and tell
them too, how much their young lady, who
was dear to them all, for her dear father's
sake as well as her own, had been distressed
at hearing of their ill-treatment."

" Be telling them, every word about it,"
replied Father Patrick, " and about what a
sweet, beautiful creature she is (for there is
none, so sweet and beautiful, in the wide
world, sorrow one) and tell them, what a
burning sin, and shame it would be, for
them, to be letting their brave lord's, darling
child, starve in prison: when if Signore
Brondelo, did but know that same, 'tis she
would find a big friend in him, as well as the
best of ye."

" One word from Lady Angelina herself,
I am certain, would do more than we could
with the soldiers," said Ledo, another of
the attendants. " If my lady would but
go on the ramparts, as she takes her walk of

a morning, .I have no doubt but any one of them would endeavour to go to Signore Brondelo, if they thought it could be of use to our illustrissima signóra."

Angelina graciously. thanked Ledo for this most welcome intimation; and, after Sigismund remunerated these men for the purchases they had humanely made for his benefit, and entreated a continuation of their assistance, they respectfully withdrew; when Angelina earnestly requested her uncle to write a few lines, without delay, to his notary, which she, early on the morrow, would attempt to prevail upon some one of the soldiers to take in charge for her.

Sigismund instantly complied, and again accomplished the effort of walking a short time about his chamber, supported by his lovely niece and Father Patrick; an exercise he several times that day summoned up sufficient energy to undertake, in the sanguine hope of it's leading to the completion of Angelina's project; and full now of the soothing pleasure of it's anticipated success, they all conversed together with some degree, of : cheerfulness ; rearing many a structure of air-built fancy, until the approaching hour of separation, when Father Patrick, recollecting the fragments of their last night's charitable present, was about to take them from the cabinet, when it darted into his mind, the probability of finding a repetition of such kindness in his room ; when, going to seek for it, he soon returned with a tray, more substantially prepared than on the preceding evening; and hid under the provisions it contained, they soon discovered a few lines, evidently written in a disguised hand, importing, " that a supply of that nature should await them in Father Patrick's chamber every evening ; and to request, in return, that the tray and appointments, when done with, should be carefully concealed in the nitch behind the statue of Hercules, in the adjoining corridor."

This grateful trio thankfully partook of this tempting repast: in their united orisons to heaven, a blessing for this secret benefactor was fervently invoked ; and, with scrupulous care, Father Patrick obeyed the directions relative to the tray; first thriftily putting all that remained of their feast into the *gabinétto,* " Against a rainy day," he said.

END OF VOL. I.

C. Robinson, Printer,
Rolls-Buildings, Fetter-Lane, London.

Lightning Source UK Ltd.
Milton Keynes UK
UKHW02n0938120218
317657UK00002B/138/P